The Unexpected Bride

Lena Goldfinch

INDIGO ROAD PUBLISHING
SWEET HISTORICAL ROMANCE

The Unexpected Bride
COPYRIGHT © 2014
Charlene Goldfinch Glatkowski

All scripture quotations are from THE HOLY BIBLE: NEW INTERNATIONAL VERSION® (NIV®) © 1973, 1978, 1984 by *Biblica*. All rights reserved worldwide. See Author's Note.

Cover images: ©*Veve Soran* (*Mountain Cabin*) | ©*Ewa Mazur* (*Horse*)

Published by Indigo Road Publishing
info@indigoroad.pub

ISBN: 0692264957
ISBN-13: 978-0692264959

Dedication

For Paul, my love.
For Jeane—Mom, Nana—our love forever and always.

One

S omewhere along the way I went off course.

Becky Sullivan kicked China into a gallop, sending the mare full speed through Farmer Tucker's fallow cornfield. Cold wind tore at her loose brown coat and whipped her cheeks to a smarting tingle. Yes, sometime in her growing up years, she'd veered off track. She leaned low over the mare's neck and dared her mount faster, ever faster.

It was no way for a young lady to ride.

No, nor could most young ladies track a pheasant through a dense dawn-lit thicket of trees. Most young ladies couldn't shoot an acorn off a branch at fifty paces. Not a "proper" one anyway.

None of that quite mattered until now. Nothing had been more important than freeing the restless energy bubbling up inside her, like a teakettle set to boil. Things changed last Monday when Jack came home from his travels with sweet womanly Melody on his arm. That was the day Becky's youthful fancies died a hard and painful death.

She was starting to think maybe Papa was right, a shocking thought in itself. Maybe there was something to his favorite quote, "The Lord's wanting 'a quiet and gentle spirit' from all womankind, not your loose-limbed hoyden ways, Rebecca Sullivan. You're a disgrace to womankind."

Papa's lectures came fast and frequent enough that perhaps

she could be excused for not taking them much to heart. But at church yesterday, the preacher held up the Good Book during the worship and quoted nearly those same words. Her heart had squeezed to a halt right then and there as she sat in her pew, and she'd sunk into the deepest thoughts.

She might've passed it off as a misunderstanding, but that night she'd waited until after her parents were abed and crept downstairs to peek into her father's big black leather Bible for herself. He forbade her and her younger sister, Rachel, to touch it. Just looking at it too long could spark a long lecture. Even knowing he looked down on women reading the Bible, Becky had to see with her own eyes what it said. That night, she fingered the leather binding with a mixture of reverence and anxiety for several moments before she turned to the page her father kept marked with a wide slice of black ribbon. And there the words were, stark on the page.

She'd wanted desperately to read more, but heard the sounds of someone stirring above. Afraid her father was about to come down and catch her, she'd stopped reading. She'd read enough anyway to know that what Papa and the preacher had said was true.

Did that make her "a blight" on all womankind?

Was that why Jack had abandoned her for that oh-so-proper, young Southern lady?

It was a worry.

Becky had quickly replaced the Bible on the kitchen table —at the precise angle her father had left it—and doused her lamp. Later, as she'd lain in bed, she couldn't close her eyes without seeing those same words again: *gentle and quiet*.

As she galloped across the field now, the anguish struck her afresh, as chilling as the nor'easter gale that was bending the dead corn stalks round her, like a sea of dull gray.

Was God punishing her by taking away her only love?

Was he trying to get her attention?

She slowed China to a walk to allow them both a chance to catch their breath. Cold air filled her lungs, so cold she ached from it. But that was nothing compared to the empty places inside of her. She could feel them growing and growing, until that was all she had left. It was time to make some decisions. Past time.

She looked up at the gathering clouds, seeing in them the face of God looking down at her with a frown that would stop a buck at a full run. It hurt to think the Lord didn't look kindly on her natural inklings—that she offended him by her nature—but there was no doubting it on a day like today.

"Lord," she whispered up to the sky, "I know I'm not all I should be." A tear warmed her cheek, and she said more softly, "And I'm sad to say it. I'm not sure if I can change my ways, but I want to please you. You know that. I want...I want... I don't know. I don't know what I want. I just know I'm not happy. So if it's your will"—she swallowed a hard lump in her throat—"then please take these hoydenish ways from me. I'll be whatever you want me to be...even if it is a proper lady." She paused to consider the threatening clouds, then added for good measure, "I should probably also apologize for not being more respectful of Papa in my heart."

She bit her lip.

She'd tried her best to please her father, but all her "Yes, Papas" only seemed to reap more lectures. All she'd wanted her whole life was one good word from that man. Maybe that was her trouble... Maybe she'd allowed his lack of praise to fill her head with bitter thinking. It shouldn't matter what any man did or didn't say. The Good Book had a thing or two to say about respecting your parents. She knew that well, since he'd quoted those words to her often enough.

So in the days that followed, Becky set out to become a proper young lady. It wasn't easy, especially on the days when her rifle—the one Jack had given to her years ago—needed to be polished and cleaned. And on the days when she took China out for exercise. Keeping to a sedate pace nearly killed both of them, but she tried. It didn't help that all of New England— or all of Pepperell, Massachusetts anyway—still saw her as Becky Sullivan, the grocer's wild daughter. Some even called her a hoyden behind her back, she knew.

Surely, her determination couldn't be faulted. She prayed "Dear Lord, please give me a quiet and gentle spirit" in the morning, in the afternoon, and late at night too. If heartfelt petitions alone could change her, she'd be a proper young lady in no time.

Seven long days later, Becky walked China through Farmer Tucker's tilled field, noticing a premonition of change in the breeze. The air was unseasonably warm, and she spotted a few crocuses stretching their eager purple faces to the sun. It seemed a fitting backdrop as any for an answered prayer.

After a much-too-tame ride, Becky returned to her father's store to work her shift. She was perched high up on a ladder stocking jars of peach preserves on the top shelf, when Melody Duncan—*Jack's wife*—walked in, wearing a perfect ladylike confection of a dress. Her arrival was about as welcome as— say—a spring blizzard catching you barefoot far from home. She stopped in front of a display of white flannel and ex- claimed softly. From Becky's vantage point, those dreamy-eyed looks could mean only one thing: Mrs. Melody Duncan was going to have a baby.

Becky gripped the ladder.

Leave. Please just let her leave now, she silently beseeched the ceiling. As Melody exclaimed some more and made no move for the door, Becky was left with an unpleasant answer to her prayer: *Evidently not.*

She slammed a jar of peach preserves onto the shelf, next to the neatly arranged row she'd been stocking. The jars rattled in protest. She was lucky she hadn't broken any. *Not exactly "gentle," Becky. Or "quiet," for that matter.* She blew out a sigh, fluttering a strand of her hair that had fallen from her topknot.

Continuing to stock the shelf was a futile delay, she knew, since she was the only one minding the register this morning. She'd have to face Melody Duncan—and offer her congratulations. She peeked under her arm, and Melody gave her a cheery little wave. Becky forced a smile.

Only a couple of weeks had passed since Jack came home with a bride on his arm. It felt longer. Surely enough time had passed for Becky to set her heart to rights, but not a day went by that she didn't wake up with an empty ache in her chest. Jack was supposed to marry *her,* but instead he'd chosen someone else. The perfect Melody.

And now Melody was expecting Jack's baby. The news shook Becky to the core.

She'd endured it when Jack bought the old livery—just two doors down from Sullivan's Grocers—and set up shop with Melody. He'd always been interested in horses, so his choice was no surprise, but having them so close made Becky's feelings of loss an ever-present ache.

She'd endured Melody coming into the shop nearly every day. That had only been the beginning of the woe though, for no matter how hard Becky had searched, she hadn't been able to find a single fault in Melody's friendly face, or her soft Southern drawl, or her gentle blue eyes, or her sweet perfectly ladylike manner...or even in that pale delicate-looking skin of hers.

Apparently the fault was Becky's. She must have some permanent mark on her soul, an inability to extend charity to the young woman below her. She should have befriended the girl, should have swallowed her jealousy and hurt. A surge of recriminations assaulted her, and she slammed another jar of peach preserves onto the shelf next to the last.

"Rebecca Ruth Sullivan!" Papa's voice boomed from the back room. "Stop banging those jars! You're going to break something."

Becky startled at the sound of his voice and nearly toppled off the stepladder. His tone was harsh and angry, the tone he most often used when addressing her. The only other tone she'd identified was the voice of quiet disappointment, which was almost always accompanied by an equally disappointed gaze. She gripped the shelf hard to keep from plummeting to the floor and bowed her head, resting her cheek against the coolness of the jars.

Please give me a gentle and quiet spirit, she prayed for the hundredth time that morning.

"Yes, Papa," she called, stifling a moan. Nothing she did ever pleased her father. The past week—had it only been a week?—she'd been on a quest to become the perfect daughter, a perfectly prim and proper young lady—like Melody. She was trying. But Melody having a baby was the last straw. She had to escape.

As Southern Belle wandered around the aisles below her, Becky strove to keep her heart from breaking completely in two. Cold air whisked around her ankles, causing her to shiver. Dipping her head, she saw Jack closing the glass-paned door behind him without a sound. He sidled up next to his wife and kissed her cheek, clearly unaware that Becky was balancing precariously above them. Did he remember kissing *her*, Becky? Did he remember that tender long-ago kiss that had led her to believe he'd marry her one day? As Becky watched him nuzzle his lovely wife's cheek—right there below her—her memory of Jack's kiss soured.

"Hello, darling," Jack whispered in Melody's ear, unfortunately loud enough for Becky to hear as she was practically on top of the pair. "I've missed you this morning."

"I've been gone less than an hour, Jack." Melody pulled away from him with a pleased blush. She gave Jack a playful swat and peeked up at Becky, looking somewhat mortified.

He had the grace to look chagrined when he caught sight of Becky and offered her a look of apology. He nodded to her. "Good day, Miss Sullivan."

"Jack." Becky refused to call him Mr. Duncan. She'd made a resolution, one that she was tempted to break, right along with her broken heart. What had compelled him to kiss Melody right *here*, practically under her feet? Under her feet, for goodness' sake.

Well, the man certainly has a right to kiss his wife, Becky told herself firmly. *But why here, Jack? Must you kiss her here?*

Perhaps a hard ride on China would cure her, she thought. She'd been so good—riding like a blessedly proper young lady since she'd made her resolution. Surely, one little hard ride would be acceptable in the Lord's sight, especially today when she needed it so. The wind in her face might just chase away her aching thoughts.

But for how long? a nagging voice asked.

As long as she lived practically in Jack and Melody's pockets, there was no hope of relief. She prayed, then and there, for a way out.

"Becky, quit lollygagging and come here," Papa yelled, interrupting her prayer.

"Yes, Papa?" She hurried down the ladder and to his side by the cash register, her cheeks burning.

Papa set his ledger on the counter and jabbed a finger into the page he had it opened to. "You entered the wrong amount here."

She bent over the page, gave a quick-but-thorough study of the numbers. When she located the problem, she quietly pointed to the correct column. He stared at the ledger for a moment, then without a word of apology, he sent her a furious look and stalked through the doorway to the office located out back.

Jack and the perfectly ladylike Melody had heard every word of her father's rebuke, of course. Every word he'd blasted across the store. Becky stiffened her spine—standing tall and straight, her chin held high—and looked over her shoulder. There they were, the two of them, their gazes riveted on her. Melody had this look of pity and discomfort on her face, clearly embarrassed on Becky's behalf.

Becky turned and briefly squeezed her eyes shut to gather herself. Then she moved behind the counter with as much composure as she could muster and rang in their purchase: a length of the softest white flannel that Sullivan's carried— obviously meant for baby clothes. That's all anyone ever bought this particular fabric for. It was no secret.

"Congratulations," Becky murmured. It was the hardest word she'd ever spoken, made harder by the fact that Jack must have known it. How could he not? He had the grace to look discomfited.

"Why, thank you, Miss Sullivan." Melody blushed, her

cheeks practically glowing.

After they said their goodbyes and left the store, Becky stared down at the bolt of baby flannel on the counter before her. There was only a small square left, not even enough for the tiniest baby dress—not enough to put back on the display table.

She should set it aside though, perhaps tie it with some twine and mark the price down.

But she couldn't move.

She stood there for an eternity, fingering the flannel. It was soft and perfect—light as dandelion fluff. Despite the fact that everyone called her a hoyden, Becky had always wanted a baby someday. She loved children.

A baby.

She held the fabric to her cheek, filled with an unspeakable longing.

Who would marry her now? Certainly not any of the young men who'd returned to Pepperell after the war. Many hadn't come home. Too many. And she couldn't think of a single one who would've chosen to marry her anyway.

But to stay here? She looked around, seeing shelves of goods stacked to the ceiling, table upon table of neat displays—the same as always—and the street outside, carriages rumbling past... The same, the same, the same. She didn't know how she could bear it any longer.

Glancing over her shoulder at the door to Papa's office she hesitated, then quickly hid the remnant under the counter, her heart pounding like a wild thing.

Late in the night while the house slept, Becky retrieved her bundle, slipped a few coins inside the register, and crept back up to the room she shared with her younger sister. Careful not to disturb Rachel, who was thankfully still snoring delicately on the far side of the bed, Becky tucked her little treasure into the back of her linen drawer, wincing when the lid creaked.

She fell asleep praying.

So then, when Mr. Melrose Preston arrived in town the very next afternoon, Becky was convinced her prayers from the night before had been answered.

He went door to door and shop to shop handing out leaflets. Becky overheard him telling her father about the opportunities to be had for any young women who might be willing to travel to Seattle, Washington Territory. He even preached an impassioned matrimony plea at the Town Hall that night. Becky slipped away from the house to listen, hoping for her answered prayer. Longing for escape. And Mr. Preston's fervor swayed her. She signed up to marry a man named Isaac Jessup, sight unseen.

Two

Not one week later, Becky bustled around her room, packing for her voyage.

"But, Becky, what do you know about this Mr. Preston? Or this Jessup man?" her mother asked for the thousandth time, wringing her hands.

"What's left for me here, Mama?" Becky asked. With Jack married, they both knew the answer: *nothing*. "And you know Papa wants me gone, the sooner the better."

"Becky! I know no such thing. Don't be so quick to judge your father. There's much you don't know about him... about what he's done for you. Or the sacrifices he's made..." Mama's eyes took on a look of anguish. She stood there, biting her bottom lip, as if debating whether she should confide in Becky or not. That she had something to confide was obvious. Her gaze slid away to the window, and she wandered across Becky's room to look down on the street.

"Tell me, Mama," Becky whispered, feeling a measure of dread and certainty overtake her. There was *something*—she'd always known it, always suspected. "What is it?"

"Your Papa and I were courting, when—ah—a situation arose precipitating our wedding in haste."

The walls closed in around Becky. A buzzing sound filled her ears.

What?

"What are you saying, Mama, that you were...expecting?" Becky couldn't have been more surprised if her mother had said they'd found her—the infant Becky—under a mushroom.

"What?" Mama turned to her, clearly flustered, her cheeks turning a rosy pink. "Oh, no, Becky. No. It was Papa's sister, Marilyn. She was the one who was...expecting. Well, the Boston Sullivans can't abide by scandal—that's a known fact—and Mari's beau had run off at the news. So your papa was called upon to 'handle' the situation. To save the family from social ruin, we rushed our own wedding and moved here to Pepperell to start the business, and to raise you as our own once you were born. And Mari was sent away to live with your great-aunt Margaret in Philadelphia."

"Auntie Mari?" Becky stared at Mama's back in silence until she finally turned to meet her gaze. "Auntie Mari was *my mother?*"

"Yes." Mama quickly looked away again.

Any hope that Becky had mistaken her mother's words or that this was some sort of bad dream evaporated with that one softly spoken word.

The floor seemed to tilt away from her. She collapsed onto the top of her newly packed trunk and stared vacantly at the ceiling.

"Don't ever doubt you're a Boston Sullivan, Becky." Her mother sounded sad, almost bitter. "And don't ever doubt my love. I have always been, and shall always be, your mama."

Mama's words were meant to reassure, but they only left Becky feeling empty. She'd never really known her aunt Mari. She certainly hadn't known her as a mother. And she was gone now. She'd died of consumption about five years ago.

Tears welled in Becky's eyes, blurring her vision.

She brushed them away angrily, willing her hurt away. What use was it crying now?

Mama was still wringing her hands, not daring to look at her.

She appeared lost, something Becky wasn't used to. Her mother had never been a particularly strong woman—she always had an air of concern about her—but she was always refined, always in control.

Becky stood and went to her.

"Of course you are," she said softly, taking her mother in her arms. It was a rather awkward embrace, since they'd never been particularly affectionate—not like Mama and Rachel were. Those two were like two peas in a pod.

Becky swallowed.

So this was why. It explained so much. *Like why Mama always let me go my own way.* Why she'd simply thrown up her hands at Becky's hoydenish ways and not put up a fight.

The truth certainly explained the way Papa was with her. He'd left everything he'd ever wanted because of her: Boston, an established family business, his freedom... Why, just about everything.

The *sacrifices* he'd made.

No wonder he resented her.

Well, come tomorrow he'd be free of her. She'd soon be so far away from him he might even forget she existed.

Becky made a fist and clutched it to her stomach, trying to hold herself together.

Unfortunately, she didn't think the hole in her heart was going to be so easily mended. If she wanted to start fresh and build a family of her own—finally find a place she belonged—she'd have to guard her actions. Her future was at stake, and every step she took from now on would determine what kind of life she'd have.

She'd disappointed enough people.

Papa, who'd given up so much.

Mama, who hadn't known what to do with her.

And finally, Jack, who'd wanted a wife, but found her wanting.

It was time for a fresh start. A new Becky.

A new *Rebecca*.

Or else there was going to be one more man who found her lacking, who would discover that Rebecca Ruth Sullivan wasn't all she was meant to be.

Three

"Miss Rebecca Sullivan!"

Becky's head jerked up to find Mr. Melrose Preston, the leader of the expedition, scanning the crowd impatiently. How many times had he called her?

"I'm here." She waved to him, leaning to one side around a strapping young man and a woman in a wide skirt.

Mr. Preston inclined his head and waited for her to scurry over. "Mr. Jessup hasn't shown up," he said, checking the list in his hand once more.

Not here?

Why? Where was he? Had he changed his mind even before he met her?

Acid sloshed in Becky's stomach.

"The hotel's full up," Mr. Preston continued, "so I'm going to have to put you up with the Pearsons. For now, until we track this Isaac Jessup down."

"Oh." Becky clutched her carpetbag tightly to stop her fingers from shaking. If ever she'd felt like a child alone, it was now in this strange new land.

Mr. Preston instructed her to wait where she was and strode off, evidently to talk to the Pearsons, whoever they were.

"Becky." Meggie, a girl she'd befriended on board ship during the long journey, touched her elbow and gave her a sad smile. "I just wanted to see you before I left. And I wanted to say good luck to you."

Becky squeezed Meggie close and kissed her cheek. "Good luck to you too. I hope your William appreciates what a fine woman you are," she said, meaning every word. If anyone deserved a good life it was Meggie, such a sweet girl. She was just a year younger than Becky, but seemed even younger. After months of commiserating and confiding on board, Becky felt closer to her than she'd ever felt to her own sister.

Meggie blushed shyly. "And your Isaac too."

Becky watched as Meggie walked away toward a young man, tall as he was lean, who looked about twenty. The two climbed up into a wagon behind an older couple. His parents, Becky supposed. She felt a twinge of envy at the sight of them together. Meggie had met her William.

Where was *her* Isaac?

Becky craned her neck to look around, but all the men who'd come to meet the ship had been paired off already.

Oh, Lord, what've I done?

She'd committed to marrying a man sight unseen.

Had she come all this way for nothing?

She gripped the handle of her bag and forced herself to take in a few deep, steadying breaths.

She had the oddest sensation of still being on board the ship. Though the ground was steady, it felt like it was undulating beneath her. Like the rolling decks of the ship she'd left behind. She wasn't going to miss that ship—that much was for sure. After spending three months being tossed about by waves and storms, she was heartily sick of the sea and everything in it.

Would she ever feel normal again? she wondered.

While she waited anxiously for Mr. Preston to return, Becky sized up the town. So this was Seattle. It was nothing like

Pepperell, with its white clapboard buildings and brick-paved roads. This place looked more like a lost civilization. It was small—not that Pepperell had been particularly large, but this was even smaller. It had an intimate cluster of town buildings, but everywhere to the left and right was a wilderness. Towering snow-capped peaks jutted into the clouds, dwarfing the collection of stores and houses. And the sky above was the most incredible deep blue. It seemed to go on forever. The air was crisp too, like a drink of cold water.

Becky soaked it in, willing her nerves away.

She was in the middle of all this beauty, surrounded by the best of nature's glory. This place seemed an untamable land. It almost didn't seem real, but then on the muddy ground near her, she saw a few hardy flowers peeking up between clumps of green grass. Their purple and yellow faces offered a cheerful welcome. The only real welcome she'd received to her new home.

As promised, Mr. Preston returned, and he escorted her to the Pearsons' home, which, though modestly sized, spoke of money.

"Preston." A tall, well-dressed gentleman answered the door.

"Mr. Pearson." Mr. Preston cleared his throat, his eyes averted from Becky. "This is Miss Sullivan, the one I told you about."

Mr. Pearson gave her a dismissive nod and immediately pulled Mr. Preston aside. The two of them held a private conference inside the foyer, while she stood like an awkward uninvited lump on the front porch. Finally, they nodded at each other and introduced her to Mrs. Pearson, a starchy-looking woman who immediately gave Becky the impression that she didn't much appreciate having a house guest thrust upon her.

"Well, Miss Sullivan," Mr. Preston said, "welcome to Seattle.

The Pearsons will see to you now. I wish you much happiness."
He nodded as if this sealed the matter and quickly took his
leave.

See to me?

What did that mean?

Becky stared after his departing figure, unable to shake
off the feeling that she'd just been deserted.

Mrs. Pearson looked Becky over and compressed her lips.
Her cheeks turned a purplish hue, like two indignant plums.
"Well, Abe"—she turned to her husband, her fists planted
against her hips—"this is a fine mess."

As if Becky weren't standing right there, hearing her every
word.

She wished more than anything to disappear into the
floorboards.

A fine mess?

Perhaps it was. She'd left her family, despite her mother's
pleas, and now she was putting the Pearsons out. Guilt hit her
belly like a cold gulp of water, leaving her chilled.

Mr. Pearson pulled his wife aside. Becky couldn't hear the
hushed argument that followed between them, but the meaning
was clear enough: she wasn't wanted here, and Mrs. Pearson
didn't care if she knew it.

"Miss Sullivan"—Mr. Pearson turned to her, assessing
her with cool, blue politician eyes—"I hope you find Seattle
to your liking." With a curt nod, he scooped up her bags and
turned to carry them up the wide stairs.

He was leaving her alone with his wife?

"Thank you for your hospitality, Mr. Pearson," Becky
called after him with a tiny frown. She swallowed and addressed
the imposing woman before her. "I hope I'm not putting you
out." Her voice was hushed with worry.

She was beyond the point of weariness, her legs threatening to give way. She had traveled around the world, basically, and had no husband-to-be to show for it. Never had she felt so alone or out of place.

She only wanted to sleep. A bed, a pillow, cozy sheets. A floor under her that didn't move.

Perhaps then she could think.

Perhaps then it wouldn't feel as if her world had just toppled into the sea.

"My husband is sending a messenger up the mountain tomorrow to let your man know you're here." Mrs. Pearson's unspoken words came across loudly enough: *And then we'll be rid of you.*

Becky swallowed. So her day of reckoning was tomorrow then. Would Isaac Jessup step forward to claim her as his bride?

Four

"Mr. Jessup? I've got a message here for you from Mr. Pearson."

At Isaac's brisk nod, the gangly youth standing before him handed him a folded note and quickly stepped back, stroking the mane of his sandy mare.

The boy seemed winded as if the trek up the mountain from town had been a harrowing one for him. If his slightly awed glances at the dense green firs surrounding them were anything to go by, he hadn't spent much time up here in the trees. Isaac sized him up and decided the boy was a little anxious about the sound of saws cutting through wood, as several of his men continued to work around them. That was good. It was good to be cautious where tree felling was concerned.

Isaac wondered if the boy was familiar enough with the forest not to get himself lost on his return trip, but then all he had to do was follow the stream down and eventually find his way.

He turned his attention to the note, curious as to why Mr. Pearson was sending him anything. He was an influential man, but the two had never met outside a town meeting or two, and even then the man hadn't been particularly friendly.

Isaac read the note, then squinted and read it again.

His bride had arrived and was waiting for him at the Pearsons'?

His *bride*?

"Is this some sort of joke?" Isaac stared blankly at the messenger boy.

The youth gawked back at him with a nervous swallow. "No. No, sir!"

"Well, get along then." Isaac pressed a coin into the messenger's hand. The boy obviously didn't know anything.

It was a mystery.

A mystery that could only lead to one person. His father. It had to be a joke. It sounded like something he'd come up with.

Pop would think this was hilarious. But why he'd gone to such lengths to set up a joke like this in the first place was another mystery. Pop didn't much like going into town. Maybe he'd involved some of the men then, convinced them to help out. Even worse.

Isaac looked around, but none of his men seemed particularly interested in the messenger boy's presence or Isaac's reaction to the note.

He found his father uphill a ways, on the edge of their current swath. Isaac pulled him away from any prying eyes.

"What's this about 'a bride' waiting for me?" Isaac cornered Pop with a tree at his back and nowhere else to go. He held the note out in front of his father's face so he could read it.

Pop braced himself like a fortress against a siege, his face weathered with lines, tanned from years in the sun. He wore his long white hair gathered at the back of his neck and tied with a strip of leather, as usual. Same old Pop, but Isaac thought he caught a trace of guilt in his expression.

Pop's eyes flicked over the note. He knew what it said.

Time for this joke to be over. It wasn't funny at first, but maybe Isaac would be able to laugh about it later, say, over dinner.

"I thought it best." Pop said.

Wait.

"What?"

"It's about time you married, Son. And the way things are going, you're never going to."

"You mean it's not a joke?" Isaac felt the need to sit down.

"A joke? Why would it be a joke?"

That's when it really hit Isaac. His father had sent for a bride for him. He'd actually done it. Hadn't asked him. Hadn't thought twice about it probably.

Unbelievable.

"Why, Pop? Why would you do such a thing?" Isaac felt a pulse beating extra hard at his temple.

"I did it for you—you need a wife." Pop seemed to lose a bit of his bluster.

"I'm a grown man, Pop. I'm not a child."

Somewhere down the mountain was some poor woman who thought she was about to get married to him. What had Pop been thinking? Did he actually think Isaac would just stand up with a stranger and exchange vows?

"Well, it seemed like a good idea at the time." Pop said. "Why, that Preston man had a line of men just waiting to sign up for a woman from back East. I don't know, maybe I got swept along..." His voice trailed off.

Back East, Isaac registered that detail with a frown.

"And you didn't think to tell me?" he asked.

His father bowed his head with a look of disappointment, somehow managing to look old and withered, as only his father could. But Sam Jessup was a lively sixty-five, an American frontier original. He'd no doubt live into his nineties. Isaac sensed some of that steel come back in his father's spine as he lifted his eyes and pinned Isaac in his gaze. His eyes were a steel-blue color, which seemed fitting.

"I know you weren't expecting this, Son, but I'm asking you to give it a chance. I'm not a young man anymore." His expression softened. "I want to see my grandchildren someday. I want to bounce them on my knee. Is that too much for an old man to ask? Won't you at least meet the gal—give her a look-see?"

Pop sure had a way of pulling on the heartstrings. No mercy. And it was impossible to argue with him. *Meddling old man*, Isaac thought with equal amounts of frustration and affection.

"Aw, Pop." Isaac would do anything for his father. His mother had died young, so Pop was his only family—and he'd given Isaac so much. But that did *not* give him the right to order him a bride. The last thing Isaac needed was some delicate, *Back East* woman. He was a man of simple needs, and all of them were focused on building his logging operation right now. He'd long since stifled any softer longings for a wife and family. His reasons were simple enough, which he'd already expressed a time or two. Why couldn't Pop respect that? Why'd he have to keep treating Isaac like a boy in short pants who needed his nose wiped?

Surely he'd proved himself by now. Hadn't he shown that he was a man who knew his own mind? His mind very clearly said having a woman around would mess up his logging operation. Why, it was still in its infancy. At this tender stage, the slightest disturbance could set off an avalanche of untold consequences.

A wife was definitely a disturbance, and slight didn't even begin to describe it.

Isaac became aware of an audience forming behind them, as scores of his men hovered just inside hearing range. He turned on them with a scowl. "Get back to work! I'll find you something to do if you feel you have enough time to stand around like a gaggle of geese."

The loggers fell back and hurried off to where they should've been, felling trees.

Now, see, Isaac thought, *it's already happening. I'm getting testy with the men.*

Wasn't that a sure sign of "untold consequences"?

He turned back to his father with a sigh. "If I wanted a wife—and I don't—I certainly wouldn't have sent off for some citified, 'Back East' woman. Don't you trust me? Don't you think if I wanted to I could have picked a woman myself?"

His father arched a brow. His eyes were filled with a look of obvious challenge. Thankfully, he didn't say anything.

"Forget it. I'll go set things straight." Isaac stalked off toward their cabin. He'd have to wash up, comb his hair, change his shirt, get the horse saddled...

Over the din of saws and cracking wood, he heard his father call out, "Hold on now. What does that mean—set things straight? Don't go off and do something foolish."

Isaac stifled a snort. *Don't go off and do something foolish?* Pop had no right—no right at all—to talk about not acting foolish. A citified, Back East lady? What had Pop been thinking?

Trying to cool himself down, Isaac slowed to a deliberate stroll as he neared the cabin and took his own sweet time getting ready and saddling his great bay gelding. By the time he finally set out to meet the woman waiting for him, he had a speech in the making:

There's been a mistake. I'm terribly sorry.

He continued to practice and refine his choice of words as his mount picked its way down the mountain path through the towering pines to the Pearsons' place in town. But his speech froze in his throat like a lump of river ice when Mrs. Pearson presented him to a petite young woman and introduced her as "Miss Rebecca Sullivan."

He removed his hat out of politeness and said, "Isaac Jessup." But that was all he got out, for as he stared down at the young woman, he promptly lost his words. She was so...*tiny*. Her face seemed exceptionally smooth and pale to him, almost like she was a porcelain doll and not a real woman. Her hair was a nice reddish-gold color, he thought, except she had most of it scraped back into a rather severe schoolmarm's bun. On any other woman, the style would have been down-right unflattering, but on her...it wasn't, maybe because a few strands had gotten loose and were curling softly against her cheeks. It made her look somehow softer, more delicate. He didn't much care for that starched-up charcoal-gray dress she had on, or the overly wide skirt that seemed like it would get in the way of her doing just about anything, but he had to admit she looked pretty despite the awful color.

Every inch a proper young lady.

She stared up at him with a pair of soulful eyes—greenish-gray, maybe?—and it seemed to him her expression was one of vulnerable expectation.

She's anxious. Afraid even.

Why wouldn't she be? What did she know about him, a stranger?

Why had she come?

He tried to imagine what would prompt a woman to leave her home, travel all that distance, all to marry up with a man she'd never met. It didn't seem quite—comprehensible. In fact it seemed a little desperate.

She must have fallen on hard times.

Something about her tiny form facing him so bravely

stirred up an uncomfortable desire to protect her. How could he possibly go back and tell his father he'd sent the girl away without giving her a chance? How could he look into her questioning eyes and send her away?

Isaac ducked his head in confusion.

All his hard resolve began to melt off. So Pop had sent for a bride without asking him? His father meant well, and the thought of him going to his grave without seeing his grandchildren tore at Isaac. Pop had never asked much of him.

Isaac stared down at his hat in desperation.

What was he thinking?

He couldn't let Pop have his way.

He firmed his weakening resolve and set his jaw. He was sensitive to Pop's desire for grandchildren, but he didn't have a choice in the matter. He had a business to grow, men who were counting on him. Their livelihoods—not just his and Pop's—depended on him succeeding.

He had to send the girl away. There was no call for him to feel guilty either. He hadn't sent for a bride. Hadn't asked for one.

He closed his eyes briefly against the sight of her.

She was clearly more than her weight in trouble. Best to get it over with fast.

Five

$\mathcal{B}$ecky blinked at the man standing before her in the Pearsons' foyer. He stepped closer, until she was staring level with the vee of his brown leather vest. It was the kind of vest she'd expect a man of the West to wear: serviceable, a bit weathered. She took notice of his tanned throat, square jaw, and a mouth that was now set in a firm line. Dark hair. A nice straight nose. A rather handsome man, when you added it all up. Youngish, but not as young as she was. Quite a bit older than that. Twenty-three or -four perhaps? And he was so *tall*. Exceptionally tall, and not just because she was on the short-ish side. He was the kind of tall that would put him a head over most of the men she knew. He practically loomed over her.

She swallowed uneasily.

He's here to meet you, Becky, just like you're here to meet him.

He wants you here. He wouldn't have sent for you if he didn't.

She tipped her head back and met his eyes resolutely. She even attempted a small smile. "A pleasure to meet you."

"Miss Sullivan," he said and extended his hand, "pleasure to meet you too."

So formal. Almost...cold. Which completely went against the impression she'd had of him a moment ago. She was sure she'd seen something else in his eyes: interest. Maybe even sympathy. Kindness. But now that was gone. Like he'd put up a wall.

27

Don't be silly, she told herself. *He's likely just anxious.*

Becky slipped her hand into his, and he shook it firmly. She blinked in surprise. What a strange way to greet her. He was her husband-to-be, but that was more of a business hand-shake, like someone you might meet at a social function, someone you never expected to see again. It wasn't like she'd expected him to scoop her up in a warm embrace—that would have been too forward, of course—but he could have kissed her hand. That would have been perfectly acceptable. She shrugged ever so slightly and dismissed the thought.

Mrs. Pearson cleared her throat, looking as put upon as ever. "Excuse me while I fetch some tea," she said and strode off toward the kitchen.

It was left to Becky to lead Isaac Jessup into the parlor. After seating herself beside him on the Pearsons' strawberry chintz settee, she found herself at a loss for words. He seemed similarly afflicted, and an awkward silence fell between them.

"Miss Sullivan, there's been a..." His voice trailed off, and he suddenly looked a trifle unwell.

"Call me Be—" She stopped, remembering her resolution to be a perfectly prim and proper young lady. She'd always thought of herself as Becky, but that name didn't fit anymore. "Please, call me Rebecca."

And with that the words were out.

She wasn't Becky anymore.

It was like losing one more piece of herself.

How long would it take until she was entirely gone?

"Rebecca," Isaac repeated with a slight frown, as though testing it.

He hadn't smiled at her once, which gave her the distinct feeling he wasn't entirely pleased with her. She tried to push aside her mounting insecurity. She'd done her best with her appearance. Gone completely was the hoyden of Pepperell, Massachusetts. She'd carefully wound up her hair into a tidy knot and selected a perfectly ladylike gray dress—complete with a hooped crinoline, perfectly ladylike slippers, and white gloves. She folded her hands demurely in her lap.

Jack Duncan had spurned her for a perfect lady, and a perfect lady she'd do her best to be for this Isaac Jessup. He would, after all, be her husband soon. She shifted restlessly at the thought. No matter how she tried, her heart still belonged to Jack. She wasn't free to love Isaac Jessup, the man perched like a great oak next to her. Sneaking a peek at his profile, she noticed him staring off toward the window, as though searching for something to say. Maybe he was a shy sort of man. Not that he appeared to be, but it was entirely possible.

Well, she needed to set him at ease was all. She cleared her throat and flashed a glance into his deep brown eyes, which were now looking right at her. He certainly was handsome, if you liked your men tall, strong and dark-haired, which she didn't.

An image of Jack's fair hair and slim build flashed through her mind.

She bit the inside of her cheek, completely mortified to have brought Jack to mind when her husband-to-be was sitting right next to her. That had to stop.

It wasn't fair to Isaac. Didn't he deserve a woman who could love him?

But then, what man ordered a bride sight unseen and expected true love?

Perhaps the best they could expect was to become close companions, perhaps even friends. And maybe that was enough. They didn't have to be head-over-heels in love to build a family together. She was determined to be a good wife. She'd respect him and help with—whatever help he needed as a logging boss. His books, maybe? She was good with numbers. She wasn't much of a cook, but she could try. And she'd wear the corset that cinched her waist, these uncomfortably tight gloves, and the dratted crinoline that felt like she was wearing an umbrella upside down...whatever she needed to do to appear the impeccable lady. If that was what a man looked for in a wife, well, she'd do her utmost.

A gentle and quiet spirit, she reminded herself.

Becky, the wild hoyden, was gone.

"I'm not expecting a love match, Mr. Jessup," she finally said.

He frowned and cleared his throat. "I see you're a—uh—practical young woman, Miss Sullivan."

So they were back to formal names. That was her doing, she realized. She'd just called him Mr. Jessup.

Becky pressed her lips together to stop a frown. He thought she was *practical?* No, not by nature, she wasn't. If she was practical she would have been able to forget Jack the moment she found out he was married. She would have been able to set thoughts of him completely out of her mind. But they were still there, taunting her. Her shoulders drooped a little, as she was swept back to the moment she saw Jack and Melody buying flannel in Papa's grocery store.

They were going to have a baby.

What practical woman would keep thinking about that?

Becky grasped the tiny, square remnant of baby flannel in her gloved hand. She couldn't feel its softness, but her memories of it were so strong she almost could. Her heart swelled with a longing so sharp it hurt. What practical woman would have kept this? She closed her hand more tightly around her precious scrap. Well, there was no use hiding what she wanted from this marriage, was there? Isaac deserved honesty from her, and she would give it to him. Squaring her shoulders a little, she lifted her chin.

"I hope we can be friends, but, to be honest, what I really want from this marriage is a baby." There, she said it. Her words broke through the silence with all the force of a crack of lightning.

A baby? Isaac almost fell off the seat. She certainly got to the point quick enough.

"Is that right?" His head spun, making word retrieval a trifle difficult.

"Yes, and though the Pearsons have been—hospitable—I'm afraid I've overstayed my welcome here. So, if you're agreeable, I'd like to arrange the wedding as soon as possible."

Tell her, tell her now, he urged himself. But the whole thing had been dumped on him that morning, and he felt swept along like a log headed downstream.

What have you done, Pop?

He wanted to bury his head in his hands and take a moment to think, but she was looking at him again with those expectant, hopeful green—gray?—eyes, and he heard himself replying, "That shouldn't be a problem."

Not a problem? Had he lost his head?

First of all, she was far too delicate and fragile to endure such a rough life. He'd be watching her all day to make sure she didn't get hurt, or worse, killed. How could he run a logging operation that way?

"Would you agree to three days from now?" she asked.

"That sounds fine." That was his voice he heard. He'd

31

lost command of his senses again. Had he just agreed to marry a stranger in three days?

After he returned home to the cabin that evening, he found Pop waiting with an expectant expression.

"So I'm getting married, Pop."

"You are?" he exclaimed, jubilant.

"It would seem that way," Isaac said. Inside, his heart was heavy as a rock. Some of his dread must have shown on his face for Pop gave him a hard look.

"Son?"

Isaac waved him away. "A touch of headache."

His father nodded. "Maybe you should get some rest. Go to bed early. It's been a lot all of a sudden, I 'spect."

"It certainly has been," Isaac said dryly.

"Watch yourself, Son."

Isaac chuckled at his father's warning.

"I was hoping as much," Pop said. "Had a team of our strongest lads come by this afternoon. Adding a room off the back. Someplace private for you and your lady."

Of course. Because why wouldn't he *add a room on the cabin* without waiting for Isaac to come back?

That was it.

"Goodnight, Pop." Isaac ducked behind the potato-sack curtain that separated the sleeping area from the main room. *Let Pop stay up and celebrate by himself,* he thought. Meanwhile, he needed some time alone to think.

He sat on the edge of his bed and dropped his head into his hands. He hadn't lied about the headache. The pain hadn't let up since he left the Pearsons' house. Whatever time that was. He'd completely lost track of time.

Aw, Pop, what have you done?

Pop hadn't seemed all that surprised by his news. In fact,

he'd already organized a crew to add a room onto the cabin. Unbelievable.

Isaac shook his head in disbelief, imagining a rough-framed structure protruding off the back of the cabin.

He was marrying a woman he didn't know.

In three days.

He dug his fingers into his scalp. What did he know about women? His whole life had been work. After his mother died about fourteen years back, his father had sold off their Colorado parcel, and they'd spent years wandering across the Western frontiers looking for a home. They came to Seattle a little over eight years ago, when he was sixteen.

At first, they'd worked for another logging outfit, stayed there a few years learning the ropes, saving every cent of their money, and since then they'd bought land. They were focused on building their own logging operation. But that hadn't come without a price. All that hard work left no time for a social life. Not that there were any acceptable women to be had in the logging camps up here. The only unmarried women available were of questionable repute.

And Isaac had been raised on the Bible. As a God-fearing young man he'd stayed away from "that type of woman"—well, except for one time. He remembered with shame the young woman who'd taken in wash and "serviced" the men at their first logging camp. Rosie had been a worn shell of a woman at nineteen. He'd slipped into her tent on his seventeenth birthday to "prove his manhood," as the other boys had urged him to do, egging him on. Rosie had welcomed him into her tent without the slightest sign of surprise. He remembered how she'd taken his hand and led him over to her dingy pallet on the ground. They'd had to duck because the roof of her tent sagged down on the sides. He hadn't seen through her false eagerness at first. He'd been so nervous, his heart pounding, struck dumb by equal parts excitement and terror. And shame, even then in the moment. He'd hesitated, listening to the squawk of his conscience. That was when he'd looked into her faded blue eyes and really *seen* her. He'd seen past what he'd been thinking of doing. Seen past her brazen, come-on look and only found emptiness underneath. His desire had fled in a hurry, leaving behind only feelings of guilt and pity.

He'd stolen a quick kiss and hurriedly pressed a coin into her hand. Backed away. She shrugged it off with a puzzled frown, tucked the coin into the pocket of her skirt, and returned to scrubbing a tub of wash. She hadn't shown the least flicker of emotion.

He'd ducked out of the tent to breathe some fresh air. He remembered it was an effort just to stand upright, he was shaking so hard, as if he'd run up the mountain.

So he'd never *been* with a woman—not for more than that one stolen kiss anyway—in all his years. He was twenty-four now, boss of his own business. His men looked up to him. But he didn't know a thing about women. And now he was marrying a stranger. In three days.

He returned to the cabin to find his father already snoring in the narrow bed next to his. Thoughts of marriage and a woman with reddish-gold hair and green eyes soon swirled into a fog as sleep claimed him.

Six

In a one-room shanty just outside Seattle...

Icy rain leaked through the gaps in the roof, chilling Jem Wheeler's face and soaking his sheets. He shivered and tried to remember a time when the roof didn't leak. He was sixteen now, and it seemed like raindrops had been splashing against his skin his entire life. When he was really small, he'd wake up in terror feeling cold water on his face. Back then, he'd thought the ceiling was gonna cave in on him. Even though he knew now that it would hold, he still lay awake, uneasy. Waiting.

The front door crashed open, and he saw the shape of a man standing in the doorway, not much more than a shadow in the night. The shape staggered in, coming toward his bed. Thunder cracked, making Jem jump, then there was a moment of deathly quiet.

He jerked upright, his pulse deafening in his ears. "Pa?"

"Hush up, boy!" The slurred command sounded like a gunshot. It was Pa, drunk again. He struck Jem across the jaw with the back of his hand.

Something broke inside of Jem. He finally snapped, like a branch bent back too far.

"No, Pa! You hush up!" He scrambled out of bed and shoved Pa away.

His father stumbled backwards. He roared in anger, swearing. A flash of lightning lit the room. Jem saw the glint of metal

in his pa's hand. It all happened so quick. Pa rushed him before
he could get out of the way. Pain lashed across his chest. It
was hot at first, then icy cold, all over.

"Git on out of here, boy!"

Pa's string of cusses weren't anything Jem hadn't heard
before, but he was already at the breaking point.

"I hate you!"

"You good for nothin'! Go on. Git!"

Jem didn't wait for a second swipe of Pa's hunting knife.
He ran out the door. For a second, he glanced back, hating to
leave his one treasure behind, but there was no way to get it
now. He ran through the storm, feeling the safety of the black
night immerse him.

He was done with Pa. He was done with Pa's cussing. He
was done with Pa's drunkenness. He was done with Pa's beat-
ings. He was finally on his own.

Seven

The Pearsons' household was quiet with sleep. The sound of thunder woke Becky, returning her to her anxious thoughts. She'd be a married woman soon. Shivering from the cold and perhaps something else as well, she rubbed her feet against the sheets to warm them. She turned her head into her pillow, but sleep eluded her. Doubts had plagued her on the long voyage to Seattle—three seasick months with nothing else to do but think. She'd doubted her sanity, her common sense, her judgment.

His name had convinced her to come.

An Isaac for her Rebecca, as if God placed his approval on the match.

But perhaps God hadn't been telling her that at all.

Maybe she'd made it up in her mind. Maybe she'd just wanted to believe it so bad. She'd wanted to leave.

A soft sigh escaped her lips.

It was a little too late for doubts now.

Yesterday, Isaac's height had dismayed her. She smiled to herself, remembering her relief as she'd met his dark brown eyes for the first time. They were nice eyes. Warm eyes. The eyes of a good man—if you could tell by a man's eyes alone. Isaac seemed like a good man anyway, and they'd have the next few days to get to know one another.

He was so different from Jack. Where he was dark, Jack was fair.

Jack was lean, blond, and handsome. For years, he'd

taught her everything a proper young girl shouldn't know: from riding bareback through the orchard to shooting a rifle. He'd showered her with attention. Her first and only kiss had been with Jack Duncan. She'd dreamed of having a family with him, a house full of children and laughter. How she'd loved him. She remembered the night she'd found out he was back from the war and pressed her face deeper into the pillow, mortified afresh.

When she'd heard the news, despite the cold, she'd hiked her skirts to her knees and run from Sullivan's Grocers all the way to the Duncans' family orchard. She banged on their door and pushed it open, so embarrassingly eager, not even waiting for so much as a hello. She'd seen Jack first. He was standing just inside the doorway, looking somehow different—older, more a man than a boy. She'd told herself that was why he hadn't grabbed her up immediately and swung her around. He'd become a man, and a gentleman at that.

"Jack!" She launched herself into his arms, wanting to show him how much she'd missed him with the strength of her embrace.

"Becky, it's good to see you," he said, sounding oddly subdued.

He should have been as excited as she was.

Why wasn't he?

Was he hurt? Wouldn't someone have told her? She didn't see any signs of injury. No scars, no bandaged anything.

"Jack?" Becky searched his face as he gently set her aside, wondering why he looked so much like a discomfited suitor.

"Jack?" A young woman with a soft drawl had claimed Jack's sleeve. Her white dress had a hooped skirt that had filled the hall, and her shining black locks had been caught up with perfect white bows. She was the loveliest lady Becky had ever seen.

Becky had also never seen a dress quite like that before. It had made her feel somehow inferior. Unsophisticated. And confused, because nothing made sense. Who was she? What was she doing here?

A relative maybe. But Becky didn't know of any relatives they had in the South. A distant cousin?

Why was she holding onto Jack's sleeve as if she had the right to?

"Miss Rebecca Sullivan, may I present Mrs. Melody Duncan... my wife."

Jack's strained words slowly penetrated Becky's fog. Her heart had been breaking, but she'd somehow forced her cold limbs to obey her command. She'd offered Jack her congratulations, given a welcoming smile to his lovely wife.

How her face had hurt.

She thought her cheeks might break.

She couldn't get out of that house fast enough, but Jack's mother had begged her to stay for dinner. It had been the longest night of Becky's life.

And letting herself wallow in memories like that wasn't going to help her sleep tonight.

Becky burrowed deeper into her pillow, trying to clear her mind. But her thoughts continued to spin.

Was Papa glad to have her gone?

She'd never been able to please him, no matter how hard she tried. Even her efforts to help him with the books got turned around on her. She never knew what to do whenever she found out he'd made a mistake. If she pointed it out, it only made him mad. If she left him to find it himself, he thought she'd done it. She'd seen the flicker of interest in his eyes when she'd brought up the notion of leaving with Mr. Preston. He'd wanted her to go, and she'd wanted to be gone more than anything. Thinking about Papa was only turning her inside out, so she pushed those thoughts aside as well and tried to sleep.

A half-dream finally claimed her: She was in the water, floundering in a roiling sea. Lightning flashed and lit up the night sky. A shadowy figure beckoned to her. The figure became Isaac, but as he reached his hand to rescue her, Jack called her name from another shore. She turned to him, but a woman dressed all in white was pulling him away. Becky tossed about throughout the night, her bedclothes wrapping around her like seaweed.

Eight

I saac picked at the cords of his loose-fitting leather vest to avoid looking at his father, whose jaw was stuck out in that obstinate way Isaac found so annoying.

Backing toward the door of the cabin, Isaac bumped into the crate of hooks and chains his father kept just inside the door. He glared at it. How did Pop expect him to bring a woman to this old ramshackle hut?

"You know, if you don't want her, there's a slew of men around here who'd appreciate having a wife."

Isaac realized the truth in his father's words, but the thought of Rebecca going to another man made his brow buckle.

"No, I've committed to a date. I won't go back on my word now—and I wouldn't want to put the Pearsons out." He glanced at his father.

"Put the Pearsons out? Right, Son." Pop chuckled.

Isaac gave a frustrated tug at the knotted cords and ducked his head to avoid Pop's too-observant eyes. He'd resigned himself to marrying the woman to please his father, but part of him wanted to see Pop wriggle a bit.

Problem was, he was the one doing the wriggling.

"Go on, boy. Go see the little gal. We can handle the work here—don't you worry about that." His father pushed him out the cabin door, tossing his coat out after him.

"All right." Isaac sighed in defeat and headed to the lean-to to saddle his horse.

Rebecca. He toyed with her name in his mind, imagining

her reddish-gold hair, her delicate face, and huge green eyes. As he rode toward the Pearsons' place, he kept thinking he was making the biggest mistake of his life.

He continued on his two-hour journey down the mountain into town, lost in his thoughts.

From the second story of the Pearsons' house, Becky pressed her forehead against the window in her room, her gaze skimming the horizon. The peaks of the Olympic Mountains towered around like sentinels, protecting this place, protecting her. It was a fanciful thought perhaps—the stuff of fairy tales. When she'd finally left the ship and stood on land, she thought the sea would never bring her pleasure again, but now, as she looked down on the choppy waters of Puget Sound, the sight was simply beautiful. She sighed.

A spattering of wagons and carriages rumbled by on the deeply-rutted dirt road below. This was the most populated area of Seattle, but it was by no means a big city. She scanned the horizon where the mountains rose up. There was a lone figure on a horse—barely more than a dot. It had to be Isaac. She'd watched him disappear over that same rise yesterday. Gripping the curtains, she watched him now as he rode up to the front of the Pearsons' house.

Who was this man who was to be her husband?

She studied Isaac's back as he tethered his horse under her window. He turned, and she saw his black greatcoat was hanging open in front, revealing a black leather vest underneath. He paused to tuck in the back of his white shirt, running his hands around the waistband of his dark brown trousers. He didn't exactly look like a mountain man today. He'd polished himself up a bit, like these were his Sunday, going-to-church clothes. She thought he looked a bit nervous, which was just as well. She was too. She dropped the curtain before he could look up and catch her. She dashed to the mirror to check her face. She smoothed down her dark green dress, hoping it was suitably proper. She'd worn petticoats today. Should she have chosen the crinoline instead?

Becky hurried downstairs toward the foyer and almost ran straight into Mrs. Pearson on her way up. Her hostess gave her an irritated wave, indicating she should continue down and entertain Isaac.

Isaac was below them, pacing the foyer floor.

Why hadn't Mrs. Pearson shown him into the parlor to wait? Becky simply didn't understand the woman. It was as if she were going out of her way to be impolite. Maybe she was. She'd made it clear from the start that she didn't want Becky here.

Becky gripped the banister tightly, realizing with a tiny burst of panic that she'd left her gloves in her room. Some lady. She continued down the stairs at a more sedate pace and greeted him brightly, "Mr. Jessup—" That sounded ridiculous, seeing as they were going to be married, so she added faintly, "Isaac."

He spun toward her and snatched off his hat.

"Miss." His frown revealed he too felt strange. "A pleasure, Rebecca."

They exchanged uncomfortable smiles.

She led him into the Pearsons' parlor, where they maneuvered themselves onto the long, ornate settee. Mrs. Pearson eventually brought in a tray of tea, served it into dainty china cups, and left them to help themselves to the apple tarts she'd baked. As they ate, an uneasy silence hung in the room, broken only by the mantel clock.

Two days, it taunted Becky with each persistent tick.

Theirs would have to be a swift courtship.

Isaac cleared his throat a little and said, "You're from Massachusetts." It was more a statement than a question. More awkwardness. It sat uneasily between them like a third person, someone who refused to leave.

Becky tried not to think it would be a permanent problem. How could they possibly get along if they couldn't even talk to each other?

"Yes. Pepperell. My father owns a store there."

"Ah." There was a wealth of meaning in that one syllable, and he seemed self-conscious as he studied his boots. He gave her a quick, sidelong glance and said, "My father and I own a logging operation."

His tone was slightly challenging, as if he expected her to run the other way. Becky stared at him, puzzled. He'd been upfront about his business in his letter, so why now was he acting like he expected her to be put off by his occupation?

"Yes, of course," she said. "I remember that from your letter."

"My letter?" His eyes widened slightly, then he nodded quickly. "Right. That's right. My letter. Then you probably also know we've been in Seattle about eight years."

It was all so odd. Had he forgotten what he'd written? Maybe so. It had been many months since he'd sent it off.

"And your mother?" she asked, curious that he hadn't mentioned her.

"She died when I was ten." He paused, his gaze fixed on the view of the mountains outside the window. His memories obviously pained him, and Becky regretted bringing up the subject.

"I'm sorry," she said. "You must miss her terribly."

At her words, he looked steadily into her eyes. "I do." He seemed surprised at the admission, like he hadn't allowed himself to think about it for years. "She was quite a woman— a real lady." His voice trailed off, but admiration shone in his eyes. He smiled slightly.

"I think I miss Mama most," Becky said quietly. "My father, well, there's always been a wall between us. I never really understood why." *Until right before I left home*, she added silently, frowning. She was tempted to sink into memories, but lifted her chin. "My sister, Rachel, will likely keep them busy— she'll be fifteen this winter."

Becky suddenly realized she would probably never see her little sister again. She'd never see her become a woman, never see her nieces and nephews.

Isaac seemed interested in learning more about her family and Pepperell, so she told him what she could, how she'd worked in the grocery store. Things like that. She wished she could explain Jack. It seemed like he deserved to know something about him. But putting it into words was impossible. There was nothing she could say that would sound right, so she looked out at the mountain view through the window. "It's so beautiful here. What's your home like?"

At Rebecca's question, Isaac tried in vain to picture the young woman next to him in his cabin. It wasn't much to speak of. In fact, the breeze cut right through it in the winter. She didn't belong in a place like that, even if they were adding on another room. The image just didn't fit. She belonged back East in some big, fancy house—not in some old mountain cabin barely holding together.

She was tiny, seemed like such a delicate creature. Seattle Territory would swallow her whole. Like the frontier had taken his mother from him. It was a disturbing thought, one he didn't wish to dwell on.

He cleared his throat. "The land is magnificent. The mountains are spectacular, as you can see. There's glory all around, but...our cabin is small. It's nothing fancy. My dad has a crew of our men building an addition right now. They're doing quite a job—should be done right soon." He faltered and felt heat rising up his neck, realizing the men were building the room he was supposed to share with *her*.

"I look forward to meeting your father," Rebecca said, and she seemed sincere enough.

"I'd like to bring you up to meet him tomorrow." Isaac looked into her eyes. They were definitely green today. Cat eyes. He thought of the way she moved, refined but fluid, with sort of a feline grace. "You could stay the night in the new room, and the next day we can have the wedding there." He swallowed on the last words, forcing them out. "Pop will serve as chaperone."

"That sounds fine. You know, this may sound funny, but when I met Mr. Preston, and he showed me your letter requesting a 'God-fearing woman,' I felt as though God had a hand in it."

"Is that right?" Isaac said. More like Pop had a hand in it.

Some of that dry humor must have come out in his voice or in his expression, because she looked at him a little oddly, as if she were trying to decide if he were laughing at her. He quickly wiped the humor from his face.

He remembered Pop saying he'd prayed for the right woman. But why would God choose to bring him this tiny female?

Isaac looked thoughtfully at their hands, lying side by side on the seat.

His own hands were big, with broad, square knuckles, and sun-darkened skin. Hers looked small and pale in comparison. His palms perspired, and he clenched at the fabric of the settee to dry them. Every instinct within him told him to take her hand in his, such a small thing. And as they fell into another one of their long, awkward silences, he knew he had to.

She was going to be *his wife*.

He closed his fingers over hers, and his mouth dried to ashes. Her skin was so cool and silky smooth against his work-roughened fingers. A jolt of awareness skittered across his skin. It scared the tar out of him.

Isaac traced her face with his eyes. He caught the fresh scent of her soap—something lemony. Nothing flowery or exotic. The simplicity of it eased some of his anxiety. Maybe she wasn't as starched-up and fancy as she looked.

Who was he kidding?

She had a Dresden-doll face, tiny porcelain hands, tiny everything. She'd need constant protection. He'd have to watch out for her on the mountain or she'd get eaten alive. A hearty, frontier woman would have been more suited to share his kind of life, not someone who'd likely faint at the sight of a bear.

Becky enjoyed the feel of Isaac's warm fingers around hers, but it brought up the strangest feeling, as if she was being disloyal to Jack, which was completely and utterly absurd. Jack was married to another woman.

But he was still her first and only love...

Becky moistened her lips. She hadn't expected Isaac's touch, not at all, and didn't know what to say or do now. All she could think about was how different he was than her first impression of him. Standing in the Pearsons' foyer yesterday, he'd looked like he could take down just about any man in a fight. But the way he held her hand was so gentle. Tentative, even. Maybe he was afraid of scaring her. That must be it. Beneath that rough exterior of his hid a man of warmth and sensitivity. Respectful. She couldn't say how she knew it, but she did. She also knew he worked hard. His hands bore all the signs of countless hours of manual labor. And his eyes were sincere.

She smiled at him self-consciously.

"Will you marry me, Rebecca Sullivan?" Isaac asked and gripped her fingers. The searching look he gave her left her strangely rattled.

Had he really just asked her to marry him, even after she'd traveled so far to be his bride?

"Yes, I'll marry you, Isaac Jessup," she answered quietly. It wasn't like theirs was a love match. Even so, it was nice to be asked.

Nine

The next day, Isaac rode with Rebecca up the trail leading to his cabin. Whenever he looked back at her, he was concerned with the way she was perched on the sidesaddle. She looked unhappy, as if she feared she might slide off any moment.

He turned back and closed his eyes briefly.

Evidently, she didn't ride much. It was a skill she'd need on the mountain. There were no carriages here, no brick-paved roads—just rocks, packed dirt, and exposed roots. He focused on the trail ahead, stuffing his misgivings down, determined to make the best of it. He'd given her his word—given Pop his word—and he wouldn't back out now. Even so, he checked every now and then to make sure she hadn't fallen off.

Becky followed Isaac up the mountain on a spirited, chestnut mare with a dark mane. She regretted telling Isaac she rode sidesaddle back at the livery. She hated sidesaddles, but hadn't wanted to spoil his impression of her as a proper young lady. Her skirts and voluminous petticoats formed a lump under her, making it worse. It felt like she'd never ridden before. And the mare knew it. She was a feisty little thing who'd reached back to nip at Becky's skirts several times.

Her mount whinnied and tossed her head.

Oh no you don't. Becky scowled and took a firmer grip on the reins. If she'd learned anything from riding China, it was to never let a horse think it was the boss.

She wished she could ride astride like she did back home, bareback, with the wind whipping through her hair. Thoughts of home made her glad she'd had a chance to post a letter to her mother before they'd left town. With Isaac living so far from town, she couldn't help wondering when her next opportunity to send another letter would be.

The mare settled into a comfortable walk, and Becky bent forward to pat her neck and whisper a few praises. The mare twitched her ears back and preened. Saucy little thing. Becky smiled.

Soon she was lost in the beauty surrounding her. The trees towered above them all around, getting taller and taller, wider and wider. It seemed as if they were reaching into the sky and blocking the light. They'd entered a secret under-world—one of fragrant pine needles and cool mountain air, air that snuck in through the seams in her coat and dress. The smell of pitch and earth was soothing, and she felt a sense of belonging that surprised her. This was a land she could come to love.

The far-off noises of wood cracking and men yelling out were the only signs of logging she'd heard along the way, but it was quiet here.

"What kind of trees are these?" she asked in a hushed voice, not wanting to disturb the peace.

Isaac looked around, pride of ownership evident in the straight set of his shoulders. He seemed so at home in this place. "That's red cedar there. White pine, Sitka spruce, hemlock." He pointed each out to her and then paused at the base of a giant trunk. His head tilted way back, an expression of awe crossing over his features. "And this is a Douglas fir."

Becky stared at its huge base, wider than her father's store front. She let her gaze travel up the trunk to the prickly limbs hanging above them at a staggering height. "It's beautiful."

"I'm glad you think so." He gave her a quick smile and nudged his huge bay gelding up the path. The skid loaded with her trunks skipped along behind him, making clunking noises as it went over the rocks and roots.

Finally, they came to a weathered shack in a clearing. She peered more closely at the building as Isaac pulled his mount to a halt and dismounted. There were two little windows flanking the front door. What looked like curtains on the inside.

Her stomach dropped.

Was this his *house*?

She hadn't expected anything grand, but this? Her sense of majesty crashed like a felled tree. He must have caught her look of disappointment for his cheeks reddened. Becky felt a twist of shame at her reaction—this was his home after all.

Isaac grasped her waist and swung her down from her mount. Becky stood on legs that trembled from the effort to stay on the unfamiliar sidesaddle and watched as Isaac led the horses to a lean-to. He tethered them, removed their saddles, and gave them a quick brush down. After shaking a helping of hay out for them and filling their water trough, he swiftly unloaded the skid, stacking her trunks in a neat pile on the cabin's porch. All the while Becky had itched to help with the horses. She could have at least helped with brushing down her mount, but she hesitated to offer and then the opportunity had slipped by.

The quiet was broken by the sounds of hens clucking in a chicken coop off to one side of the lean-to. *They must keep them for eggs*, she thought, as there didn't seem to be enough hens to supply them with roasters as well. She also heard the sound of hammers thudding and the rasp of saws, coming from the rear of the cabin.

Isaac approached her with an uncertain-looking smile.

"Here we are," he announced simply. Was that a sigh of resignation?

She forced a smile. It wasn't what she'd expected, but she'd make the best of it. Big houses with fancy stoops had never meant that much to her anyway.

"Pop's got a crew of loggers out back finishing up the addition," he said, talking over the noise. He led her inside and pointed out a newly hung door at the back of the cabin. "That's what all the racket is."

An addition.

He meant a new bedroom. Theirs.

"Oh." Her voice was barely a squeak.

She stared around the cramped one-room cabin with dismay, and corrected herself: two-room cabin. A huge black stove in the corner consumed much of the kitchen area. The air was close and warm, and smelled of burnt pine pitch. A small table with three ladder-backed chairs hugged one wall. On another wall stood a pair of twin beds made of rough logs, with an old wooden trunk separating them. Pieced-together potato sacks hung from the ceiling, and a loop of leather cord held the simple makeshift curtain against the wall. *They must close it at night when one of them is sleeping,* she thought.

This was to be her new home? It made her parents' cramped apartment seem like a palace. She was all too aware of Isaac standing at her side, his expression guarded, yet a little expectant.

"It's—it's nice," she stammered lamely. "Cozy."

"It's small, I know," he apologized miserably and cast a

disgusted glance around the room.

The door to the addition opened behind him and a tall, wiry man ducked through. He was much older than Isaac, but the square jaw was much the same, as was the nice straight nose. He had the most startling white hair Becky had ever seen, pulled back into a queue at the back of his neck. His skin was deeply tanned, and when he smiled at her, crinkles appeared at the corners of his eyes. It was clear he was accustomed to long hours in the sun.

"Rebecca, this is my father, Sam Jessup," Isaac introduced his father with what seemed like an air of relief.

Becky looked up at the man. His silvery-blue eyes sparkled as they met hers, and he thrust out a large hand toward her. She took it in both of hers and smiled in delight. He was a character from a Western dime story, complete with fringed, leather shirt and a pair of faded denim trousers with a hole in the knee.

"It's a pleasure to meet you, Mr. Jessup."

"That's Sam to you, gal." He patted her hand, as if pleased at her welcome. Then he spoke in an aside to Isaac. "I can sure pick 'em—right, Son?"

"Pop," Isaac said, dragging the name out, his tone filled with exasperation.

Becky watched their interchange, puzzled at Isaac's look of warning and Sam's expression of wounded innocence. And what did Sam mean by "pick 'em"? What a peculiar thing to say. Pick what?

"So, tomorrow's the big day," he seemed to take great pleasure in the announcement.

"Right, Pop, tomorrow." Isaac was wearing that slightly sick look again, the same look she'd spied on his face that first day in the Pearsons' parlor. He hustled her away from his father, leading her by the elbow to the back corner of the cabin. "This is the kitchen," he pointed out the obvious, with what she took to be a hint of desperation in his voice.

"Yep, and it's time to eat," Sam announced. He approached the great, black stove with a sense of purpose.

When he lifted the lid on the pot, Becky almost fainted at the smell. Boiled beans. She'd had enough boiled beans on her voyage to Seattle to last ten lifetimes. The smell alone was like a slap. She closed her eyes briefly to steady herself, then swallowed as the floor began to pitch like the decks of the ship beneath her feet. Her head felt too light, as if she were falling.

"You look right peaked." Sam glanced over at her with a look of concern.

Peaked? He must mean hungry.

"No, sir, not really." She was frantic now, but feared offending him. "I ate before we left the Pearsons'." *Five hours ago,* she added silently. Isaac had arrived several hours after breakfast to lead her up the mountain, and she'd felt a few hunger rumbles on the way, but now all her stomach did was churn.

"Nonsense. You'll eat with us. There's plenty." Sam shoveled out globs of thick, brown mess into three wooden bowls. "Now, make yourself at home."

Isaac held out a chair for her, and she sat, biting back a groan. She was doomed.

Sam set a plate of salted pork in the middle of the table and scooped a helping onto the top of her beans—just like every meal she'd been served aboard ship. Her stomach rocked. Her lips pressed shut of their own accord. Staring down into her bowl, she shook her head in an imperceptible refusal.

She couldn't eat it. She just couldn't.

The men took their seats and, after Sam gave the blessing, they both tucked into their meal with enthusiasm. Isaac's eyes were filled with question as they met hers. She smiled back grimly and lifted a tiny portion to her mouth. She forced her lips open and tried to imagine a feast of roasted wild turkey and new potatoes as she clamped down on the fork with her teeth. The undeniable taste of boiled beans and salted pork met her tongue—waxy, briny, slippery...

Every night she'd spent with her head hanging off her bunk over a pail came back to her, making her eyes water. She bit her lip in despair, pushing away from the table with a jerk. The hot air in the cabin thickened. She couldn't get a breath. Suffocating. She hurried desperately toward a door off the kitchen area and hoped it led outside. Swinging it open, she spied the privy and stumbled across the yard toward it. She escaped inside, promptly losing her breakfast. As she sagged to the floor, too weak to stand, the miserable smell of the place assaulted her.

What must Isaac and his father think of her, tearing out of their home without even a word of apology?

She moaned and pushed against the door. It wouldn't budge. As she pounded on the rough boards with her fists, a marble of panic lodged in her throat. She was stuck in the privy. The foul air choked her. She pressed her nose into a long crack in the door and tried to snuffle in some fresh air. With renewed energy, she heaved her body against the door and fell out onto the ground in a flurry of skirts and petticoats. When she raised her head, she saw a pair of men's work boots—Isaac's boots. Funny she would recognize them.

"Are you all right, Rebecca?" he murmured. His deep rumble of a voice sounded concerned.

Her cheeks burned. Her face was likely a bright shade of red. His hand appeared before her face, and she stared at it a moment, undecided. She swallowed her embarrassment and took it.

"I— The door was stuck," she mumbled, refusing to look up at him.

"It does that sometimes. You've got to give it a good push." He lifted her easily to her feet, his dark brown eyes searching hers, evidently trying to decide if this was a one time thing or if she was a sickly sort of person in general. She thought she detected a sense of awkwardness in him, as he stepped back to lead her into the cabin. Probably wondering what he'd gotten himself into.

And here she'd always prided herself on her sturdy constitution.

Becky sighed as she watched his back, brushing the dirt off her skirt and trailing after him.

Sam had a glass of cold water ready, which she accepted gratefully. They were both truly kind, not questioning her about her hurried dash out of the cabin. Isaac seemed almost overly kind. She caught his concerned gaze sweeping over her face several times. He was likely thinking her a complete hoyden. After she finished her drink, Isaac retired to the back room, saying he had some work to do. As she sat with Sam listening to his stories of the frontier, she relived her race for the privy in her mind, burning with mortification.

So much for all her efforts to appear the perfect lady.

While Pop kept Rebecca company, Isaac helped the crew finish nailing down the roof over the addition. When they were done, he waved them away, back to the logging camp, and set about a thought-provoking task—building his marriage bed. As he adjusted the support ropes for the mattress, his nerves tightened with each twist and pull. He knotted the rope and sat back on his heels, wiping his brow with a handkerchief. Tomorrow he was getting married, to a woman who was more a stranger than a bride. He groaned. Indecision tugged at him. Why had he committed to marrying her?

He lifted the new feather-tick mattress and tossed its cumbersome bulk onto the rope webbing. It was a good bed, he decided, giving it a look of satisfaction. He tucked in the white linen sheets he'd bought at the general store in town this morning before fetching Rebecca from the Pearsons'. At least he had money to provide for a wife, if not a lovely home. As a logger in this wild mountain country, all he could offer Rebecca was a hard life and lonely days.

Why, it wasn't even safe up here in the mountains with the wild animals and all...

He rested one hand on the headboard—gripped the wood.

What was he doing? She obviously couldn't take care of herself, could barely stay in a saddle, and from her strange behavior at lunch, she had a delicate constitution to boot. And yet he couldn't imagine backing out now. He couldn't imagine letting Pop down either. His father's wishes were simple, and when Isaac was being honest with himself, he admitted he'd always wanted a family someday. He just hadn't pictured it coming together this way.

There had been times he'd thought about it. Usually he pictured himself going into town, maybe having a place there, which made no sense. Why would he do that? But in his scenario it had somehow made sense. He'd imagined courting a woman there, maybe. They'd fall in love. They'd eventually marry. They'd *know* each other. But that wasn't an option now—never had been. It had been a dream. Nothing more. His wedding was tomorrow afternoon, and he'd committed to it.

Ten

As Jem approached the Jessups' logging camp, a mixture of wariness and optimism built in his chest. He'd heard tell of Isaac Jessup being a fair boss. Evidently, he knew the business and had risen from the bottom of a logging crew to owning an operation in a matter of years.

That's where Jem needed to be.

He'd learn the business from the top man firsthand, and with a little sweat and a lot of luck, he'd be someone of consequence someday too. If only to show Pa he weren't no "good for nothing."

Jem cussed under his breath at the thought of his pa. He tried to forget all about him as he strode with purpose toward the Jessups' camp cookhouse. The place looked deserted, which was odd for this time of day. Usually the loggers would be getting ready to sit down to their chow about now. Forcing his impatience down, he took a calming breath. No matter. He'd wait. He had all the time in the world.

Restless energy prevented him from sitting on a fallen log outside of the cookhouse, so he paced back and forth.

All the time in the world seemed too long to wait.

Jem smacked his palm against the huge tree stump taking up a good deal of space in the camp clearing. He liked the pounding feeling going up his arm and through his entire body. He'd been so numb for years, feeling anything was a nice change. The rough bark under his skin felt good and right—like he was connected to this place.

This was his future all right.

He could almost taste it.

Even so, his goal loomed before him like an insurmountable peak. He had to climb it was all. He had to find a way—*any* way—to be better than his beginnings. And Pa need never know what he made of his life. No, not ever.

Jem never wanted to be in the man's company again. Not even for one more day.

All that mattered was seeing it for himself.

That'd prove Pa wrong.

Eleven

The wedding the next day was simple and quick. Becky felt more like a spectator than a bride as she clutched her simple bouquet of wildflowers. Isaac had surprised her with them just before the ceremony, making her blush. He stood beside her, reminding her again of a great oak towering over her. Before them was a weathered old miner, who also served as a preacher to the logging camp. Their vows were simply and quietly spoken, but felt strange, committing their lives and love when they scarcely knew one another. In the blink of an eye, she was a married woman, complete with a simple gold band.

A group of loggers with droopy handlebar mustaches and red suspenders jostled together in the tiny cabin. At first, the men seemed to hang back a little, nodding respectfully to Becky and looking at Isaac as if he were every inch the boss-man he appeared. At one point, they collectively appeared to gather their courage and took turns punching Isaac in the arm and whispering into his ear. He laughed with them ruefully and occasionally glanced in Becky's direction. He looked uneasy to her, which didn't inspire much confidence.

A burly man with red hair took his turn punching on Isaac's arm. He had a great booming voice that carried like a carnival leader's, so it caught Becky's attention from across the room. "Should've had old Sam fix me up with a bride too. She's a looker—sure you won't change your mind? I could use a wife—"

She grew absolutely still, transfixed on the man's face, and yet trying desperately not to let anyone know she was watching him. Listening.

That she'd *heard*.

But she had.

"Brody." Isaac wasn't speaking nearly as loudly, and his voice probably wouldn't have carried to her across the room if she weren't looking directly at him, watching his lips move. She also saw how he tried to silence Brody with a stern look.

"I wouldn't mind getting a surprise like that one day," another one of the men said, thrusting a jug of whiskey into Brody's hands and spilling some of the golden brew onto the floor in the process.

Becky watched as Isaac grabbed the jug and shoved the dangling cork in place. He tossed the jug back to one of the laughing loggers and growled at them. "Save it, men."

She scarcely registered the events going on around her. An image of Sam teasing Isaac yesterday came to mind and claimed all of her attention.

I can sure pick 'em—right, Son?

That's what he'd said. It hadn't made sense at the time.

Sam's words whirled in Becky's head.

And then everything fell into place.

The room tilted around her in the heat. The heady smell of spilt whiskey was nauseating. She'd nearly bent her bouquet of wildflowers in two she'd gripped them so hard. They were ruined now, wilting anyway. She might as well throw them out...

Isaac's father came right up to her then. Maybe he'd been watching her all this time. "You all right?" he asked.

"Just tired, I guess. I think I'll—" She gestured weakly to

the door at the back, the one that led to the new addition they'd built. For her. And Isaac.

Isaac.

He hadn't sent for her.

He hadn't wanted any of this.

It all made so much sense now. Every look he'd sent her way. The doubts she'd felt coming off him.

She was such a fool.

She'd come all this way. Thought it was an answer to prayer.

But how could it be?

Sam had sent for her. Not Isaac. What grown man would want to marry a woman *his father* had picked out for him?

Sam must have seen her dart one more stricken glance at Brody and Isaac, for he winced ever so slightly, enough for her to notice. Enough to realize it was all *true*.

"He may have been reluctant at first, but..." Sam's voice trailed off at the disbelieving look she sent him.

She had to get out of here—now.

Becky flashed an apologetic smile at Sam, because no matter what he'd done or why, she found she couldn't stop liking him. Before he could say anything else, she escaped into the room at the back where she'd slept last night—the room she was supposed to share with Isaac tonight. She looked around numbly. The space was scarcely big enough for the large double bed and one wardrobe, both of which looked new. The wardrobe looked broad enough to store her things and Isaac's as well, but the doors hung a bit crooked. His men were hopefully better loggers than carpenters.

The thought failed to make her smile.

Probably because she kept circling back to the fact that Isaac hadn't sent for her.

She sank onto the edge of the bed. Their marriage bed. She stared at nothing for a long while, the ruined flowers in her lap, her gaze fixed on the wall, making shapes out of the wood grain:

A cloud. A whale. A swirl. Maybe smoke.

Jack hadn't wanted her and now Isaac too? She'd been *foisted* upon him—that much was evident. Would she always be Isaac's obligation? He seemed a moral man—he probably married her out of duty, to please his father. She moaned and bowed her head.

I'm an unwanted bride.

She was about to throw the crushed wildflowers out the window, when she stopped and, with a sigh at her own sentimentality, placed them in her trunk, on top of everything else she'd brought from home. She undressed quickly, throwing on her nightgown, hardly conscious of her actions. But there were men in the other room. She felt their presence, heard chairs scraping across the floor. The sound of male voices and laughter. At least someone was happy. She crawled into the bed and covered herself with the white sheet. It looked new, crisp and a little stiff. She crossed her arms protectively over her heart against the pain, refusing to cry. Her tears seemed frozen inside. Now, more than ever, she missed Mama. The dim shadows outside deepened to black as she stared out the lone window. Despite her confusion, she registered the sounds of the men dwindling to a murmur.

Isaac would come to her soon.

She lay, lifeless and sad, imagining a very different wedding day, marrying someone who wanted her—who would love and cherish her. An image of Jack's face floated into her mind. But Jack had chosen Melody. She sighed.

It was stupid to think about Jack now.

It had been stupid since the day she'd found out he was married.

Stupid heart.

It didn't know any better.

Her eyelids grew heavy, and she eventually began to drift away...

Once the last of the men emptied out of the cabin, Pop pushed Isaac into one of the rough ladder-backed chairs surrounding the kitchen table and pulled another across from him, straddling it with his lanky thighs. He rubbed his palms over the knees of his best denims, as though relishing whatever he was fixing to say.

"Son, I realize you know the particulars about babies and such, but there's more to loving a woman than bare facts."

This ought to be interesting, Isaac thought with a sick wrench of his belly. Embarrassment was sure to follow.

"An untried woman needs a tender touch, and keep it sorta quick tonight— not that you're likely to go long with it being your first time and all—"

"Aw, Pop." Nothing he said could have made Isaac feel more like he was seventeen again. His neck burned with a creeping heat.

"I'm not blind, you know. Anyways, it may be a week or so before your wife can enjoy the act—leastways, that's how it was with your mama and me, but then she turned out to be a generous lover." Pop's eyes grew wistful.

"Do you have to talk about Mama that way?" Isaac groaned.

"What? Don't tell me I've raised a prude?" His father's

shaggy, white brows lifted inquiringly. Pop was frontier to the bone and had the disconcerting habit of speaking his mind.

"No, no. Anything else you feel the need to say?" Isaac tapped his fingers nervously against the table and stole a glance at the door at the back of the cabin.

"Well, one more thing, I guess, and I'll be off." Pop rubbed a hand along the back of his neck, his eyes lit with wry amusement.

"You're leaving?" Isaac couldn't keep the hope out of his voice.

"Yep. I'm not staying the night, Son. In fact, I'm planning on staying with Brody for a spell. This way you two can get accustomed to married life for a while—without your father in the next room."

"Thank you." There was relief in that at least. "One more thing?"

"Oh, yeah. It's not all about you—remember that." Pop gave an emphatic nod. "Well, I guess I'll head out. You go on in—"

Pop was leaving. In two seconds he'd be out the door.

And Isaac would be alone.

With Rebecca waiting in the other room.

"Pop," he said, stopping him. "I don't even really know her. We're still strangers. It's sort of awkward. Don't you think I should wait a while before—you know?" Isaac asked, filled with the most excruciating embarrassment he'd ever felt in his life. He'd get over it though. This was his father. Who better to ask?

"What better way to get to know her?" His father's voice was flat, his gaze dead serious.

"Pop!"

"What did I say?" Pop was all innocence. "You'll see. It'll

66

all work out, Son. This Rebecca's the right gal. Remember I told you I prayed God would send the right woman for you?"

He'd prayed about it, but never thought to ask Isaac if he wanted a bride? That would seem the next logical step. Isaac shook his head in disbelief.

"Oh, Pop." He pushed his chair back from the table a bit and faced his father with a feeling of grim determination.

"You're not going into battle, Son. Relax. This part might be a trifle awkward, I'll grant you that, but once you get the hang of it—"

"Out. Get out of the house." Isaac was up out of his chair so quick he nearly toppled it backwards. He pointed toward the door.

"All right, all right. I know when I've gone too far," Sam said with a chuckle. He swung his leg over the back of the chair like he was dismounting a horse. He grabbed up his hat from the nail by the door and jammed it onto his snow-white head. For a moment, he simply stood, looking at the door, then he turned with a misty-eyed expression and tugged Isaac to him for a quick hug.

"I only want the best for you, boy. I hope someday you'll see that."

"I know, Pop. I'm not sure I can say thanks yet, but at least I think I'm coming to understand your thinking." Isaac tried to put his father at ease, certain he'd never understand what had possessed his father to send back East for a bride. A bride who was waiting for him through the back door. He glanced at it apprehensively, and his father gave him a little push in the right direction.

The sound of Pop's laughter echoed as the front door closed behind him, and Isaac stood alone facing the door to his new bedroom.

Twelve

*I*saac found his new bride sleeping. Perhaps it was the sign he'd been searching for. He'd felt uncertain about consummating the marriage since they didn't know each other. So maybe this was his answer. They should wait awhile—get to know each other.

He'd just drifted off to sleep, when a soft, feminine voice woke him.

"You're back?"

What an odd question, Isaac thought. Was he back?

"Um, yes?" he said, suddenly fully awake.

"I missed you, darling."

Darling? Isaac's heart skipped a beat at the unexpected endearment.

"You have?" he asked warily. Something wasn't quite right with her voice, her manner. Like she was talking in her sleep, maybe.

"I thought you'd never come back."

"Is that right?" He stilled as she leaned close, her breath tickling his ear.

"Jack..." Her whisper was strangely demure seeing as her lips were now trailing across his cheek.

Jack?

It took all Isaac's will to hold still and not explode from the bed.

"Who's Jack?" he asked carefully, so as not to wake her.

Her sleepy laugh warmed his cheek.

"Oh, Jack." Her lips gently brushed his, the slightest touch, really, but it felt like a fire. "Darling."

She'd said it twice now—*darling*—and both times it soured his belly.

"So, you love this 'Jack' fellow?" he asked, appalled at the slight croak in his voice.

"Love you? Of course I love you. You're my sun, moon, and stars." She punctuated each celestial being with a little kiss.

Had this *Jack* taught her to kiss? Isaac groaned silently, ashamed to find himself enjoying each soft kiss, despite the fact that he wasn't her intended target—*Jack* was.

"Dance with me?" She hummed a few sleepy notes, enough for him to recognize a lively waltz.

He froze as she rested her hand on his shoulder. The touch of her fingers against his nightshirt. They burned right through.

His wife loved another man.

His blood slowed to a trickle, like an icy mountain stream.

"Wake up or go to sleep, but either way, no more kissing." He pushed her resolutely away. "Go back to sleep," he repeated more firmly. It was the tone he used with his men when something urgent needed done. The tone they jumped to.

She rolled over and snuggled into her pillow with a sigh.

"Yes, Mama," she mumbled, at which point she promptly began to snore—a delicate, feminine-sounding snore—but she was asleep nonetheless.

She'd obviously done this sleep-awake talking before. Somehow he felt she should have warned him about that.

A burst of anger hit him hard and fast on the tail of that thought.

She should have told him *a lot* of things.

She'd come out here to marry a stranger—to marry *him*, Isaac—when she loved another man? Why? Tonight, in her sleep, she'd laughed playfully, *kissed* him, and seemed a different person altogether. If she'd been widowed, wouldn't she have said so? Of course she would have. Besides, she seemed too young to have been married. So who was Jack?

Who are you, Rebecca Sullivan?

Rebecca Jessup, he corrected himself.

And then he thought: *I'm married to a woman who's in love with another man.*

The realization took the heat out of his anger fast. All he felt was empty.

If she loves this Jack fellow, how can she ever come to love me?

The pain of that thought revealed one thing: he'd begun to hope they could build a loving marriage like the one his father and mother had enjoyed. Sure, he'd started out with thoughts of pleasing Pop, but to Isaac's mind marriage was a lifelong commitment, one he didn't take lightly. Somewhere along the way, he'd resolved to give it his all. And he'd let himself indulge in some imaginary tender feelings for his little wife. Heaven help him, he'd dared to imagine she might come to care for him too.

Her loving another man changed all that. Their whole marriage was one big glaring mistake.

Well, he obviously couldn't touch her now. It wouldn't be right, would it?

Of course not.

Maybe someday she'd forget this Jack. Maybe he'd fade from her memory in time...

How long would that take?

If ever.

Isaac stared sightlessly up at the ceiling until, at last, he managed to sleep for a few hours perhaps.

When he woke again, he found Rebecca turned toward him, her eyes wide open, staring at him.

Becky watched her husband, amazed at the sight of a man sharing the pillow next to hers. From the light peeking in through the curtains, she knew it was certainly morning. Her wedding night was over. She barely remembered anything, save a vague memory of a kiss or two...?

Or had that been a dream?

One thing was sure—Isaac had shared her bed last night, because he was here, right beside her, fixing her with the most intense stare. It was like he was trying to pry a confession from her. As if she'd done something wrong.

She wrinkled her brow, wondering what she'd done.

He gave an embarrassed sounding cough as her gaze wandered to the open neck of his nightshirt. She quickly averted her eyes.

Had he tried to wake her up last night? Her cheeks warmed at the thought of him watching her sleep. What a strange and awkward marriage they'd tumbled into. She looked into her husband's deep brown eyes, eyes holding a hint of reproach. She nearly groaned aloud. The perfect wife wouldn't have slept through her wedding night, would she?

"I'm sorry for falling asleep last night. You should've woken me up." She gave him a shy, apologetic smile and snuggled down into her pillow, waiting for him to respond.

How very, very strange to have a man beside her. She may as well have been walking down Main Street in her nightclothes—

that's how strange it felt.

On the heels of that thought she remembered what she'd learned last night. Isaac hadn't sent for her. Sam had.

She should ask him. She should ask him straight out if he wanted to be married to her or not.

She moistened her lips. Tried to form the words.

How could she?

Time would tell, soon enough, wouldn't it? She could at least try to make the best of it.

Isaac shifted under Rebecca's inquiring eyes. He had to confront her about this Jack fellow.

So…who's Jack?

Is there anyone back home—anyone important *I should know about?*

But he couldn't get the words out. It was all too humiliating.

She never claimed to love me. In fact, she'd said she didn't expect a love match. Was that why? Because she already loved another man?

The little smile she was giving him turned his belly all soft and warm. She had no call to smile at him that way when she loved another man.

He had to do it.

He had to swallow his discomfort and ask.

Get it out in the open.

Clear the air.

Okay then.

Anytime now.

Turning onto his side toward her, he propped himself on

one elbow and rested his head on his hand. He stared at her for a moment and asked, "Who's Jack?"

"Jack?" She stiffened a little and moistened her lips.

"Yes, *Jack*. I think you know who I mean?" At her miserable looking nod, he continued, "Didn't you think I deserved to know that your heart is consigned to another? *Before* we got married?"

"I... I..." She stammered, and her brow wrinkled in confusion.

He waited. His heart seemed intent on hammering as loudly as his construction crew banging on the roof a couple of days ago.

Her throat worked and, after a minute of looking around the room as if for answers, her gaze met his, and she nodded jerkily. "You're right. You had a right to know. And I—and I'm sorry. My heart's not free. That—that's true. I won't lie."

"I see." He felt his jaw clench with equal parts anger and hurt.

"And what about you?" she whispered.

"I'm not in love with anybody."

Something flickered in her eyes, recognition of what he'd just said, but some other expression he couldn't read. Some womanly thing probably. How should he know?

"I—"

"Never have been," he added for good measure. Which probably revealed more than he'd intended, he realized belatedly.

"I mean, what about you not sending for me? What about that?"

She had a point there. He hadn't told her.

He still didn't feel like bringing it out in the open.

Now look what you've done, Pop. See? What a fine mess.

"I—"

"Exactly," she said, a slight militant glint in her eye, as if she wasn't going to let him get away with anything. Good to know.

"I'm sorry," he said. "Maybe I should have said something." It was a small admission. "I was just trying to spare your feelings."

She pressed her lips closed. Maybe she was trying to hold her words back. He also got the impression she was waiting for something, for understanding to catch up with him, and it did.

To spare her feelings.

That's what he'd said.

And she hadn't told him about Jack for the same reason.

It wasn't nearly the same. He told her that with a level glance.

The look she gave him seemed a little wounded, as if he'd hurt her. And that wasn't at all what he'd intended.

His conscience tweaked him. Okay, maybe a little. But just the smallest amount.

Because *loving another man* was on an entirely different scale than the secret he'd kept from her. Entirely different. What Pop had done, they could've laughed about that one day, years down the road when they were happy, with a handful of children running around.

And now he had a headache.

He'd meant to stay home today, to spend some time showing her around the area, maybe taking a walk down by the stream together. He'd envisioned quite a different day, but now he couldn't bear hanging around and pretending all was well between them. He needed some space to breathe and to think.

"I've got work to tend to today. Understand? I'll leave you

74

so you can dress." He quickly pushed the covers off and jerked on his pants, which were lying over the chair next to the bed. He spared a thought to be grateful that his nightshirt came down over his knees, sparing them both more embarrassment. He flicked a glance at her, seeing her wide-eyed look of apology. Before he could say something he regretted, he grabbed up his work shirt and marched into the other room so he could finish dressing in privacy, leaving Rebecca to do the same.

About twenty minutes later, he watched as she prepared breakfast. The black stove dominating the corner had been his mother's. It belched up clouds of smoke occasionally, true, but it got the job done.

He noticed that Rebecca seemed a bit jumpy with the skillet, and she'd burned the first round of flapjacks. It puzzled him, and he frowned at her back as she ladled out another batch with a big wooden spoon. Her excessively full skirts seemed out of place in the tiny cabin, a constant reminder that she belonged in some city somewhere, not up here in the forest. But, to his mind, even a city girl should at least know how to cook. Or maybe she came from one of those houses where servants did all the work? That didn't bode well. Pop had made a mistake this time, for sure. How could a woman used to having servants do her bidding survive in a place like this?

His wife loved another man, and now she couldn't cook either.

Oh, this is getting better and better.

Rebecca placed a sad stack of blackened flapjacks before him, and he tried to offer her a grateful smile. He'd need about twice that amount plus a rasher of bacon to make it to noon, but he kept the thought to himself. He stuck his fork gingerly into the cakes and was rewarded by an ooze of batter.

"Oh, no! Let me put them back on." She looked frantic.

"No, don't bother," he said quickly. "That's how Pop makes them." It wasn't quite a lie. Pop couldn't make a decent flapjack either. He'd hoped she could at least take over the cooking duties, but that looked like it wasn't going to work out so well.

Isaac forced himself to eat the soggy cakes and pushed back from the table, squelching a groan.

"I'm, uh, going to go check on my men." He ducked his head, avoiding those vulnerable green eyes staring at him. It didn't feel right leaving her here alone. Plumb wrong, actually.

"Don't worry about me," she said. The way she lifted her chin made him feel she was just trying to put a brave face on it. "You've got work to do."

"Stay near the cabin. It's not safe to go off wandering," he warned, hesitating for a moment. Perhaps he should stay?

Stay and do what? Go for a walk with her? Pretend nothing had happened?

A band of pain tightened around his skull.

No, not today. He couldn't. He needed to get away—if only for a little while—to clear his head. He turned away and headed for the door.

Becky watched his lanky swagger as he crossed the room. He bumped into a huge crate of chains and kicked at it with the toe of his spiky-bottomed, calked boot, but he didn't bother to move it. Did they like living in this mess? Or maybe they just never had the time or energy to clean it. She stared as he closed the door behind him, leaving her alone.

As soon as the wooden door latch clunked into place, she sagged onto her chair, defeated. She groaned with embarrassment. Her first day as a wife and she'd neglected her wifely duties in the bedroom, admitted to his face that she loved another man, and now she'd failed to make him a decent meal. It was that ancient monster of a stove—it was impossible to control the temperature.

Isaac hadn't kissed her goodbye. It was a small stray thought that hit her from nowhere.

And why would he?

After her confession early this morning, he probably couldn't stand the sight of her. The day he'd held her hand in the Pearsons' parlor, she'd come to hope they could at least share some affection. She quelled the sharp feeling of loss that struck her. They were married right and proper now, and he was her husband. She'd be a good wife to him, a real helpmate—well, once she mastered that beast of a stove.

If only he knew how much she wished her heart *was* free. If she could somehow blink and make it happen—make herself *not* love Jack—she would, but that was impossible. That wasn't the way the heart worked, was it? She'd tried often enough to know it wasn't possible to wish love away, even an inconvenient love such as hers, the kind that wasn't returned. The one-sided kind.

The realization left her feeling unfit to be Isaac's bride. He wanted something more than she could give him. When he'd questioned her about Jack, she'd yearned to deny she was in love with someone else, but what else could she do except tell him the truth? To do any less would be showing him a lack of respect, and he'd been kind to her so far. Generous even. He'd paid for all the expenses for her journey out here, hadn't he? Or maybe Sam had, seeing as he was the one who'd sent for her, which a whole other headache. And, looking around, it seemed to Becky that neither one of them had a cent to spare.

Surely Sam had expected a woman to come whose heart was free. Isaac certainly had expected it. She'd seen as much in his face when he'd asked her about Jack. Accused her, more like it. He'd expected her to be honest with him up front.

She'd failed again.

She'd tried to point out that he hadn't exactly been fully honest either, but the look he'd given her had told her quite clearly what he thought of that: it wasn't the same.

He wasn't in love with anyone.

He *never* had been. That's what he said. Meaning he'd come into this marriage with his heart unattached. Completely.

Becky rested her forehead on the table, feeling a hundred failures weighing her down.

No matter how hard she tried, she just couldn't seem to fit in anywhere, could she? No. At home, Papa, Mama, and Rachel had been like a matched set of gold beads strung on a fine chain, and she'd been this one mismatched, ceramic bead. When she'd been removed from the chain, the family had finally seemed complete—like she'd never really belonged.

There was a good reason for that. She knew that now. Mama had told her their secret. She'd finally understood why Papa acted the way he did toward her. Because she wasn't his. Her mother was a woman she'd known only as Auntie Mari, a woman she'd barely known when she was alive. And she didn't even know who her real father was.

Becky forced her head off the table and looked around the tiny cabin, taking in the sooty wood floor and piles of unwashed dishes lying on every flat surface, left over from the wedding party yesterday. The place desperately needed cleaning. Here was one way to make herself useful to Isaac. Pushing away from the table, she gathered all the filthy dishes into the sink. Only then did she realize there was no pump. Isaac had given her a pitcher of fresh goat's milk earlier for the batter, so she hadn't needed water, hadn't noticed the missing pump. She groaned. At least at home there'd been a pump at the sink, a decent stove, and real furniture.

Heading outside, she found a water barrel next to the back door, but some large animal must have overturned it during the night, for the water had already seeped into the earth, making it slick and muddy. She resolutely traced her way back to the stream she'd crossed with Isaac on their trek up the mountain and hauled buckets back and forth to refill the barrel. She was strong enough for the task, but it wasn't long before she abandoned the perfectly proper crinoline she'd worn to impress Isaac. He wasn't around to notice the lack of fullness to her skirts anyway, and the stiffened hoops got in the way.

It took her nearly an hour to scootch and pull the heavy box of chains from the cabin all the way to the lean-to, but when she was done, she felt a sense of true accomplishment. The pretty coffee-brown filly she'd ridden up the mountain was still in the lean-to, and Becky stopped to give her a quick brushing. She'd miss the saucy mare when Isaac took her back to town. And he would for sure now, after what happened last night. She sighed and searched the coop for fresh eggs, but didn't find any.

Rubbing a sore spot at the small of her back, Becky went back inside to finish straightening up. By the time she finished, she was filthy. It looked like in the process of cleaning she'd transferred all the cabin's grime to her dress and skin. She desperately wanted and needed a nice hot bath, but that was impossible. There was no way she could fill the tin washtub with water. Absolutely no way. Every little muscle and tendon ached. She could barely move without cramping up.

Besides that, the stove was still a daunting challenge, one she was too tired to tackle. So she made do with a bucket of cold water to wash her hair, and rubbed her face and arms with a grayed cloth. The sad material must have been white once. To make matters worse, each trip to the privy that day had been a struggle with the blasted door, which kept trapping her inside the stuffy darkness.

Isaac had successfully avoided his father all morning, not the easiest of tasks. But with his father's focus on training the newer teams, he'd been able to stay out of sight by working with the more senior members of the outfit. Isaac was starting to think he might be able to slip away unnoticed, until he finally ran into his father late in the day.

"Just what do you think you're doing?" Pop demanded. Behind him came the ominous crack of timber, and then a shower of limbs and fragrant pine needles.

The crack echoed in Isaac's head.

"Working." *Best to keep it simple. Less to argue with.*

"You mean to tell me you left that little gal alone—the day after your wedding?" Pop shook his head in disbelief, and Isaac stiffened as his father's steel-blue eyes skimmed over him. It was clear he didn't like what he saw. "I raised you, Son, but if I didn't remember every minute of it, I'd be starting to wonder."

"Pop, please, just leave it?" Isaac turned and saw a Douglas fir downhill a ways, which two of his men were fixing to fell. He squinted and could see one of the men was Tanner, but he didn't recognize the other one. There was something about the young man—really not much more than a boy—that didn't quite sit right with Isaac. He started to move in their direction.

"Hold up there, Son." Pop placed a hand on his arm.

Isaac glanced over his shoulder to find his father scowling, the planes of his cheeks and the corners of his eyes creased with concern. Isaac turned back to him.

"Aw, Pop. Things are fine. We just need some time. Can you give us some time?"

Pop slowly nodded, but he looked hurt. Isaac wouldn't have hurt him for the world, but if he gave his father even a piece of the story Pop'd be digging at him with questions, like a persistent badger, until he had the whole of it. Isaac wasn't prepared to tell him the whole of it yet. Especially since he hadn't quite wrapped his mind around the situation himself.

"Thanks, Pop." He gripped his father's shoulder and looked him in the eye, letting him know there wasn't any big disaster to worry about. Or at least he made an attempt. Seeing a flicker of acceptance in his father's eyes, Isaac strode off to inspect the new youth's footing.

As he moved down the slope, he paused to check the progress of the peeler crew, a team of men who were stripping the bark off the felled pine, so it could slide more easily down the mountain to the Skid Road. From there the logs would eventually end up in Port Gamble, the sawmill where Isaac sent his logs to be cut and shipped. After satisfying himself that the work was progressing on schedule, he continued down the mountain.

As he approached the two-man falling team, he eyed the placement of the new young man's springboard to see if it was steady enough to support his weight. Up close, Isaac could see he was only about sixteen or seventeen, with the broad shoulders and muscled arms of a much older man. His dark bangs fell into his eyes, a hazard, but he seemed eager enough. Isaac took note of his awkward stance and decided he lacked experience.

"Tanner?" Isaac looked curiously at his logger standing beside the tree with the saw, an oilcan in his hand.

"Boss." Tanner acknowledged him with a respectful nod. "This here's Jem Wheeler. Came in yesterday."

Isaac looked up briefly, giving the young man a hard stare to let him know he was being sized up. He turned back to Tanner. The rough, taciturn man was one of his most experienced fallers, but in Isaac's present mood, he felt the need to be all over everybody.

"No one asked me about that," he said. "Did Pop bring him on?"

"No...your father wasn't around much yesterday. And, well, with your wedding and all, I figured you was too busy for a such a trifling crew decision." Tanner frowned, his manner now a mite edgy. "You got a problem with me, sir?"

"Just checking," Isaac said. He liked and admired Tanner, always had. He was a hard-working man—and had never been anything but respectful. And now Isaac had essentially called his judgment into question. Tanner didn't deserve that.

The logger nodded and climbed up on his springboard.

Isaac hesitated. An image flashed through his mind: Jem lying on the ground, his fresh face pale and lifeless. Maybe he should see to training Jem himself. "You're the finest faller I got, Tanner. In fact, why don't you go down and help Harper finish up? Almost quitting time, isn't it? I'll see to Jem."

"Yes, sir, Mr. Jessup," Tanner said. He hopped down from his perch and walked off, his body stiff-backed and proud.

Isaac stared after him for a moment and then turned to oil the falling saw—a ten-foot long, two-handled saw that he and Jem would use to slice through the thick trunk. But first they needed to cut a swath with the axes, so he hauled himself onto the springboard Tanner had already set up on the other side of the tree and grabbed the ax Tanner had left embedded in the trunk. Isaac soon lost himself to the rhythm of alternating chops, as he and Jem took turns at the tree. The steady thwack of metal against wood felt satisfying. This he could do.

After they formed a satisfactory undercut, Isaac looked over at Jem. "Ready to saw?"

"Yessir."

Pulling the saw was backbreaking work, but Isaac hadn't started out as the owner of a logging operation. He'd worked his way up from a peeler to a faller, back when he was about Jem's age, in fact. Back before he and Pop had enough capital to finance their own outfit. The steady sawing action left his mind a little too free to think about Rebecca and this man named Jack, who she'd admitted she loved. The thoughts doubled his efforts on the saw, until he feared poor Jem was going to fall off his springboard from sheer exhaustion.

Isaac showed Jem how to drive in the wedges to deepen the undercut so the saw could move freely, and after several more hours of tedious work, they were ready to make the final back cut.

When they were almost through cutting the backside of the tree, they called out a warning to clear the area.

"Jem," Isaac yelled over at his young falling partner.

"Boss?"

"Remember, loose branches come down fast and hard. When I say go, leap as far as you can and scramble on out of range. You hear?" Concern made Isaac's voice come out harsh and edgy.

"Yessir, boss. I've heard of 'em widda makers." Jem swallowed long and hard and ran a hand through his black hair.

"Well, we call them 'widow makers' for a reason. Don't ever forget that."

Jem swallowed hard again, and his face, if possible, paled more.

Good, Isaac thought, *he should be sober. He should be sober and quick.*

As they made their final cuts, the screaming cracks of a tree ready to fall pierced the air.

"Go!" Isaac leapt off his perch and took off running through the trees. The huge fir collapsed through the thick canopy of limbs above, sending a shower of branches to the ground. He turned back to watch in horror as a heavy limb landed on Jem's back, trapping him underneath.

"Jem!"

The tree landed with a reverberating crash. Isaac couldn't see the boy. He sprinted over, climbing over fallen limbs, scraping his hands and shins. There he was, an arm. Isaac hauled the heavy branch off him, praying as he pulled it off. *Please let Jem be unharmed.*

As soon as the branch rolled off him, the young man levered himself up on his elbow and grinned at Isaac. His eyes were alight with excitement.

"We felled 'er, boss."

"I told you to get out of range." Isaac laid into him, hard and fast, his heart still racing painfully in his chest. "This isn't a game, boy. You could've been killed. Now, go! Get on back to camp," he ordered, pointing, then leaned his hands against his thighs and just breathed. He was shaking.

"Sorry, boss."

Isaac could see Jem hanging back in his peripheral vision.

"Just get on back to camp." Isaac said, struggling to speak

in a more measured tone. It had all happened so quick. It could've been worse, much worse. Jem looking cowed and very young, but he still didn't seem to fully get it. How could he? He was young. He'd survived. He had a story to tell his friends. Isaac could almost hear him bragging about it now.

Isaac shook his head. All he wanted to do was yell at the boy, but he snapped his mouth shut. Sending Jem away was the only way to protect him from a fresh outburst, so he waved the youth on.

He kept an eye on Jem as he slunk off in the direction of the bunkhouse. But what he really saw was that branch falling, taking Jem down, trapping him.

For the next hour or so, Isaac pushed his men harder than usual. The incident with Jem was weighing on him. And all the thinking about Rebecca loving this Jack fellow only added to his strain. As he was packing up to head home, he saw some of his men walking through the trees ahead, their voices carrying back to him.

"What do you think's got into the boss?" That was Tanner's voice.

"Maybe there's something amiss with the new Missus," Harper whispered back a little too loudly, for Isaac could hear him fine.

"I don't know, but we're gonna break like twigs if he keeps pushing us so hard."

"You got that right." Their voices grew fainter as they moved away.

Isaac watched with a pang of guilt as his men trudged off in the direction of the logging camp. They looked weary. He had pushed them hard. It wasn't right to take out his frustration on them... Tomorrow, if he was still feeling foul, he resolved to go off on his own and do something satisfying, maybe split a pile of logs, before he joined his men.

He wandered back to the cabin with all the excitement of a man headed for the gallows. Delaying the inevitable, he stopped to haul a couple of buckets from the stream. Then he carried the water around to the back of the cabin, stopping short when he found the barrel full. He was sure the barrel had been almost empty yesterday. He shrugged. Pop had probably come by to fill it up. Isaac would have to remember to thank him for his thoughtfulness. Maybe it would ease the sting of their conversation earlier. If things ended up working out with Rebecca and she stayed, he'd like to dig a well and put in a pump. He was already working out the plans when he heard the door creak open.

He looked up, and his weariness lifted at the sight of Rebecca standing in the doorway. She'd come out to meet him. Maybe that meant she'd missed him a little after all. Seeing a woman outlined in the lamplight was nice, but strange, like finding some exotic flower in a field of weeds. Her waist-length hair was damp and swung thick and wavy about her, surrounding her tiny frame like a golden cape. No, it was more like copper and gold mingled together, hanging loose around her. She looked like an angel.

For a long moment, Isaac could only stare, filled with a longing to touch her cheek, her hair, breathe in the scent of her soap. He shook himself and met her gaze. Spiky, gold lashes framed her eyes. Were they blue or green? Right now they looked bluish-green, like the sea. They seemed to change from one to the other, depending on her dress.

She was a pretty woman, all told.

And she loves Jack, he reminded himself.

"Isaac?"

"Yes?" he asked cautiously, aware of her air of hesitancy,

as if she had something bad to announce. Maybe she had to tell him she was leaving. She couldn't do this after all.

What would he do then? Could they get an annulment, or would they be trapped: forever married but not?

"I wanted to ask you about...the privy. It's the door. It keeps getting stuck."

The privy?

Isaac felt his shoulders stiffen, a reflexive response. He'd worked hard all day. There'd been the incident with Jem too. The terror that had coursed through him. He didn't need a list of things to do. He was bone-tired. He dropped the buckets to the ground next to his boots, sloshing the water in his haste.

"The privy?" he asked.

"Could you fix it?" She wrinkled her nose.

He grimaced. Her wife loved another man, couldn't cook, and now she wanted him to fix the door to the privy. It was a start, he guessed, but not a very good one.

Later that evening—after another disappointing, blackened meal—Isaac sat back in the chair next to the fire and gave the spotless cabin an appreciative glance. The place was clean—that was something at least. She'd even moved Pop's box of chains. He'd held his hat and thanked her for that—for all she'd done—and she'd brushed aside his comments with a pretty flush.

His mind wandered to the decisions he needed to make about Rebecca and their marriage. He dragged a palm over his weary face and sat up, listening to her quiet, singsong hum carrying across the room. Her uncertain glances flicked over him now and again. Listening to her, he could feel a scowl tugging at his lips and brow. Why did she have to hum that blasted waltz? It only reminded him that she'd come here loving another man. Maybe he should send her away before things got any more complicated. Things were complicated enough.

After all, he'd only heard about Rebecca a few days ago. The weight of what had happened since then pressed down on him. It had happened so fast, and he'd had no preparation time. He liked to think things through more. Jumping into things just felt wrong. It wasn't in his nature. So maybe he should wait a few days until the air cleared a bit before making any more decisions.

Suppressing the huge sigh that longed to escape his lips, he tightened his jaw and decided then and there to sleep in his old bed. Rebecca's heart wasn't his...a fact he needed to remember every time he was tempted to touch her. Draw her close. Kiss her. Mentally shaking himself, he looked away from her and stood. No, he wouldn't touch her.

As Isaac's scowls grew, Becky wondered what he was thinking. Was he thinking how inept she was at even the most basic womanly tasks? The lame excuse for a breakfast this morning, the equally poor offering for dinner this evening. Her shoulders slumped. How did she ever think she could pass herself off as a proper lady?

"I think it best if I sleep out here," Isaac said, "while things are unsettled between us. Sharing a bed won't solve any of that." He nodded decisively and stood.

He was sleeping out here? He didn't want to share her bed. After one night, he was abandoning their marriage bed. Some wife she'd turned out to be.

"I understand." Her voice sounded small even to her own ears.

"Goodnight, Rebecca." He sounded firm and determined, and maybe a little sad. He paused and glanced at her over his shoulder as if waiting to see how she'd take it. She wondered if he even cared.

"Goodnight, Isaac."

He gave a quick nod and disappeared behind the potato-sack curtain that separated the sleeping area from the rest of the room.

The room went cold, as if someone had left the door open and a draft had come in. Becky shivered. She stood and pushed the little three-legged stool she'd been sitting on into its spot in the corner next to the stove and picked up the lantern. She wandered into the room off the back of the cabin and shut the door behind her, feeling as though she was shutting the door on her marriage. She'd only been married one day, and she'd already failed to be a passable wife.

She shouldn't have pestered him about the privy door right when he was coming home. It had been on her mind, but she should have stopped herself when she'd seen the weariness on his face. She hadn't been thinking. Well, she'd been thinking, but only about herself and what she wanted.

That wasn't the worst of it though. There was Jack. Now that Isaac knew about Jack, that had changed everything.

She'd seen the truth in Isaac's eyes tonight. He regretted marrying her...that much was obvious from his scowls. She sank onto the bed, her heart nearly breaking all over again. She cared more than she'd like to admit what Isaac Jessup thought of her. More than anything, she wanted him to like her. Staring down at her hands, the ones that had ruined the last two meals, she resolved to do better. That stove was an awful monster, but she'd do her best to master it. She'd make him breakfast in the morning, and it would be better. Something wonderful to erase her burnt, soggy flapjacks and the charred sausages she'd served up tonight. It couldn't get any worse.

She smiled wryly to herself.

Maybe she could make something fresh for dinner—a pheasant, or whatever other fowl they had around here. She'd have to employ some of her more unladylike skills to accomplish the task though. Hunting was something she was quite good at, thanks to one Jack Duncan. Not that she wanted Isaac to know that. She'd have to go out while he was off working. With any luck, he'd think one of his men had dropped some game by.

She kneeled at the foot of the bed and opened her trunk, taking a moment to finger the drying bouquet of wildflowers that Isaac had given her on their wedding day. They were a crushed mess, but she still couldn't bring herself to throw them out. So she set them to one side and dug around until she found just what she needed. She took out the rifle Jack had given her on her fourteenth birthday. The gun was weighted perfectly for her size and had a strap just the right length for hanging across her back while she rode. She rubbed a finger slowly over her name scratched into the handle. Jack had even added a crude flower engraved in the wood underneath the "B" in Becky. The weight of the gun felt comforting and familiar.

Yes, this would do quite nicely.

Thirteen

The next morning, as she'd promised herself, Becky set out to master the awful stove. After fending off the few hens in the coop next to the lean-to, she carried the precious eggs she'd found back to the kitchen. By watching her skillet carefully, she was able to turn out a platter of cheerful, yellow-faced fried eggs and a tall stack of nearly decent flapjacks. The grudging look of approval on Isaac's face turned to appreciation with the first bite.

His eyebrows rose a notch. "They're good," he said and grinned.

Her whole body relaxed, only then making her realize how tense she'd been, wanting so much for him to like them. She smiled back, noticing how his brown eyes seemed to gleam a little.

"I'm glad you like them," she said. Last night she'd slept alone in the wide bed. Even after only one night together as a married couple, she missed his tall frame stretched out beside her, his dark head resting on the pillow next to hers. At some point since she'd met him—maybe even on the voyage over—she'd felt this desire to make him happy. Breakfast was such a small thing, but his appreciation meant so much.

He tucked into his meal, and she sat across from him, happily eating her breakfast. She caught herself humming one of her favorite tunes, but at Isaac's swift glance, stopped short.

Why had his eyes gone cold?

Maybe he didn't appreciate music at the table. She pressed her lips tightly together to remind herself not to hum anymore, and then finished her breakfast quietly. A little light had gone out of the day though.

This getting used to living around another person wasn't the easiest thing. Would there ever come a day when she understood him? When he understood and maybe even liked her?

Well, it wasn't as if he *hated* her. He'd been kind and thoughtful. She'd noticed first thing this morning that he'd made an effort to fix the door to the privy.

Isaac pushed his chair away from the table and carried his plate over to the basin. Scratching the back of his head, he turned to her. His mouth opened and shut and opened again. She was suddenly nervous, wondering if he had something difficult to tell her.

"I'm going off to work," he said, looking a mite uncomfortable about the fact. Did he think she expected him to entertain her all day? "You best keep near the cabin, Rebecca," he added.

"All right, Isaac." She matched his tone of formality, wondering if he'd start every day with the same warning. The thought brought a small smile.

She followed him outside to the lean-to and watched as he saddled his horse.

"I expect you'll have to take Siren back to the livery soon?" She stroked the brown mare's velvety nose. The horse nickered softly and bumped Becky playfully in the shoulder with her head. What she wouldn't give to keep her. The little mare had a lot of fire, and they'd seemed to be of one spirit from the first. Having her around had eased the pain of missing China a bit.

"Take her back?" Isaac looked over his shoulder, met Becky's eyes briefly, and then turned back to his horse. "She's yours now."

"Mine?" she repeated dumbly.

"That's right."

"You got her for me?"

"Of course."

He'd bought her a horse.

A horse of her own.

Quick tears stung her eyes. Staring across the clearing at his meager cabin, she felt another pang of guilt. Isaac couldn't afford to buy her a fine mare like Siren. He'd been cornered into marrying her, and now he felt obligated to buy her a horse, when he obviously couldn't spare a cent. "You didn't have to do that."

He turned to her and stepped closer, one wide hand settling over her shoulder. "What's this? Tears?" He brushed the moisture from her cheek with his thumb. "You need a horse, Rebecca. But don't go off riding alone. There are wild animals up here, and I want you close to the cabin." He squeezed her shoulder gently, then released her and swung around to face his big gelding again.

She stared after him as he quickly mounted and rode off down the mountain with a parting wave of goodbye. His unexpected gift and brief tender touch had both charmed and humbled her.

She stroked her beautiful new horse's nose and spoke to her softly, "Siren, my darling. You look game for riding bareback."

Becky felt a glow of anticipation. A little ride wouldn't hurt anything. She remembered Isaac's repeated warning and promised herself she'd stay close to the cabin. No, that wouldn't hurt anything at all. With a nod, she marched back to the cabin to clean up the breakfast dishes.

It didn't take her long to set the kitchen to order and

change into her riding clothes: a faded cotton shirt, a pair of boy's trousers that she'd once secretly bought from Papa's store, and an old pair of riding boots that eased on and fit snugly around each foot. Her bulky, dark-green wool jacket and a brown felt hat completed the ensemble. She was ready to ride. Siren was a sidesaddle-trained mare, and maybe she'd never been broken for riding astride. Well, Becky would find out soon enough.

She untethered the mare, slipped the bridle on, and led her around the clearing, keeping her hands in contact with her glossy hide at all times. Then she gradually leaned her weight more and more against her side, looping first an arm and then a leg over the now skittish mare's back. And then she was up! She gripped the reins firmly in her hands and murmured little sounds of approval to the mare to soothe her.

"That's a good girl," Becky praised softly. She leaned low over Siren's neck and rested her cheek against the bristly hair of her mane.

Siren snorted and tossed her head. She danced away, giving a little buck of protest. Becky slipped to one side and nearly fell, but years of training kept her glued to the mare's back. Careful not to prod her unhappy mare, she righted herself and patted Siren's glistening neck.

"Nice try, darling, but I'm not going anywhere." Becky couldn't hide the admiration from her voice. The mare was simply doing her job as she saw it.

When her shenanigans didn't loose the rider from her back, Siren stretched back her long neck to give Becky's trousers a nip with her teeth.

"Now, where did you learn such bad manners?" Becky snatched the fabric from the horse's mouth and kept soothing her mount with her hands and voice, until the mare settled into a circling prance.

For a while, Becky let the horse go her own way as she became accustomed to carrying her weight without a saddle. When Siren finally switched to a resigned trot, Becky sat up. Using her legs and a light pressure on the reins, she guided the horse into a wide arc around the cabin.

Triumph!

She grinned and wished she could shout out—loud and long—but she didn't want to startle Siren. And she certainly didn't want Isaac to think she was calling out for help.

Once she gained a little more confidence, Becky led the mare into the trees. She guided Siren carefully through patches of spring mountain snow and down the path toward the stream. Once they arrived, Becky indulged in a drink, cupping her hands and scooping the icy water to her mouth for a refreshing taste. Siren seemed to enjoy her drink as well.

Giving her new horse a proud pat, Becky looked around the forest. The towering trunks made her stare up, agog at their sheer height and breadth.

"Siren, would you look at this place?" she whispered. "It's like God's own cathedral in the woods." Each tree, root, and stream seemed to reach out and bring her closer to heaven. A deep, peaceful feeling poured over her. She stood there, simply soaking in the majesty around her. The quiet solitude allowed her to reflect on her troubles. Isaac had been kind to her this morning, even though she'd admitted to his face yesterday that she loved another man. His scowl had told her clearly the news didn't sit well with him—that, and the fact that he'd abandoned the marriage bed. She felt again the same intense desire she'd felt last night to mend things between them. Being here in this amazing place made her think anything was possible.

Turning to Siren, Becky ran her hands over the mare's

sleek coat, feeling the thrill of ownership. Isaac couldn't know how precious a gift he'd given her.

Father God, thank you for my horse and for this beautiful mountain. She thought of Isaac too and how she'd already disappointed him, and added, *And help me be a good wife for Isaac.*

There was the barest movement of brush, a shadow in her peripheral vision. The hairs on her arms stood up on end.

Someone or *something* was watching her.

A hulking form charged from the tree line.

A big blur of brown.

Becky didn't wait to see what it was—she just leapt onto Siren's back and spurred the horse toward the cabin.

Ducking through the branches took all her concentration. Luckily, Siren seemed to have a sixth sense about where to land each hoof along the rooted path, as if she'd memorized the terrain on their trip down. Becky, barely aware of their flight, fought off the sensation of fear crawling up her spine. As they neared the clearing, she looked back long enough to catch sight of a huge brown grizzly rearing up. His paws and claws looked big enough to kill her with one swipe. Likely they could.

Gun. No gun.

She could kick herself for being so foolish as to have left her weapon back in the cabin. What use was it to her there, propped against the foot of the bed?

The bear stood on his hind legs and sniffed the air. With a roar of warning, he turned back and lumbered into the forest.

Not taking any chances, Becky rode to the back of the cabin, quickly tethered Siren, darted inside, and grabbed her rifle. Returning to the winded mare's side, Becky stood guard for an hour, her gaze fastened on the line of trees surrounding the small clearing. Finally letting down her guard, she returned

Siren to the stable. The mare had worked up quite a lather, so Becky gave her a good rubdown and covered her with a blanket. She'd just returned to her bedroom, stripped out of her riding clothes, and was washing up when she heard the distinctive sound of spiked boots clicking across the front porch. Frantically, she hid her gun under the bed and kicked her lather-soaked trousers and hunting coat underneath as well. She jerked on a petticoat and a plain day dress with fumbling hands.

Isaac pushed through the front door and looked around, surprised to find the main room of the cabin empty.

"Rebecca?" he called softly, not wanting to startle her.

The door to the back room was slightly ajar, and he pushed it open slowly, his eyes widening at the sight of his wife's back. She was fastening the top button of her dress, reaching behind her neck to do it up. The bedcovers were rumpled too, as if she'd recently gotten up from a nap. Maybe delicate, city-bred women needed more sleep than other folks? The thought of her tucked, warm and sleepy, in the bed sheets flashed in his mind. He shook off the image. She loved another man, he reminded himself. The thought stung his pride anew and sent the images of her soft womanly form curled up in bed scurrying from his mind.

"Uh, are you all right?" he asked.

She jumped like a child caught with a finger in the frosting.

"Isaac!" She spun toward him, her eyes wide and startled, as if she hadn't heard him come in. She still had that flushed-cheeked look of sleep, and there was another expression in her eyes he could only describe as panic.

"I came to check—to see if you were faring all right."

The truth was he had several bad moments imagining her cornered by some wild beast. The thoughts had haunted his morning, making it impossible to focus on his work. He'd done his best though. After splitting a huge pile of logs and stacking them on the skid to bring back to the cabin, he'd finally given into his need to make sure she was safe.

"Oh, I'm fine." She still had a guilty look on her face and quickly turned to straighten up the bedclothes and fluff the pillows on their bed.

Their bed? That was a laugh. He'd married into a life of celibacy it seemed. His days weren't much different now, were they? Except now he had a dainty female to worry about. It wasn't fair. Marriage was supposed to mean love and having a woman he could call his own, in every way. But Rebecca didn't really belong to him, not when her heart belonged to another. A flicker of resentment sprung up in his heart, making him square his jaw and stiffen his shoulders.

"Well, so long as you're all right..." he trailed off and stepped back a couple of strides to a safe distance.

"Oh, stay for lunch." She whirled toward him again, pushing a loose strand of hair from her face.

He couldn't say no with her hopeful eyes trained on him like that. And he noticed how pretty she looked with her reddish-gold hair braided and pinned up. A few loose strands framed her cheeks and made her look wholly feminine. Dipping his head in a curt yes, he helped her stoke up the fire and hauled in a fresh bucket of water from the barrel outside.

While Isaac finished some chores he said he needed to complete in the lean-to, Becky worked on lunch. She could still feel her heart thumping too fast in her chest as she cooked. If he'd come home any earlier, she would've been outside with Siren in the forest. Or he might've caught her with her gun in hand, guarding Siren from the bear. Explaining her absence from the cabin or her stance by the back door would have been interesting, to say the least.

Should she tell him about the bear? Her shoulder muscles seized up into a knot just at the thought. How could she tell him anything? If she did, she'd also have to admit she'd ridden to the stream with Siren when she'd promised to stay near the house.

He wouldn't like that.

He'd like it even less if he found out she'd seen a bear.

Instead she hid a sigh of relief that he hadn't caught her, making sure to check her skillet frequently and not get caught up in her thoughts. Encouraged from her success at breakfast, she was determined to serve Isaac a good, non-blackened meal.

Isaac returned and sat at the table. Feeling inordinately pleased with her success at the stove, Becky placed a platter of evenly browned venison sausages and quick cornmeal rolls before him.

"Thank you again for my horse." She smiled at him. "She's a real beauty." Did he have any inkling how much his gift meant to her?

"You have to have a horse up here," he mumbled, as he munched on a roll.

His expression of pleasure filled her with delight. He liked it. She opened up a can of pickled beets she'd found in the kitchen cabinet and scooped some onto his plate.

"Aren't you going to eat?" He pulled out the chair beside him so she could sit. Before she could answer, he'd already tossed a roll and a couple of links of sausage onto her plate from the platter in the center of the small table.

Becky perched on her chair and cut up her sausage and roll into neat little ladylike bites. Remembering Melody, Jack's genteel Southern bride, Becky even sliced the pickled beets into perfect little wedges, speared them with her fork, and nibbled at them as delicately as she could. She'd had her fun this morning riding bareback on Siren—she'd even had a brief face-to-face encounter with danger to liven up the day—but now it was back to the business of being a wife, and that meant being a lady. Her efforts to appear the perfect lady didn't stop her thoughts from wandering to her plans to hunt this afternoon. She'd made a mistake this morning forgetting her gun. That wouldn't happen again.

Isaac tucked into his meal with pleasure, but he couldn't keep his gaze from drifting over to Rebecca now and then. She was sitting as pretty as you please, as if she were visiting the Queen of England for tea. A sinking feeling hit him. She belonged with a proper, citified gentleman, not with a rough logger out here in the wilds of the mountains.

Was this Jack fellow of hers a tailor? Or a banker maybe? Probably some highly educated fellow with a decent home, complete with an indoor water pump. Maybe he even had one of those shiny white porcelain baths with the gold claw feet. Folks in fancy houses had things like that. Isaac swirled the cooled goat's milk in his glass and chugged it down in a rush. He pushed away from the table, unhappy with the turn of his thoughts, and wiped his mouth on his sleeve. He stopped mid-swipe when he saw the startled expression on Becky's face.

She likely was used to a man with manners too.

"Thank you kindly, ma'am."

Ma'am? Becky jumped up, her heart sinking at Isaac's stiff-sounding words. What had she done now?

"Will you be late this evening?" she asked, confused.

"I— Probably. Yes." He backed toward the front door and yanked it open. "Stay near the cabin, Rebecca."

"Of course." Becky watched him leave.

She crossed the room and leaned her forehead against the door Isaac had just shut, half-wishing he'd stayed so they could go off hunting together as she'd done with Jack for so many years. In fact, she longed to have just a few short minutes where she could just be herself with her new husband, to not have to pretend to be something she wasn't. She even half dreamed about him liking her the way she was. Wouldn't that be nice?

What a fruitless thought. Hadn't she learned her lesson? No man wanted a hoyden for a bride. Jack had taught her that.

After waiting to make sure Isaac was good and truly gone, Becky gathered up her rifle from under the bed and got to the business of hunting their evening meal.

Well after dark that evening, Isaac dragged himself up the front steps of the cabin. His boots felt heavy. Even his hat felt heavy. His resentment had returned and festered all afternoon, until now he didn't even want to see Rebecca again. He hadn't signed up for a wife in the first place. What he wouldn't give to offer Pop a piece of his mind. He'd been tempted to do just that earlier, but his conscience had made him hold his tongue. What use was it railing against Pop? Isaac was stuck with the problem of Rebecca. And that was exactly how he felt—*stuck*.

As he poked his head through the door, he heard the sound of her humming loudly to herself. The tempting scent of roasted fowl made him dizzy with hunger. His stomach gave an answering growl.

Straightening a bit at the welcome smell, Isaac entered and hung his hat on the peg near the door. He pushed out of his muddy boots too and set them against the wall underneath his hat. His coat he threw over the rocker next to the fire to dry off the chilly spring mist that had clung to him on his ride home.

Home.

The smell of a home-cooked meal certainly had a way of softening his attitude right fast.

He looked into the kitchen area. Rebecca was bustling about in one of her ridiculously wide skirts. She bent and stretched in a graceful ladylike way, as she set plates on the table and arranged cups and forks just so. She may not have been frontier-sturdy, but he had to admit he liked the look of her standing there.

"Evening." Isaac cleared his throat, noticing how she jumped and spun toward him. At least she stopped humming that little tune she seemed to like so much, the one that reminded him of Jack.

"Isaac." She sounded nervous, and he noticed her twisting her hands together at her waist. "You must be hungry after working all day." She smoothed her skirt and checked her hair, which was neatly plaited and rolled into a bun at the base of her neck.

"Pop come by?" he asked, looking at the roasted feast.

She just smiled at him, which he took to mean yes.

"Must have been busy hunting this afternoon. I wondered where'd he gotten to." He eyed the spread of food on the table, his mouth watering in anticipation. "We're getting low on venison. I've been planning to go out hunting myself soon. Mighty nice of him to rustle up a bird for us, all trussed and ready to go."

At Isaac's words, Becky let go the breath she was holding.

"Mmm," she mumbled noncommittally. Never mind the hours she'd spent flushing out that wild pheasant, then cleaning and cooking it. Isaac assumed his father had brought the game, which neatly solved her problem of having to explain where the meal had come from. She smiled vaguely and ducked her head so he couldn't see the guilty blush that was warming her cheeks.

Seeing her husband's eager expression had made all the work worthwhile, but part of her wished to take the credit for her skill with a gun, in her ability to provide a hearty meal for the towering, hungry man at her side. Well, humility was a virtue, right along with patience, and Isaac would scarcely approve of her toting a gun and riding bareback through the forest.

After they'd seated themselves at the table and Isaac had polished his plate—twice—Becky rushed to clean up, her eagerness to please spilling out in restless energy. She could do this.

Her double life would simply have to remain a secret.

After dinner they sat for a while. Isaac pored over his ledger, and Becky sewed an edge around the new cleaning cloths she was making from some scraps of fabric she'd brought in her trunk. She felt at peace sitting there with him. The silence in the air was a comfortable, companionable one, and even though she didn't much like sewing, she found the task satisfying tonight. Relaxing.

Isaac yawned and stood, tucking his notebook under his arm. "Goodnight." He backed toward the potato-sack curtain. "Gotta get up early and milk the goat."

"Isaac," Becky said, looking up at him uncertainly, "I know we got started on the wrong foot, but I want you to know I want to be a good wife for you."

He swallowed at that and pulled on his collar.

"I— Thank you. Well, goodnight." He gave her a brief solemn nod and ducked behind the curtain.

Becky stared across the room, as if by looking she could bring him back out to talk to her. How could she ever become a wife in truth when he ran off every night? A married couple shared a bed. How long would Isaac choose to sleep alone? He hadn't seemed to understand her little hint about being a good wife either. She couldn't possibly ask him straight out if he ever intended to make theirs a real marriage. Could she? She shrugged. This was only the second night he'd slept out here, so perhaps she should simply wait and see. Surely he couldn't hold Jack over her head forever? She walked slowly into the room at the back.

Much later, after lying awake for over an hour, Becky couldn't shake the feeling that her marriage was in trouble. Maybe she was being foolish. They barely knew each other, so maybe they just needed more time to get to know one another.

But when she finally fell asleep, she dreamed of running after an elusive dark-haired man—a man she desperately needed to catch, but who stayed out of reach.

A little over a week later, Isaac headed out to the lean-to as he did every morning. As usual he pondered over his life in these early morning hours, when all was quiet and tinted with a muted blue. The mountains rose up all around him, and as he crossed the clearing, he felt like he was the only person in the world in that moment. Except he was all too aware that he *wasn't* the only person in the world. Rebecca was always on his mind. What was he to do about her?

Pop continued to stay with Brody. Except for dropping off the occasional bird he'd brought down, he kept to himself, perhaps hoping that in time everything would work itself out. Isaac suspected that was his father's hope anyway. He wanted grandchildren, he'd said. Rebecca had said early on that she wanted children too. It seemed like he was the only one standing in the way of their plans.

It wasn't like he didn't want children. He actually liked children—the few he'd been around—and had always thought he'd be a father someday. He might have pursued finding a wife earlier, but the business had consumed him. It took a lot to build something from the ground up, and he'd put his all into it.

Perhaps it was pride standing in his way now, but the idea of taking Rebecca as a true wife while her heart still belonged to another... Well, it didn't sit right. It didn't sit right at all.

The lean-to was chilly and not for the first time, Isaac considered boarding it up proper and calling it a barn. He sat on the stool and began milking the goat, all the while mentally preparing for the worship service they planned to go to later that morning. The scriptures he'd read first thing that morning were fresh in his mind, and his prayers kept returning to the problem of Rebecca. One inner voice urged him to send her back home, but another voice spoke of commitment. He'd said vows before God to love and keep her till death do them part. Those weren't words he was willing to dismiss lightly.

"What's her name?" His wife's voice was suddenly in his ear, quite close.

Isaac jumped. The goat bleated at him.

"Sorry, girl." He patted her side and resumed milking her with slow, careful hands. He glanced over his shoulder toward the subject of his thoughts.

Rebecca stood watching him, leaning over the rail and peering in at them with curious eyes. He was surprised to see her out this early. She usually left him to his morning chores, and most times he'd get back inside the cabin and find her preparing breakfast.

"What's her name?" she repeated.

"Name? The goat?" He looked at the goat dumbly. It was a goat. He'd never gotten much further than that. She gave them a daily supply of milk, but other than that she was generally a nuisance. She liked to butt down the stall door. And whenever she got loose, she'd eat what few vegetables he was able to grow in the summer. She also liked to nip at his shirts and under-things when he hung them out on the line. If he was lucky. Most times she'd tug the whole line down and drag it through the mud.

"Yes, the goat," Rebecca said, a pleasant-sounding smile in her voice. "Don't tell me she hasn't got a name?"

There was something nice about hearing a woman's voice

in the morning. It reminded him a little of when he was young, and his mother had chatted with him in soft tones while they ate breakfast. As if speaking too loud would jar them too quickly out of whatever dreams they'd had the night before.

Rebecca's soft voice put him much in mind of those times.

"All right. I won't." Isaac focused on his milking.

"She doesn't have a name?" Rebecca pressed. "How can you have an animal that doesn't have a name?"

"Never gave it much thought. She's good for milk, but other than that she's nothing but trouble, always munching on the laundry."

"Well, then I think your choice is clear. Either you call her Milky or you call her Trouble." Her teasing tone brought a reluctant smile to his lips.

"Well, then, if I have to choose, then I guess she's Trouble." The real Trouble was standing behind him, her elbow propped against the top of the rail, her chin cupped in one dainty hand.

"Can you show me how to milk her?"

He glanced back at her in surprise.

"I can do it. I know I could." She looked so earnest, like she really wanted to try.

He scanned her doubtfully. He could see the outline of her skirt through the gaps in the stall door. That silly hooped skirt she was wearing would take up nearly a whole stall.

"...and that way," she continued, her tone half practical, half tempting, "I could milk the goat in the morning, and you wouldn't have to get up so early. I could feed the chickens too."

Her offer brought to mind their conversation from about a week or so ago. He knew she was curious about their sleeping arrangements, but if he slept with her, his commitment to her would be doubly binding.

It was too complicated. And it wasn't something he felt comfortable talking about with a lady. And especially not with her. It just didn't seem proper somehow, even if she was his wife.

The truth was she was just his wife on paper.

"Would you show me?" She was persistent—he'd give her that.

He stood and swept an arm out toward the stool. "Be my guest."

She unlatched the stall door and swung around the edge, somehow pressing her wide skirt through the narrow opening. Lifting the hem slightly, she managed to seat herself on the low stool, her skirt making a wide circle around her like a fabric-covered birdcage of some sort. With a little laugh, she gazed up at him with expectant eyes. He gave her a nod, and she turned back to the goat purposefully. He was reminded of the women he'd seen once as a boy in a newspaper office, their fingers poised over their typewriters. Where had that been? San Francisco? It was so long ago, he couldn't remember.

After a moment, Rebecca placed her hands gingerly on the goat's teats and pulled. When her effort produced nothing more than an irritated bleat from Trouble, her face scrunched up in disappointment.

"What am I doing wrong?"

"Like this." He crouched beside her and covered her small hands with his, showing her the proper amount of pressure and rhythm to produce a steady stream of milk.

"I did it! I mean, we did it." Her bright smile nearly knocked him over.

He stood abruptly and brushed hay from his trousers.

"Practice a while," he said. "I'll go stoke the fire in the stove." He hitched his thumb over his shoulder in the direction of the cabin, turned, and trotted toward the front door, calling himself a fool to put any weight in her beautiful, bright smile. The woman loved another man—he'd do well to remember that.

As Becky carried the full bucket of milk to the kitchen, she felt a tiny thrill of accomplishment. She'd proved she could still play the lady while helping Isaac with the chores. The silly dress was a hindrance she'd gladly do without, but images of the perfect Melody waltzing through Sullivan's Grocers in a lovely white dress reminded Becky of her purpose.

Living on a mountain had seemed strange at first, but she'd come to love the crisp air. She loved the view outside too. It took her breath away whenever she looked at it. It truly was the most amazing place. The only things she missed about living in Pepperell were the trappings of comfort: readily available food at the grocers, hot running water, a tub... And she missed her mother and Rachel, some nights rather dreadfully. Did they miss her too? she wondered. Did anyone in town miss her? Did Jack?

She shouldn't even think about him. It was wrong now. She was married. She had Isaac. Somewhat.

Today was Sunday. Back home, her family was probably getting ready for church, if they hadn't gone already. The difference in time was still a puzzle she hadn't worked out. The previous week, Isaac had conducted a short private service for just the two of them, but today he was taking her to the logging camp. It had been an adjustment being all alone so much, even though back home she'd spent quite a bit of time escaping town and riding China through the farmer's fields. But it was different not to see anyone at all—except for Isaac, of course—and his father, who occasionally stopped by to check in on her. Mr. Jessup—or Sam, as he liked her to call him—was a nice man. He made her laugh.

While preparing breakfast, she stole glances at the potato-sack curtain serving as a door to Isaac's room. She heard water swishing and the sound of metal tapping against ceramic, telling her he was shaving.

He'd left his big black Bible open on the table this morning. Having spent the last week with him, she was starting to learn his routine. He'd get up before dawn to read the Bible. After that, he'd go out to the barn to milk the goat. While he was gone, she'd start on breakfast and eagerly read from the Good Book, knowing he'd return any moment to set the milk bucket next to the basin. She'd never had her own Bible. Papa had jealously guarded the family Bible, preferring to choose the passages he wanted to preach to them each evening before dinner. So it was a treat to read it herself every morning. After Isaac returned with the milk, he usually took his Bible back to his room, emerging moments later ready for breakfast and a day's work at the logging site.

This morning, she'd joined him in the barn to help with the milking, and she'd been glad to find the Bible still out on the table when she returned to the kitchen. Maybe she could read a little while she waited for her flapjacks to cook through.

He'd marked a passage with a scrap of paper, and she read the words, "To obey is better than sacrifice..."

With a frown, she pushed back a strand of hair hanging in her eyes and tucked it into the knot at the top of her head. Of course. What else would a man be reading who was chafing against his duty?

And right now his marriage to her was Isaac's duty.

Becky pursed her lips thoughtfully as she flipped the flapjacks to brown the other side, determining as she did so to make the best of things. At least this morning they'd be spending the whole morning together, she realized with a hopeful little smile.

What was a logging camp like? She had nothing in her experience to form a picture of the place. A giddy feeling quickened her heartbeat at the opportunity to venture past the confines of the cabin and its immediate surroundings. Except for the times she went out hunting, she generally kept to her promise to stay close to the cabin, not wanting to risk another run-in with a grizzly.

Though she'd been tempted to explore beyond the stream many times, Isaac's warning to her every morning to stay near the cabin reinforced her commitment to her promise. She couldn't very well nod at him and go off and do exactly the opposite of what he asked. Her conscience bothered her enough as it was for riding off on Siren to hunt fresh game, but as long as she was careful, and as long as Isaac gave his father the credit, she didn't see the harm in it. They'd run out of venison sausages several days ago, and—at least this way—she could keep those wretched beans in the sack.

All her thoughts fled as Isaac pushed through the curtain and walked toward her. He certainly looked handsome with his face freshly scrubbed and shaven, his skin smooth-looking and tanned from hours in the mountain sunshine. The ends of his damp hair curled against his neck. As he stopped beside her, she felt small and delicate—an unfamiliar feeling that wasn't altogether unpleasant.

"We need to eat quick-like in order to get up to the service on time."

She nodded. Reaching for his Bible, Isaac paused a moment, moved his scrap of paper back into position, and looked at her, a question in his dark brown eyes.

Her heart fluttered. "Would you like milk in your coffee?" she asked quickly to distract him, even though she knew he liked it black. She wasn't sure, but based on how her father felt about his Bible, she didn't want Isaac to know she'd been reading his every morning.

"No, thanks." He closed his Bible and rubbed a loving hand over the worn leather binding.

They ate their meal in silence. As Becky washed the dishes, Isaac helped dry them with a kitchen towel. Sharing the simple task with the man at her side gave Becky a warm feeling of belonging she hadn't felt in years, maybe not since Jack had left for the war. Holding the feeling close, she excused herself and ran to her room to replace her hooped crinoline for a trio of ruffled cotton petticoats. The effect wasn't nearly as dramatic without the crinoline, but she could hardly ride a horse in the stiff monstrosity. She exchanged her slippers for a pair of practical half boots, tied her bonnet tightly under her chin, and buttoned up her warm, navy-blue wool cape.

With a flutter of excitement in her stomach, she hurried back to the main room to join Isaac for their trip to the logging camp.

Fourteen

saac watched with growing concern as Rebecca sat her mount beside him. The mare was too spirited by half, but Rebecca had told him she rode sidesaddle, and this mare had been the only sidesaddle-trained mount available. A more placid horse would have suited her better, he felt, but he hadn't had any other options. At least Rebecca seemed to like Siren well enough. In fact, she'd seemed quite touched that he'd bought her a horse. Unfortunately, she didn't appear entirely comfortable riding. That was too bad. He would have liked to take her riding through the mountain paths. Maybe he could teach her to ride astride? She'd likely be shocked if he mentioned the idea, he was sure, but her balance would improve greatly.

That is, if she stayed here much longer.

Lord, he prayed, *what direction do you want me to go here? I feel so confused. Do you want me to keep Rebecca here and make her my wife in truth?* His stomach did that funny little knotting thing at the idea. *Or should I ask her if she wants to return to Massachusetts to mend things with this Jack fellow?*

It was a terrible thought, one that filled him with dread.

You're a coward, Isaac told himself with a deep sigh. He couldn't even bring up the subject of Jack with the woman. He should ask her to tell him more about the man and why she'd come here instead of staying with him. Had the man died in the war? She hadn't spoken of him in the past tense, but sometimes people slipped and spoke of the dead as if they were still living. He remembered doing that after his own mother had died. Glancing over at Rebecca concentrating so hard to keep upright in the saddle, he couldn't bring himself to say the words: *Tell me about Jack.* Just thinking of saying it aloud gave him a serious case of heartburn.

His attention turned to the trail. They'd be at the logging camp soon. What would she think of it?

Why did he care?

He tried to picture the camp in his mind, tried to see it through a woman's eyes. A city woman's eyes. Logging was his life. He'd poured drops of his own blood into this soil, trying to build a successful business. He had a ways to go yet, but his dream was taking shape before him every day. Though his peers scorned his tactics, he refused to clear huge swaths of trees, preferring to thin out small areas and then moving on to the next. This made the work longer and less profitable, but left the mountain's beauty more or less intact.

His investments in the mills down in Teekalet were likely to reap benefits in the not-too-distant future. He liked to think things were going well enough. He straightened a little in his saddle.

It didn't matter what Rebecca thought. Sure, it would be nice to see her face light up with admiration at what he'd accomplished, but in the end it only mattered what he thought, and not anyone else. At least that was what he told himself.

As they broke through the stand of thick, tall trees into a clearing, Becky brought Siren to a halt and stared around at what looked to be a neighborhood of tents and several long rectangular log cabins, set amid huge tree stumps, impressive in their own right. Some of the trunks looked wide enough to be the floor of an entire house, or a good-sized room at least. It was really quite amazing to see. She never would have imagined such a thing.

Isaac reined his horse in and looked back at her. He was staring at her so intently, as if he expected some response from her.

"It's quite a place." This didn't seem to be exactly what he wanted to hear, but he gave a slight smile, and jerked his head toward the largest log cabin.

"Worship is over there in the cookhouse." He kicked his horse into a slow walk over to the building. After dismounting and tethering his bay to a post, he tethered Siren too and turned to help Becky down. She couldn't seem to find her balance sitting today in the awkward sidesaddle position, especially with her skirt and voluminous petticoats bunched up under her. So it was a relief to have her feet planted firmly on the ground. She enjoyed the brief sensation of being in Isaac's arms before he released her and turned to open the cookhouse door.

Inside proved to be a long spare room with two columns of simple wood-plank tables and benches. The windows along each wall helped illuminate the room with bright spring sunshine, but the air seemed old and thin, possibly due to the number of loggers already packed onto the benches. They all seemed to turn as one man, gawking at her with unabashed curiosity. There wasn't another woman in the building, but then she remembered Mrs. Pearson saying as much.

Becky felt much like a rare beetle on a pin being twirled about for a group of entomologists. Except the entomologists in this instance were big burly men with suspenders and beards. They also looked a little hungry, as if they hadn't had breakfast yet. Either that or they were interested in her as a woman. She edged closer to Isaac, felt his hand at the small of her back, warming her in a way, as if he'd claimed her. That alone gave confidence to her faltering steps. Her chin lifted higher, and her lips relaxed into a more natural smile.

Isaac led her past the staring eyes to the other end of the room near a makeshift podium. She sat on the bench next to Sam, who grinned widely at her.

"Glad to see you, gal. Son." He nodded first to Becky then to Isaac.

"Pop." Isaac nodded back and took his place next to Becky, his big black leather Bible balanced on his knees.

"Good morning, Sam," Becky greeted her father-in-law, admiring his slicked-back white hair, tied at his neck with a leather cord as usual, but seemingly with greater care today. His silvery-blue eyes scanned hers for an instant, leaving her feeling slightly exposed again, but in a different way, for his eyes were kind and his half grin contagious. She smiled.

"My son been treating you right, gal?" He whispered loudly enough for Isaac to hear, and his son scowled at him.

Becky noticed how Isaac shot a quick glance at her as though waiting for her reply.

"Just fine, Sam. Thank you." She couldn't very well tell him she hardly ever saw her new husband. Couldn't tell him Isaac slept in the other room. How could she? It would be nice to open up about the state of her life and marriage with someone. Another woman preferably—ideally her mother— but Sam actually looked like the sort of person you could say such a thing to and not get an offended reaction. Just not now, of course.

Becky glanced down at her white-gloved hands and loosened her grip on her reticule when she noticed how tightly she was grasping the bag.

"Preacher here yet?" Isaac leaned forward to address his father.

"Saw him out and about trying to rustle up a few more pew warmers."

"Pew warmers?" Becky couldn't resist a little chuckle at his description.

"Well, if you have to drag 'em here they're not doing much more than warming the bench, I say."

"Now, Pop," Isaac protested, "some folks just need a little more encouragement."

"I reckon."

Their exchange was interrupted when a man shuffled up front with a stiff, sort of running gait Becky was coming to associate with the loggers who took the logs down the Skid Road to the mill. She sometimes saw them in the distance while she was hunting. This man's face stirred up a blurry memory of her wedding day, and she recognized him as the preacher who'd performed the ceremony.

He conducted a brief lesson, complete with a solemn communion, led them in some hearty, somewhat rowdy hymns, and then called on Isaac to read a scripture.

Becky watched with interest as Isaac stood and strode to the podium to replace the logger-preacher. He opened up his unwieldy Bible, found his place, then read with a forceful voice, "The God who made the world and everything in it is the Lord of heaven and earth and does not live in temples made by human hands, as if he needed anything, because he himself gives all men life and breath and everything else... He determined the times set for them and the exact places where they should live." He stared out across the room of attentive faces. His eyes seemed to bore into each man.

Silence stilled the room. Not a logger coughed. No one wiggled or even scratched.

He continued in a softer voice, "God did this so that men would seek him and find him, though he is not far from each one of us. 'For in him we live and move and have our being.' As some of your own poets have said, 'We are his offspring.'" His words reverberated in the quiet of the room.

Becky desperately tried to remember each word. It wasn't the passage she'd expected him to read. Though she felt certain the message could change her very life, she wasn't able to grasp it at that moment.

Isaac's face split into a wide smile, and the whole room seemed to take a breath as he returned to his seat. The preacher took his place at the podium to thank Isaac and to close the service with another round of energetic singing and a prayer.

Meanwhile, Becky's gaze slipped again and again to Isaac's profile, assessing him anew. She felt the respect his men had for him. A sense of wifely pride filled her. Her first impressions of him being a good man took on renewed weight.

After the last song, the men hanging near the door deserted the room rather quickly, but the others milled around talking and laughing. Becky felt odd to be the only woman in the room, so she kept to Isaac's side, waiting for his cue as to what they would do next.

He turned to his father. "I wanted to thank you properly for the game, Pop."

Becky's stomach clenched. She darted a quick glance at Sam's rather bemused face. "Yes, thank you, Sam." She pleaded silently with her eyes for her father-in-law to play along with her.

"It was nothing." His cryptic reply didn't give her secret away and seemed to satisfy Isaac for the moment for he looked away, as if searching for someone. Sam's brows lifted slightly at her, his eyes curious, and Becky sensed he'd return to the subject the first chance he got.

"Brody, there you are." Isaac's greeting served to turn Sam's attention from Becky to the burly red-haired man charging toward them, and she felt a momentary sense of relief.

"Well, if it ain't the lovebirds." The loud booming voice was unmistakable. She immediately placed him as the man who'd inadvertently revealed Isaac's reason for marrying her in the first place.

Becky's memories of that moment drained the joy from the worship service and replaced it with sober reality. Isaac had married her out of a sense of duty to his father. She was nothing more to him than an obligation.

"Been seeing too much of you lately, Jessup, working like a man possessed. Ain't tired of your new wife already are you?" Brody laughed.

Becky saw Isaac's strained smile, and it hurt her, as if he'd come right out and said he didn't want her. His actions had said as much when he'd left the marriage bed after one night. The air seemed suddenly staler, the press of bodies stifling. The room rocked and swayed like an all-too-familiar ship cabin. Becky had to get outside and see the sun—breathe in some crisp mountain air.

"Would you excuse me a moment, gentlemen? It's rather warm in here." She forced a smile at the men, not focusing on their faces, but casting the comment out as she pushed through a cluster of loggers and made her way to the door. Without looking back to gauge Isaac's reaction, she stumbled through the door into the blessedly cool, shady air of the pines.

Breathing deeply settled her nerves a bit, but her heart

still ached from thinking of her troubled marriage. There didn't seem to be another course except the one she'd set for herself over the past couple of weeks: Be the perfect lady for Isaac. Help out in whatever ways she could.

Was there perhaps more she could do?

If so, what?

Leaning her shoulder against a massive tree stump, tall as a full-sized apple tree back home, Becky felt rather than heard someone come up behind her. *Isaac.* Her heart beat a little faster, and she swallowed before turning to face him. She blinked at the sight of a young man approaching her with a cocky grin. He was young and handsome with midnight black hair and blue eyes. Stopping a little too close for comfort, he leaned against the roughened bark next to her, a stalk of new grass bent between his slightly crooked teeth.

Moving the grass to the side of his mouth, he spoke. "Howdy." He looked her over with considerable interest.

Becky squirmed under his gaze. "Hello."

"Name's Jem."

"Pleased to meet you, Jem. I'm Becky," she replied out of habit, belatedly realizing she should have introduced herself as Rebecca.

"Becky, eh? I like the sound of that. Becky, Becky, Becky. You the new washwoman?" His impertinent gaze swept over her person again.

"I do some wash, I guess, but I wouldn't call myself a—a washwoman," Becky stumbled over her words, confused. His question seemed to have a double meaning, but for the life of her she couldn't imagine what he could possibly mean.

"No, I wouldn't reckon you would." His grin widened, and he bobbed the stalk of grass up and down between his teeth.

Becky wondered if this was meant to impress her.

"Have you worked here long, Jem?" she asked politely.

"Not so long. Not sure I'm staying much longer either."

"Oh, is that right? You don't like it here?" Her curiosity was piqued now, and she looked at him with greater interest.

"Naw. Let's just say, if I was running this place, the men wouldn't be going without their pay for weeks on end. No, siree, I'd have this place running ship-shape, not on the verge of collapse any minute."

"On the verge of collapse?" Becky looked around at the simple logging camp. It wasn't fancy by any stretch of the imagination, but she'd thought the loggers seemed content here. Perhaps that was a front they put on when the boss was around? "The business is in trouble?" she asked, remembering the state of Isaac's old cabin and how guilty she'd felt about him buying her a horse. Her guilt doubled understanding now that his business was suffering. He couldn't afford to support a wife if his own men were going without pay.

"Don't go high-tailing it outta here, now." Jem slid a knuckle down her cheek, causing her to jerk back and frown at him sternly. He didn't seem much more than a boy, maybe seventeen at the oldest. Who did he think he was? "I'm just saying things could be better," he said. "That Jessup feller has his head in the clouds if he thinks this business will survive longer than a year, but—for now anyways—the men are hanging onto his promises. I don't give much weight to promises myself, but if a pretty thing like you is setting up shop here, maybe I'll hang around a spell longer."

"'Setting up shop?' What on earth—?" Becky's question was interrupted when the cookhouse door swung open and Isaac stalked over, his expression none too pleased.

"Jem."

The young man jumped and spun around. He spat out the blade of grass and swiped his mouth with his sleeve. "Boss." Where before he'd been leaning lazily against the tree stump, he now stood stiffly at attention.

"Missed you at worship today," Isaac said, looking Becky over quickly as if to see if she were unharmed and in one piece.

"Ah, had washin' to do." Jem's gaze shifted away to the ground for a moment.

Isaac came to Becky's side and wrapped an arm about her shoulders. She resisted the urge to lean against him.

"I see you've met my wife," he said.

Some unspoken message seemed to pass from him to Jem.

"Your wife?" Jem's brows shot up, and he darted a look at Becky. He took a step backward and kicked at the stump with the toe of his calked boot. "Uh, yeah, we met."

Isaac dropped his arm to his side and fidgeted with the edge of his pants pocket. Becky missed his warmth immediately. Now that she'd cooled off from the stuffy cookhouse, she was feeling the brisk air and realized she'd left her cape and bonnet on the bench inside. At least she'd kept her reticule with her. It was still dangling from her wrist.

"Well, then, Jem," Isaac said, "how are things going on the peeling crew?"

"I'm a faller, boss." Jem stood up straight, his broad shoulders stiff and proud. "It's what I'm meant to be."

"Not until you prove to me you've got what it takes to be a faller, young man."

Jem's jaw worked as he stared at Isaac. "I've got what it takes, boss." His gaze flicked from Isaac to Becky and back again, his stance defiant. "I'm better than peeling crew, and you know it."

"What I know is you nearly got yourself killed the other day. It's my responsibility to keep you safe, son."

"You ain't my pa," Jem shot back. With a quick jerky nod to Becky, he took off at a jog.

Troubled, Becky watched after him as he disappeared into the trees. "You were hard on the boy," she said. Jem may have been closer to her age than anyone else she'd met at the camp—maybe just a few years younger than her—but calling him "boy" seemed to fit. He put up a front, but there was something sort of younger-than-his-years about him.

"Near got himself killed." Isaac turned his attention to Becky, and she found herself staring into his dark brown eyes. "You feeling all right?" His concerned gentleness threw her into confusion.

"I'm all right."

"Not feeling poorly?" He looked away and scuffed the toe of his boot through the scattered pine needles.

"Feeling poorly?" His question brought to mind her mad dash to the privy on her first visit to the cabin. He probably thought she had a delicate constitution. Her cheeks must be a flaming pink by now. They certainly felt like they were afire. "No, I'm right as rain."

"Oh, well, I just wanted to make sure you were all right." He cleared his throat and banged the heel of his hand against the huge tree stump. "I guess we ought to be getting back to the cabin."

Sam pushed through the door of the cookhouse and joined them. His glance was curious and a little suspicious as he looked back and forth between them. "Becky, it was right nice to see you this morning. I hope you're feeling better now?" He whisked her cape over her shoulders and handed her bonnet to her.

She accepted them with a smile of thanks.

"I'm fine." She hadn't thought her cheeks could get any hotter, but they did. What must Isaac's father think of her? First, there was the dash to the privy, then escaping from the wedding reception, and now slipping out of the worship service. He must think her quite rude.

"Well, I'll be 'round this week with 'the game.'" Sam clapped his hands together once and looked at her with what could only be described as glee.

"Oh, right, 'the game.' Thank you, Sam. Stop by any time." Becky tugged her bonnet on and tied the ribbons firmly beneath her chin, not liking the way her fingers trembled. She'd gladly wait a lifetime for that visit but had a feeling her father-in-law would be on her trail come sun-up.

"Good afternoon, Son. You look after this little lady, now."

"Good to see you, Pop." Isaac placed a hand on his father's shoulder for a moment. He headed over to the horses, un-tethered them, and led them to where Becky and his father stood.

After mounting their horses and waving to Sam, they had a silent ride returning home. Becky's thoughts spun from the worship service to the conversation she'd had with Jem. Isaac seemed to have the respect of his men, but if they were going without pay, that respect would wear thin quickly. He could be faced with men leaving to go to other outfits, perhaps even the collapse of his business. From the little she knew of him already, his business meant everything to him.

Once they arrived back home, Becky gave the rundown cabin a thorough inspection, which only reinforced her belief that he needed help. She was good at figuring, and had always had a good head for numbers, keeping Papa's books back home.

Perhaps she could help Isaac with that. She straightened her shoulders with resolve.

She'd ask him tonight.

As Isaac brushed down the horses in the lean-to, he kept thinking of the day he'd spent with Rebecca. Having a woman at the camp had seemed strange at first, but not unpleasant. Just when he was thinking maybe his wife could fit somewhat into his life here, she'd turned green from the confined quarters and run outside. Had she found the cookhouse too rough for her taste? Or had it been his men—hard-working honest fellows, who were admittedly rough around the edges? He'd sensed her discomfort with their stares.

Though he'd wanted to follow directly after her, Pop and Brody had needled him mercilessly with questions after she left. Pop had even hinted broadly that she might be in the family way already, but Isaac had managed to fend off the meddling old-timer, without revealing any details of his strange marriage. Then he'd found Becky in a cozy conversation with Jem. The youth was handsome enough to turn a girl's head, even if he were a little young for a woman Rebecca's age. Seeing them standing so close together though had irritated Isaac mightily.

Had she forgotten she had a husband?

Placing his arm around her shoulders had been a knee-jerk reaction that discomfited him now. What was the point? Her heart was back home with her precious Jack. Perhaps she was better off returning home so she could be near her love... an unpleasant thought.

He tossed the brush onto the shelf across the stall and smoothed Siren's sleek coat with his hands. Siren seemed right at home in her stall, and he was already growing accustomed to her welcoming whinnies in the morning. And no matter how much he denied the fact, Rebecca was also starting to carve a spot out for herself in his heart. But letting her into his heart at this point was absolutely unacceptable.

He gave the mare a pat and fetched a bucket of water to fill the horses' trough.

Jem presented another set of problems. The youth seemed hotheaded and unwilling to take direction—a deadly combination in the logging business. He acted like he had something to prove. Moving him to the peeling crew until he proved himself—in the right way—had seemed the only fit course at the time, but after Jem's behavior today, Isaac was almost certain the youth would be gone before the week's end. That was unfortunate. He wasn't a bad sort. If he buckled down and took the work seriously, he could be a great benefit to the operation.

Isaac shook out a helping of hay for each of the horses and some for the goat as well.

"Trouble." He laughed, remembering Rebecca's insistence on a name for the wily critter. She had a spark of humor that flared now and again. Just when he felt he'd distanced himself from her, she'd go and say or do something that drew him to her again.

"Isaac?"

He closed his eyes at the sound of her soft, feminine voice.

Opening his eyes, he turned to look at her. "Can I help you, Rebecca?"

"I've got supper on, but there's something I want to discuss with you." Her voice sounded small and uncertain.

Isaac's gut clenched. Was she going to tell him what had

happened with her and Jack? Good. They could finally get it out in the open. He nodded.

Leaning her back against one of the posts, Rebecca tucked a loose curl behind her ear and moistened her lips. Isaac found himself staring at her mouth and forced his gaze to meet hers. He took a step forward and leaned his hip against the opposite post, so they were facing each other, the width of the stall door between them.

"Go on," he urged.

"I was wondering if you'd mind me helping out with the books?"

Surprised, he stroked a hand across his jaw and considered her words.

She rushed on. "I helped out with Papa's books for his store and have a good head for figuring."

A woman good at figuring? Not that he knew much about women, but he'd always had the notion they weren't much interested in balancing a column of numbers. Rebecca stood before him and returned his regard with a determined gleam. Well, if she was determined, who was he to turn her away? She wasn't really his wife, not in any real way, especially with her *loving another man*, but if she could help out with something other than cooking and cleaning, maybe it would ease the sting a bit.

"When do you want to start?"

Her slow, wide smile made him swallow.

"Tomorrow. Can I start tomorrow?" Her voice was eager, her eyes bright.

"Tomorrow would be fine."

She nodded. "Well, then, I'll go check on the food. Wonderful. Tomorrow." She backed up in the direction of the cabin, then with a little wave, turned and walked quickly to the front door, disappearing inside.

His wife wanted to help with the books? The matter of Jack was unresolved, but Isaac couldn't stop the little surge of pleasure her offer produced.

That night, Becky waited until she was sure Isaac was well asleep before she went to her room. Tonight she'd resolved to have a ceremony of sorts. Before leaving Pepperell, she'd been able to say goodbye to her father, mother, and sister, but not to Jack. Such a thing was impossible given their situation, but now she felt in her heart she needed to close the door on her childhood and look to the future.

She dressed up in her riding clothes and snuck outside to take Siren for a quick midnight ride. Keeping in mind Isaac's constant warnings, she simply circled the clearing a few times. She only wanted to feel the air on her cheeks and remember those first rides she'd taken with Jack and all the memories of hunting with him over the years. She realized the girl she'd been back then had loved Jack with all her youthful enthusiasm, and she would treasure those memories forever. But Jack was a man now, not the boy she'd grown up with. And she wasn't a wild, unrestrained young girl anymore. She was a woman. She was a *married lady*, and she had to stop pining in her heart for what she could never have.

Becky circled around once more, then led Siren back to the lean-to, where she settled her back in for the night, giving her a grateful pat and a hug around her long graceful neck.

Becky returned to her room and took a final waltz around the floor. She spun in time with music intended solely for her own ears.

Goodbye, Jack, she whispered and finally fell to her bed, her face wet with tears. They were old tears, ones she'd bottled up for a long time, and now they came spilling out. She let them fall freely, wanting to get rid of them and move on. It was a release of pent-up emotion, she suspected, the grieving time she'd never allowed herself to have after Jack had come home a married man. After nearly an hour of sobbing, she felt a sense of lightness come over her and an almost overwhelming sense of freedom. Now her new life could begin.

After breakfast the next morning, Becky pored over Isaac's ledger at the kitchen table.

Isaac stood at her elbow, occasionally explaining his shorthand. "That notation there's for the mill." He pointed at an "M" followed by a squiggle.

She nodded slowly.

Everything seemed to be in order, but thinking of Jem's conversation the previous day, Becky knew there must be an error. Isaac, bright as he seemed, must have entered the numbers incorrectly, for he had much more money than could be possible. Looking around the tiny, rundown cabin convinced her she was right. The errors weren't readily apparent, so she'd have to take some time and go through the books line by line. Run the sums again. It might take a while. And when she did find the trouble, she'd approach him tactfully, of course. She'd learned her lesson with her father. Until then, she'd keep an eye on things, so he didn't make any costly mistakes. It was all she could do for now.

"Well, I think I can follow your system," she said brightly.

He handed her a bundle of receipts. "These need to be

entered."

She took them from him, feeling a jolt of awareness as his finger brushed against her palm. He coughed and jerked his hand away. Ducking her head to hide her hurt, she started to untie the string binding the receipts together.

Only, Isaac wasn't moving away. In fact, he was hovering at her elbow as if he had something to say.

She lifted her brows, curious.

"I need to head into town for some supplies," he said. He slapped his hat against his thigh, making her realize he'd been holding it for quite some time, a sign that he was indeed preparing to go out. "Would you care to join me?"

He waited with a look of expectation. Hesitation even.

Sort of like a schoolboy asking a girl to a dance.

His invitation brought a smile.

He really had a way about him, confident boss-man one minute, awkward schoolboy the next. It was really rather an appealing combination: strong and competent, but not so full of himself that you couldn't like him. It stirred her affections, and she found herself wanting to put him at ease.

She also wanted more than anything to go into town.

So she dropped the bundle of receipts on top of the ledger and stood. "Yes."

Isaac immediately stepped back from Rebecca and turned away. He set his hat on his head and then grabbed up his coat, which was hanging over the back of the rocker, where he'd tossed it last night. "I'll get the horses saddled. Can you be ready to leave quick-like?"

At her swift nod of assent, he crossed the room and

walked through the front door without looking back.

Asking her along to buy supplies had been an impulse, Isaac admitted to himself. He didn't normally make a snap decision like that, and the momentary lapse set him on edge. Her offer to help with the books notwithstanding, he'd come to realize last night that it was time to face facts. He had to resign himself to the number-one fact—that she belonged to another man, just as surely as if she were wed to this *Jack* and not to him.

Isaac scowled. To think he'd actually started to believe things were warming nicely between them. He liked her. He'd thought she liked him. He'd even let himself begin to hope a little...

And then late last night he'd tossed in bed for hours, listening to the sounds of her soft humming through the wall and the swish of her slippers across the bare wood floor.

Even now he could picture her waltzing around the small back room with some phantom lover. But it was the sound of her tears afterwards that had nearly kept him up for hours, long after she'd finally stopped and fallen asleep. She hadn't just cried, she'd sobbed. And the sound had seemed to reverberate through the thin wall between them. It was so pitiful sounding he'd been tempted to go to her, try to comfort her, but he'd decided his presence wouldn't be welcome. She'd probably find his intrusion embarrassing.

He'd been a fool. She wasn't going to forget her old love anytime soon. It was time for both of them to admit the truth. Her heart would always belong to Jack. And Isaac couldn't live with a woman who belonged to someone else. He was also all too aware that he was weak where she was concerned. If he were really being honest, he'd have to admit his feelings toward her went beyond *like*. Such a tepid word for what he felt. He hadn't let himself fall in love, but he'd become attached to her. Something lit up inside him whenever she came near. Her soft ways had a way of luring him in, and if he didn't ship her back to Massachusetts soon, he might be tempted to relent and let her stay.

He didn't relish telling her that though.

Although asking her along today had been a snap decision, the idea of sending her off well-supplied did seem the right thing to do. He'd satisfy his responsibility to the woman—he had to start thinking of her that way. Put a little distance between them. In a way, he'd be doing her a favor. She could go home and try to mend things with her beau. He'd pay the fare for her voyage, of course.

There was the matter of their own hasty marriage too, but with some discreet legal consultation, Isaac was sure—well, relatively sure—that he could get their marriage annulled. Not that he planned on marrying again anytime soon, despite his father's touching plea for grandchildren. No, it was Rebecca who would need her freedom to marry Jack. Somehow, he'd find a way to release her from this sham of a marriage.

The thought filled Isaac's mouth with the bitter taste of ashes.

Fifteen

Later in town, Isaac dropped Becky at the general store to begin shopping while he went to pick up feed for the animals. Becky was about to enter the store when she caught sight of her friend Meggie sitting in a parked farm wagon.

"Meggie!" Becky called out to her former shipmate and hurried to the wagon's side.

Meggie waved wildly from her perch. She leaned down and grasped Becky's outstretched hand. "Becky! It seems like forever."

"It does seem like forever. Where's Will?"

"He's making a deposit at the bank."

"Are you happy?" Becky asked tentatively, resting her hand on the wagon rail. Her mother would have said it wasn't polite to pry, but this was her friend. She'd been so lonely for someone to talk to, and now here was Meggie. It was like an answer to a prayer she hadn't thought to pray.

At her question, Meggie blushed a pretty pink. Her shy girlish grin said more than her softly spoken, "Yes."

"I'm so happy for you, Meggie."

"Things are tight on Will's folks' farm, but we're making ends meet. We've been married just over two weeks."

"Us too."

"What about you? Are you happy with Isaac?"

Becky hesitated, drawing in a deep breath and wishing her troubled thoughts weren't written as clearly on her face as she knew they were.

"What's wrong?" The look Meggie gave her was searching, and Becky was sure her friend didn't miss anything.

Becky looked down the street in the direction Isaac had gone. He'd also agreed to post a letter for her to her mother and had said he'd meet her back at the general store when he was through. Seeing no sign of him, she met Meggie's concerned gaze.

"Things are strained between us," she admitted.

"I'm sorry to hear that."

"Oh, Meggie, I'm trying to be a good wife for Isaac, but no matter what I do, it doesn't seem to be enough. I thought things were going better between us, but then this morning he's been different. I don't know what happened, but he seems as cold as a mountain stream now."

"Do you love him?" Her friend probed gently.

Becky hesitated. "My heart's been so caught up in Jack that I haven't felt anything for Isaac besides a growing friendship. I respect him though—I really do—and want our marriage to work."

"But...?"

"I'm just tired, I guess." Becky sighed heavily, feeling so completely torn in two. It seemed these days she didn't even know who she was anymore. "I've been trying so hard to change..."

"Change what?"

"Oh, there's this scripture in the Bible, about having a gentle and quiet spirit."

"I know that one. My mother liked that one a lot," Meggie said wryly. By which Becky supposed her mother quoted it to her when Meggie was growing up.

"I'm trying, Meggie," she said. "I really am. I want to be that kind of woman. A better woman."

"Well, that's a good thing then, isn't it?" Meggie smiled encouragingly. "You're trying."

"I suppose...but I feel so...so...*not me.*"

Meggie frowned, obviously puzzled. "You mean you have plans you want to push on him—or you keep wanting to strike out at him in some way? You can't mean that?"

"No! Of course not. I'd never."

"Then what do you mean?"

"It's just so hard, not being free to do the things I love."

"Like what?" Meggie leaned closer, placing her hand over Becky's, such a warm, thoughtful gesture.

If only we lived closer to each other, Becky thought. She'd like having a friend to talk to.

"Like riding. I love to ride fast, Meggie," she confessed. "And I'm trying so hard to be a lady."

"Well, I like to ride fast too. Sometimes. What's wrong with that?"

"I like to ride astride," Becky clarified.

"Me too! I hate a sidesaddle." Meggie grimaced. "Does that mean *I'm* not a lady?"

"No...of course not. I mean, it's *the way* I ride." Becky bit her lip, confused.

Meggie pulled a thoughtful face, as if trying to work a puzzle. Becky knew the feeling. Lately, she'd felt as if a few pieces of her own puzzle were missing. Everything was so jumbled in her head.

Had she been wrong about riding?

It seemed too late now to go back. She'd insisted on riding sidesaddle when Isaac asked her. He'd think it strange if she changed course now. Wouldn't he?

Her stomach twisted in a knot. What a tangle it all was. She didn't know how to fix it.

"I don't think that verse means what you think it means," Meggie said, her face clearing. As if that was all there was to it, a simple mistake.

She obviously didn't understand.

Becky just looked at her, disheartened. She'd told Meggie about her troubles with Jack aboard ship, and her friend had listened. She'd hugged Becky and shared her own troubles too, how her father had been killed in the war and how her mother had needed to go live with an aunt. Those late night talks had sealed their friendship. But evidently Becky had left out some crucial details about Jack, because Meggie just didn't seem to understand.

Becky sighed. It wasn't a conversation she wanted to have standing in the street. Isaac was about to return any minute.

"It's complicated," she said at last. "Maybe someday we could sit over tea and have a chat."

"I'd like that." Meggie gave Becky's hand a pat. Becky shared a look with her, both of them realizing they wouldn't likely have an opportunity to have tea anytime soon.

Knowing that, Becky felt a sudden surge of urgency. She cast a quick look down the street again and back at Meggie. "I wanted to tell you...I said goodbye to Jack last night," she whispered.

"You did what?"

"I know it sounds foolish, but I decided to put my memories of him to rest. Like a ceremony, you know? I think I can finally move on now. He's married to someone else, and that's never going to change. He's not mine, and I'm not his. I'm hoping in time I can come to love Isaac. He's such a good man."

"Then tell him so."

"Tell him? You mean, tell him outright—just like that?" Becky wasn't normally shy, but there was something about Isaac.

He had a way about him, sometimes hot, sometimes cold. She didn't always know how he was going to react.

"Go on, Becky. Tell him how you feel about him. Ask him if he'll give your marriage a chance to grow. Who knows? Maybe things will improve between you. From what you've said, he sounds like a good man. Maybe you just need to clear the air between you."

Hearing Meggie's words of encouragement gave Becky a surge of hope. Maybe offering Isaac her friendship and respect would soften his attitude toward her.

"Do you think it will work?" she asked.

"You'll never know until you try. In any case, you may plant a seed in his mind. He'll start thinking of the possibilities... I know it." Meggie gave Becky's hand a final pat for emphasis.

Will walked up to then. After an introduction from Meggie and an exchange of greetings, he climbed up next to his bride. He seemed a quiet young man. Practical. Hard-working. He wasn't talkative by any stretch, but he had kind eyes, which Becky found reassuring. As the worn wagon trundled off down the road, Meggie turned around in her seat and waved. Then she folded her hands in prayer, lifting them high for Becky to see.

Her message was clear: she was going to pray for her.

Becky's eyes smarted with tears. She definitely needed her friend's prayers. Waving back, Becky watched until the wagon disappeared over the crest of a hill. Blotting her eyes on the cuff of her sleeve, she entered the general store.

Isaac had left her with instructions to collect any supplies she needed for herself, mentioning fabric specifically, to her surprise, and groceries for the kitchen. Thinking he might need new clothes himself, she selected a length of red cotton for a summer work shirt, denim for new trousers, a couple of spools of thread, and some white linen for new underthings for herself. She then collected a selection of canned goods, along with sugar, flour, and other necessities for the pantry. She'd just finished arranging her purchases on the counter when Isaac strode through the front door and came to her side. He looked over her selection with a slight frown.

"I don't really need the linen," she hurriedly said and picked it up to return it to the shelf.

His hand covered hers, and he gently guided her to drop the fabric onto the counter with the other things she'd set aside to purchase.

"It's fine. I want you to get everything you need."

After scanning the counter again, he walked over to the display of cloth and took down a couple of bolts of cotton fabric: a cheerful yellow one and a creamy white one with sprigs of green leaves and vines. He laid them on the counter and, after getting her nod of approval, had the clerk cut a nice long yardage of each.

"How are you for soaps and such?"

She felt her cheeks grow warm at the somewhat personal question. "I could use some."

"Get what you need."

She could hear him instruct the clerk to box their purchases while she selected her toiletries. As she picked out what she needed from the limited assortment, she gulped at the prices. Isaac was spending an awful lot of money on things for her today.

She stepped up to the counter and handed her personal items to the clerk to be wrapped in paper and added to the boxes.

"I really don't need this much."

Isaac ignored her protest and lifted a box under each arm. "Could you get the door?"

"Of course." She rushed over to prop it open for him and called her thanks to the clerk. Scurrying after Isaac, she helped him arrange the boxes on the skid hitched to his bay. Her gaze caught and held on a plain brown package lying on top of one of the crates. Not recognizing it, she puzzled over its contents. With a shrug, she accepted Isaac's assistance to mount Siren and followed him on the long trip back up the mountain. The whole way, she wished she'd never told Isaac she rode sidesaddle.

Isaac waited until after supper that night to present Rebecca with his gift. He didn't know what had prompted him to buy it for her.

"This is for you." He pushed their plates aside and laid the package on the table in front of her. He'd kept it under his chair the entire time.

"What's this?" Her voice held a note of suppressed excitement. Her fingers traced the surface of the brown paper, her face lit with curiosity.

"See for yourself."

She flashed him an uncertain smile and untied the knot in the twine. Pulling back the paper, she gasped in wonder as she revealed the small Bible inside.

"A Bible?"

"I noticed how you liked reading mine in the morning."

"You noticed." Her simply spoken reply held a hint of question. Her eyes were bright and watery.

"Not tears again?" he begged.

"Thank you, Isaac." She clasped the Bible to her chest, hugging it close, like a child with a beloved doll. "Thank you."

Her sincere thanks moved him, and he felt an uncomfortable burning in his own eyes, realizing he'd bought it as a farewell gift. Unable to bring up the unpleasant topic of her leaving just yet, he resolved to tell her in the morning.

Later, as he prepared for bed, he remembered how Rebecca had sat at the table for hours poring over the pages of her new Bible, how she'd meet his eyes now and then and smile one of those bright smiles of hers, the ones that warmed his insides. She appreciated the Good Book more than anyone he'd ever known. He sat in bed propped against the wall with the covers pulled up to his chest. He was reading a few pages of scripture himself when Rebecca's soft feminine voice made him sit up straighter.

"Isaac?"

"Yes, Rebecca?"

He couldn't have been more surprised when she pushed aside the potato-sack curtain and poked her head hesitantly around the edge.

"May I speak with you?"

He cleared his throat and tried to sound offhand. "Of course."

She perched on the edge of his pop's empty bed. As she settled on the lumpy mattress, he took in the crisp white cotton nightgown she wore, noticing how it was gathered in a bow at her neck, how the cloth fell loosely about her. She propped her heels on the bedrail and tucked her feet quickly under the folds of material with one hand, hugging her Bible to her stomach with the other. Only her dainty little toes peeked out from under the hem. Covered neck to toe in white, she seemed again like an innocent bride on her wedding night.

He shook off that image. She was in love with another man, he reminded himself.

"Isaac." She started hesitantly and stopped. She moistened her lips as if she were nervous and took a deep breath.

"What is it?" he asked, her anxiety making him anxious too.

"Isaac, I'd like to talk with you about something."

He nodded mutely.

"The past couple of weeks..." Her words seemed to hang in the air for a moment. She cleared her throat and continued, "The past couple of weeks, I've come to like and respect you. I know we got started the wrong way, but I'd like to try to set it to rights. I'm sorry for all the trouble I've caused you. I know you only married me out of respect for your father—"

"I—" He sat up straighter. He wanted to deny it, but that wouldn't be the truth, and she interrupted him anyway.

"Wait. Could I please say my piece?" she asked softly, fingering the thick reddish-gold braid that was draped over her shoulder and fell to her waist.

He nodded and sank back against the wall.

"Your reasons for marrying me and my reasons for marrying you seem moot now. We're married. And, well, I'd like to make the best of it. We have the start of a friendship, I think." She paused and waited for his brief nod before going on, "Can we build on that, do you think?"

"And what about this Jack fellow?" He forced his voice to remain level, but his heart started pumping fiercely in his chest. "Do you have it in your heart to—to try to make amends with the man?" He set his Bible on the old trunk next to his bed and crossed his arms over his chest. Looking over at her, he noticed how quiet she was, not moving, not even seeming to breathe as she watched him with a wide-eyed expression.

"Jack?" she whispered, clearly alarmed that he would mention the man. "No. There's no making amends with Jack, not ever. He's married. There was...it ended up there was someone else. Another woman. And a baby on the way. So, no. There's no 'making amends' with Jack. He's married now, and *I'm* a married woman now too." She looked at him searchingly, as if wondering how he—Isaac— could have forgotten such an important detail. "What I wanted to say is I have every intention of being a good wife to you, Isaac Jessup, but I need to know if you want me for a wife?"

"Wait." He swallowed. "Jack's married?" The room seemed brighter all of sudden. His heart beat a little more steadily against his ribs.

"That's right." Her voice was soft, subdued. "And about the other?"

She didn't repeat her question, but the flash of uncertainty in her eyes told him his answer had the power to devastate her. She'd been jilted. That much was evident from what she'd said, but more so from what she hadn't said. He had no intention of adding to her pain.

"I'd like to make a go of this marriage too," he stated firmly and noticed how the stiff line of her body loosened ever so slightly.

She closed her eyes briefly, and he had the distinct impression she'd worked up her courage to ask him and was relieved at his answer.

"Isaac"—her voice was a bit strained, which immediately made him wonder what she could possibly say next—"there's one more thing. I'd like to know— That is, what were you thinking— I mean, are you planning to..." Her words trailed off in a mortified whisper. She could barely make herself look at him, that much was clear. "When are you planning to come to our bed?" she finally blurted out.

What a question!

A heady warmth flooded Isaac. He wanted to be next to her. He wanted to kiss her right then and there, maybe even tell her *tonight*. His pulse took off at an alarming rate. It was all he could do to stay where he was.

Slow down. Just this morning he was thinking about sending her away. It was all too sudden.

"It may take some time for us both to come to terms with—with everything," he said. "For now, it just doesn't seem quite right to share a bed." He suddenly felt like a bumbling seventeen-year-old, all flushed and gawky.

If his men could see him now... Well, it didn't bear thinking about.

Her gaze fell from his, and she ducked her chin low. He wondered why that made him feel so guilty. You'd think she'd be relieved. Somehow, he'd crushed her feelings. He didn't like the sensation. So he pushed his covers aside and crossed over to her, sitting next to her—close but not touching. He took her hand and squeezed it.

"It's not that I don't want that. Given time, of course." He pressed a chaste kiss to the back of her hand. It would have to be enough for now. Earlier that morning, he'd been set to ship her back home. Now, he just felt confused.

Rebecca's brow furrowed fleetingly, then cleared, and she offered him one of her full, knock-him-over smiles. "Fair enough." She stood, landing lightly on her feet. "Well, then, goodnight," she said.

Her smile dimmed bit as she walked out of his grasp, letting his hand fall to the mattress. He watched as she disappeared around the edge of the curtain.

The door to the back room soon clicked shut. Closing

his eyes, he fell back against his father's bed and finally gave voice to the groan he'd been holding back. Even now, he felt drawn to her. *Liked* her. He'd been all set to stifle his growing feelings and send her back home, but now she'd turned the tables on him by telling him Jack was married.

Her directness had surprised him. She hadn't promised him she could come to love him someday. She'd extended her friendship and no more. She'd spoken plainly with him—painfully so. Her honor drew him like no other feminine charm could have. Well, no, that wasn't quite true. He definitely found her attractive. Her unexpected question about their marriage bed had only served to remind him that he was a man and she was a woman. His heart was still pounding uncomfortably fast.

He'd have to be satisfied for now with a relationship based on companionship. Later, if she showed signs of letting go of Jack—and perhaps when his pride didn't sting so much—they could become man and wife in a real sense. On that unsettling thought, he returned to his bed, turned down the lamp, and rolled over to try to sleep.

Becky paced her room, going over her conversation with Isaac again and again in her mind. He'd accepted her offer of friendship, which was a relief, but he'd drawn a line of sorts between them as well. The only possible explanation was he wasn't sure if he wanted her for a wife. His words were coming from a feeling of duty and commitment—nothing more. Though she didn't have the right to expect it, part of her felt the tug of wanting more. She couldn't afford to be so fickle-hearted, she told herself. She'd offered her friendship. He'd accepted. End of story.

Pushing those thoughts aside, she decided to focus on what she could do to forge a new beginning between them. With a determined lift of her chin, she unpacked the red cotton fabric she'd bought for a work shirt for him and set about cutting out the pattern and piecing it together. She wasn't much of a seamstress, but she kept the lines simple, and before long she was sitting cross-legged on her bed trying to make neat, even stitches. The repetitive task of pushing the needle in and out of the fabric brought a feeling a peace she hadn't felt during all her pacing and fretting.

There was a form of contentment in doing what she could and not worrying about the rest.

After several days of newfound peace with his bride, Isaac could now go about his work without feeling guilty about it. Each evening after dinner, Rebecca sewed while sitting in the rocker and softly humming her waltz. Although the tune was an uncomfortable reminder of Jack—the man she loved—he admitted to himself that he enjoyed the domestic scene. He liked the way her hair would have loosened from its knot by the end of the day, how the reddish-gold strands curled about her face and neck.

He found himself thinking about just such a scene one morning as he stood in a recently cleared area with his father. They were supposed to be organizing their next swath for felling, but Isaac couldn't concentrate fully on the map. Thoughts of Rebecca brought up other concerns.

"Harper said there's a mean grizzly running loose," Isaac said, speaking his worries aloud, sharing the news as if he had no more than a casual interest. Rebecca was a city girl. She wouldn't know what to do if she came upon a bear. He absently worried a loose cord on his vest.

Though he'd purposefully not mentioned Rebecca, Pop took one look at his face and came right to the point. "You're going to have to teach her to shoot."

An image of Rebecca's small womanly hands gripping a rifle flickered through Isaac's mind. It just seemed...wrong.

"What?" His father's voice broke into his thoughts.

"I don't know—"

"She can't stay in the cabin for the rest of her life—now, can she?"

"No." Isaac sighed in defeat.

You just couldn't argue with Pop.

"I came by the other day and no one was about." His father glanced at him, his steel-gray eyes openly curious.

"We went into town for supplies. Need anything?"

"Thanks, I'll stop by." Pop seemed especially satisfied with the idea of dropping by the cabin. He seemed to enjoy spending time with Rebecca, and Isaac wondered what they found to talk about.

"Saw Dally at the feed store," he said, remembering. "Been a long time since I'd seen him last. He was surprised to hear I was married. Invited Rebecca and me to a dance up at his place next week." Telling Pop about Dally reminded him that he hadn't mentioned the dance to Rebecca yet. He hadn't been sure at the time if she was even staying, and then, with all that had happened since, he'd sort of forgotten about it.

"Good, good. Always liked Dally." Pop shrugged and turned his attention back to the map spread in front of them on the stump serving as their worktable. "I think we should move the crew here next. Easy access to the Skid Road." He traced a line with his finger across the page. "And not too far from the logging camp either."

"Right. Let's plan on it." Isaac drew a circle on the map and rolled it up, tucking it under his arm.

"Teach the gal to shoot, Son. You won't regret it." Pop grabbed his shoulder and gave him a fatherly shake.

"Okay, Pop." Isaac grinned at him, but felt a wave of uneasiness about the idea. The image of Rebecca with a gun didn't sit right at all, but maybe spending some time together would help their newfound peace to grow into friendship. Although, he already felt drawn to her too much for comfort.

"And you won't forget to tell your old pop if you and your bride have some particularly good news?" Pop's brows wagged suggestively.

"All right, Pop." Isaac couldn't help laughing at his father's antics, but he couldn't meet those all-too-observant steel-blue eyes. Pop could read him like no other person could. He almost wished he could assure his father that someday soon he'd be a grandfather But the jumbled mess of Isaac's mind and heart needed untangling before he and Rebecca could set off on having a baby—that much was certain. Even as he made the resolution, an image of Rebecca with an infant tucked in her arms and a sweet smile of contentment on her lips filled him with unexpected longing. He shook the feeling off.

That wasn't likely to happen anytime soon.

Watching Isaac pace the room after breakfast the next morning, Becky knew a moment of panic. He obviously had something he wanted to say, but hesitated saying it. Her mind searched for any mistake she may have made, something she'd forgotten to do. Had he discovered she'd forgotten to fasten Trouble's gate yesterday? The goat had nibbled on some of the laundry on the line before Becky caught her at it and returned her to the barn. The rascal had even taken a nip out of Becky's hem along the way, and she was still trying to fix the damage.

Had Sam told Isaac he didn't know anything about "the game"?

She continued to repair the hem of her torn skirt and watched her husband out of the corner of her eye. When he finally spoke, she jumped a little, and met his gaze with a sinking, guilty sensation in her stomach. She raised her eyebrows in what she hoped was an innocent-looking fashion.

Isaac coughed into his hand and then tugged at his collar with his index finger. "I'm going to need to show you how to shoot a gun."

Becky slowly released the breath she'd been holding and blinked at him in relief, until she realized the implication of his words. She wasn't supposed to know how to shoot a gun. She was supposed to be a perfectly proper young lady. Her cheeks cooled as the blood drained from her face. She forced a swallow. "Oh?"

"Harper's seen bear in the area." He cast her a nervous-looking glance and rushed on. "Now, I don't want you scared of your own shadow or anything, but you'll need to know how to handle a weapon. I can't always be here protecting you, so I'd like you to know how to protect yourself. That being said, you'll still need to stay close to the cabin. Some bears come looking for trash, so we'll have to be even more careful how we dispose of food."

She should have told him about seeing the grizzly that day by the stream. They were careful to bury the garbage anyway, but she should have mentioned it. Then again that would have involved telling him she'd wandered farther from the cabin than he would have liked.

"So." He cleared his throat again, looking more than a little uncomfortable with the idea. "I'll go get my rifle, and we'll head out."

"Now?" Becky knew a moment of panic. He wanted to go right now. There was no time to think it through. She'd have to plan out her strategy along the way.

He was already checking the barrel of his rifle and loading his pockets with bullets.

"I'll just be a moment." Becky ducked into her room. Her dress was a simple cotton day dress, and she'd abandoned the hooped crinoline days ago. Isaac hadn't seemed to notice the change anyway, so she'd opted for petticoats this morning. She fanned her cheeks with her hands, trying to clear her thoughts. She'd just have to pretend to be learning from scratch. How hard could that be?

On that not-so-comforting thought, she grabbed up her cape and bonnet, wishing she could wear her familiar old hunting trousers and hat.

They left the horses back at the barn and hiked up the mountain a ways. Isaac set up a row of bottles at the base of an enormous fir and jogged back to join her, all business-like. He swung his rifle off his back and gave her a demonstration of how to load the weapon properly, how to point it away from others while handling it, and how to raise it to the pocket of her shoulder and aim. Becky watched him, admiring the way he moved. He handled the weapon with such ease, obviously confident in his skill.

"Now, it's your turn," he said. She watched as he placed the hammer at half cock, opened the breech block, and removed the bullet. He snapped it back in place and handed her the weapon unloaded.

Pretending to find the weight of the gun unfamiliar, she allowed her arms to drop a bit lower than she would have normally. The gun *was* a little heavier than hers, but it wasn't that much different than Jack's, the one he'd first taught her with.

"It's heavy." She pulled her lips in and swiped them with her tongue to ease the sudden dryness in her mouth. She offered Isaac a hesitant smile and hefted the rifle a little higher. Although careful to keep the gun pointed away from him, she held it at a deliberately awkward angle.

"Is this right?" she asked.

He frowned and corrected the position by placing his hands on her forearms and shifting the gun's weight forward.

"Now, try to load it," he said.

She blinked at him for a moment, then frowned in concentration as she fumbled with the hammer and block.

"This way." His tone was patient and quiet. He guided her hands and helped her open the block. He handed her a bullet and watched as she placed it in backwards. "The other way." Still patient, but slightly alarmed.

"Oh. Sorry." She grinned at him weakly and turned the bullet around. Deciding not to press her luck too far, she closed the breech block with a nice sharp click and looked at him for his next directions.

"Good." He sounded pleased, and she decided her decision to show some competency had been a good one. "Now, the hammer." He pointed to it, in case she'd forgotten what was what, Becky supposed.

She fully cocked the hammer just as he'd done earlier, and he nodded.

"Good, now aim it at the bottle like I showed you and

shoot."

Becky lifted the barrel, aimed directly at the leftmost bottle, and then found her own target just beyond it, a bare spot on the enormous fir. Squeezing the trigger slowly, she waited until her bullet hit her target, missing the bottle completely, and then gasped. "I had no idea it would be so loud." She squinted at him as if in pain.

"Don't worry about not hitting anything your first try. It'll take some practice to improve your aim, but with time you'll be hitting those bottles every time." He grinned with an obviously forced enthusiasm.

Becky smiled weakly. She'd never played down her skill before, and it felt like lying. Maybe it was. She certainly felt a little sick inside.

"Here." Isaac took the rifle from her, reloaded quickly and expertly, and shot one of the bottles, shattering it. "See how I line up and look down the barrel?" He held the gun up to show her how to aim and handed it back to her.

After missing another few rounds, Becky hesitantly allowed herself to chip the neck of the leftmost bottle on her next, producing a shout from Isaac.

"That's it!"

She felt a burst of happiness at his smile, but knew he'd find it strange if she hit the remaining bottles. So she missed the next two and nicked the third at the base.

"We'll call it a day for now." Isaac took the gun from her, loaded it, and then hung it across his back.

"You're leaving it loaded?"

"Just to be safe." Isaac looked off into the trees. He gave her a comforting smile. "But we probably won't run into any trouble."

Becky looked off into the trees as well, remembering the

big brown beast charging after her that day by the stream, and how naked she'd felt without her gun. She still felt a little naked without it, but Isaac had proved his aim was accurate, so she followed closely after him.

As Isaac gathered up the remaining bottles, Becky bent to examine her target in the tree trunk. Her bullets peppered the surface in a tight circle. She allowed herself an unobserved moment to beam with unladylike pride. With a lift of her chin, she straightened and hid the bullet holes with her skirt before he noticed.

She wondered, rather uncomfortably, if this was how a drunk felt, hiding a bottle of whiskey behind his back. It wasn't a good feeling, especially since Isaac *wanted* her to learn how to shoot. He'd brought her here to teach her, hadn't he?

It was because of the bear, of course. And he wanted her to be able to defend herself if she was attacked.

Maybe it had been wrong to hide her true talent. Pretending to be something she wasn't left her feeling slightly sickened, like she'd swallowed something bad. Jack had taught her to shoot. But in the end he'd chosen a proper lady for his bride. So what had *she* been—a friend? More like a kid sister? Or even—she winced—a brother? She hadn't thought so. She'd thought he loved her. He'd even danced with her. Kissed her once. But maybe she'd just been practice...?

She was a tight ball of confusion inside.

If only she could reveal her true talent to Isaac... If he wanted her to learn, then why not show off her skill? She pushed the fruitless idea away. If Isaac found out how well she could shoot, then he'd also find out she'd been raised an absolute hoyden. It would color his perception of her. And he'd also know she had been presenting herself in a not-so-truthful light. She felt guilty about that—prickly little stingers of guilt that dug at her everywhere—and the idea of letting Isaac in on her secret and seeing his low opinion of her was just too mortifying.

Why did everything have to be so confusing? And why did trying to be a proper lady have to feel so awkward?

Perhaps if he brought her out shooting again, she could shoot a bottle or two, show some progress, and eventually he'd be confident enough to let her carry a gun. She wondered what he was thinking as he gathered up the bottles.

Isaac frowned with concern as he picked up the last un-broken bottle. How could he have possibly thought Rebecca could learn how to shoot a gun? They'd spent the better part of an hour practicing, and she'd made only marginal progress. More likely it was a case of beginner's luck she'd grazed those two bottles. The shots hadn't even knocked either one out of position. Looking over at her, standing so tiny and frail next to the massive tree, he felt the urge to protect her even more strongly. And now that he'd opened his heart to the idea of her staying, he couldn't help imagining what it would be like to have her as his true bride.

"My old logging friend, Dally, is having a dance up at his place next Sunday," he said casually, realizing as he said it that they were likely setting up a reel. If they went, he'd have a chance to dance with Rebecca. Everyone would expect it, with them being married and all.

What would it be like to hold her?

To know she loved him?

Now where had that thought come from?

"Oh?" she said.

"I thought you might like to go," he said, not so much a statement but a question. He felt much like a youth asking his first girl to a dance. He hadn't done much of that, he thought wryly.

"Sounds nice." She kept staring at him, her gaze soft and inviting.

Unaware that he'd moved, Isaac found himself standing before her. She looked up at him, her wide eyes full of questions. His gaze wandered down to her sweetly curved mouth. Dropping the sack of bottles beside his boot, he circled her tiny form with his arms and brought her against his chest. Before he could stop himself, he leaned down and formed his lips to hers. With his eyes closed, his senses were alive to the clean fresh scent of her lemony soap, the softness of her lips, the sound of her swiftly indrawn breath.

For a moment lost in the kiss, he could imagine she was truly his.

Memories of their wedding night flooded him. She'd kissed him in her sleep, called him "Jack," vowed her love and devotion to him... Hadn't he heard her humming her lover's tune just moments before they left the cabin?

What was he doing?

He stepped back quickly and set her a good safe distance away from him.

There was nothing like a woman sighing another man's name to sour a man's desire—even if it was only in his memory.

He apologized, his roughly spoken words taking the shine out of her expression. Berating himself as a fool, he stalked off toward the path. How could he have forgotten she loved another man? She'd offered him friendship. *Friendship. Friendship. Friendship.* Though she seemed to welcome the thought of him sharing her bed, he couldn't help feeling it was wrong to love her.

If her heart were free, why, it'd be a different matter. But her heart wasn't free. Kissing her was wrong. W-R-O-N-G.

Just as certainly, he was sure her friendship wasn't enough. It seemed like such a poor substitute for what he wanted. He wanted a real marriage. One based on love. Like the one his parents had. Why should he open his heart up, just to have it trampled on? Better to go slowly and wait for signs from her that she welcomed his love, that someday she could return it.

Unfortunately, Becky needed several more shooting lessons this next week. Spending time with her was the last thing he should do after kissing her like that, but it was a husband's duty to protect his wife.

So he'd let his defenses down today. He wouldn't weaken again.

Not until the time was right.

Becky stood for a moment staring after Isaac's retreating back. What had just happened? One minute he was kissing her—and she'd found it a surprisingly pleasurable moment given the confused state of her heart—and the next he was pushing her away.

She thought he planned to walk all the way home without her, but then he paused. He glanced over his shoulder at her and just as quickly turned away. He stood there, his straight back sending a silent message. He was waiting for her to follow him, and he wasn't the least bit happy about it. At least he wasn't abandoning her to that big grizzly, she thought with a humorless smile.

She snatched up her cape and bonnet, which she'd left in a neat pile under a nearby tree, and followed after Isaac. As if he heard her footfall behind him, he started walking at a steady pace toward the path.

How could he kiss her, all warm and deliciously soft like that, and then shut her out so completely? He'd stirred up feelings of attraction unlike any she'd ever felt before—nothing like the girlish giddiness she'd felt with Jack, but a grown-up-woman kind of feeling that completely shook her.

His actions afterward could only mean one thing: he regretted kissing her. Right?

But at some point, he'd asked if she'd like to go to a dance. She remembered that distinctly. It had been moments before his lips had begun their descent toward hers. He'd said a friend of his from another logging outfit had invited them to a dance.

Didn't that mean Isaac *wanted* to dance with her?

Could that be right?

It didn't sound right.

Certainly her heart had thumped more loudly at the prospect of spending time with him, of being in his arms as they spun in time to music. She couldn't stop going over his words and his kiss. Nothing had seemed amiss in that. Not until he'd pushed back and tramped off like a man on a mission.

She sighed.

The man was un-understandable. She smiled at the awkward turn of phrase. It wasn't quite "proper," but it fit.

In spite of his strange actions, she kept feeling a tiny thrill return again and again at the thought of the upcoming dance. Sunday, he'd said. She smiled and skipped a few times to catch up to Isaac's much longer stride. She hurried along a few paces behind him on the narrow path all the way back to the cabin, admiring the way he walked. Like he owned the place. Like the boss-man he was. Young but competent. She admired the width of his shoulders too. His back looked strong, like he was used to lifting and moving logs or something, which made sense. She knew his arms were strong just from that one quick embrace.

He certainly wasn't hard to look at.

If you liked that sort of thing.

I do. I actually think I do.

She smiled thoughtfully to herself.

And on Sunday, they were going to a dance. She loved dancing.

Sixteen

Isaac kept his promise to himself to keep his distance from Rebecca as best he could. Although he'd taken her shooting a couple more times, and each time she'd improved a little, he was still nervous about the idea of her handling a weapon on her own. The remainder of the week he'd plowed into his work with a vengeance to keep himself occupied.

Being busy hadn't erased the memory of holding her in his arms or kissing her though. Every night when he fell into bed, he was in tune with the slightest noises coming from the next room. He could almost hear the sound of her brush stroking through her hair—pictured it long and loose around her shoulders like that evening when she'd met him at the door. The clean lemony scent of her soap seemed to permeate through the walls.

He'd toss and turn, trying to bury the pleasure he'd felt holding her in his arms, the sense of being absorbed by her as he'd kissed her. No matter how hard he tried he couldn't shake the memories. Every morning was the same: she smiled at him, offered him a well-cooked breakfast, and wished him a good day at work.

And what did he do?

Like a sore-headed beast, he grumbled at her, shot her irritated scowls, and made their brief time together intolerable. The evenings weren't much different. Thank goodness Pop was still bringing by a steady supply of game, for they ate well enough. That was about all that went well. Her constant humming every single day reminded him that she loved Jack. In fact, it seemed to him that she was humming more often. A torture. The lively tune buzzed in his ears even when she wasn't around. It was a small, stupid thing, he knew, but it kept him from relenting. His heart pestered him with guilty feelings about it. He wasn't treating her right. Not like a husband should.

Not that he was her husband in the real sense of the word, an issue that didn't bear thinking on too much.

But a man protected his woman. Loved her.

Not that she'd married him with any intention of offering her love in return.

But she'd become a dutiful bride in every other sense of the word.

His mind warred back and forth. Finally, he couldn't stand it anymore. He just didn't *like* himself these days. If he didn't stop acting like a brute, then he couldn't live with himself any longer.

He needed to change. And quick. Like yesterday.

Pausing for a deep breath of cool mountain air, Isaac swiped his forehead with his sleeve and then plunged his axe into the stump he'd been using as a chopping block for splitting logs.

No. If he couldn't be decent to the woman—no matter where her devotions lay—then he wasn't the man he wanted to be. And that wouldn't do at all. He hauled the skid back to the cabin, stacked the logs next to the lean-to, and finished his other chores as efficiently as possible. The dance was tomorrow, and he had some serious heart changing to do before sun-up.

After worship service the next morning, Isaac rode with Rebecca on the long trek to Dally's camp and found the festivities already in action. He looked around with interest at the handful of women in the group and the children that were bounding about. There looked to be about a dozen children, give or take, ranging in age from babes in arms to the half-grown variety. It was hard to tell exactly how many there were of them, because they were darting back and forth. Spotting Dally, he led Rebecca over to introduce her to his old friend, who was much the same stocky young man he'd known before, except his sandy hair was now thinning a little on top and he had a few laugh lines around his eyes.

"Isaac!" His friend gave him a back-thumping bear hug. "Welcome to my little corner of the world."

"Scarcely little. This is quite an operation you've got here, Dally." Isaac looked around at the neat rows of cabins and large cookhouse, complete with a front stoop and white rocking chairs. The smell of a wood fire and meat grilling drifted on the air. "You've done all this in seven years?"

"Who would have thought two green fallers like us would end up owning their own operations someday? Boggles the mind, don't it?"

Isaac chuckled and turned to Rebecca, "Dally, this is my wife, Rebecca. Rebecca, this is Dally, an old friend."

"Not so old, not so old. Only have a few years on you, friend. Don't forget. A pleasure, young lady. I understand you just recently got hitched up with this here ruffian?"

Rebecca shook Dally's hand. "Thank you for the invitation, Mr. Dally. Yes, Isaac and I were recently wed."

"No 'Mister.' Just Dally. Short for a name I don't care to reveal." He winked at her.

Dally placed an arm around a sturdy, capable-looking brunette who joined him at his side. "This is my wife, Catherine, and these are my children. Come on over here, young'uns," he called. A bevy of children of all sizes gathered around him, and he placed a hand on each of their shoulders in turn. "This here is William, and Emily and Mary Alice—twins, though they don't look nothin' alike. This is Patrick, Henry, and the littlest one here is Bess." He hoisted a cherub-faced toddler onto his shoulder and beamed at his guests with fatherly pride.

"Six?" Isaac asked incredulously, even as he smiled politely in greeting at Catherine and their brood of children.

"And one on the way." Dally bent to give his wife a peck on the cheek. He waggled his eyebrows playfully at her, and she swatted him on the arm. Her cheeks colored up prettily, bringing a youthful glow to her face.

"Get on now, Dally," Catherine said, but her tone was light, affectionate. Seeing the contented little smile she gave Dally, Isaac decided he liked her. She was obviously a sensible, flexible sort of woman, suited to this kind of life.

Dally continued, "You never met Catherine, of course, because she brought the older children up from Sacramento after I got this place under way."

Isaac remembered Dally talking about his wife and "young'uns," but he'd never thought Dally would bring them here. Even though Pop's wish for grandchildren had spurred him into marriage, somewhere in the back of his mind he'd never been able to imagine having a family survive, let alone prosper, in the midst of a logging operation. Too dangerous. But looking at Dally surrounded by his family, Isaac saw a man who was proving him wrong.

Suddenly wishing he and Rebecca had news of their own to share, he swallowed hard. He cast a glance at Rebecca and found her watching Dally's family with a wistful expression, a sort of yearning look that made him wish they had the kind of relationship where he could give her a quick peck on the cheek, like Dally and his wife. But they didn't.

"Well, there's no shortage of food." Dally waved his children off to continue playing. "Zed's got a fine pig roasting on the spit. And we've got an apple pie contest later. Catherine will win again this year, of course. She makes the best pie."

Isaac's stomach grumbled at the mention of food. He thought he'd caught a whiff of cinnamon on the air, something sweet and buttery. That explained it. "Apple pie," he said. "Always reminds me of Mama. She made an apple pie fit for angels."

Catherine laughed. "I wouldn't call my pie 'fit for angels,' but it's just fine for us regular folks. The secret's in my canned apples," she said in a mock whisper. "Now, make yourselves at home. Today's all about having a good time."

After the feast and wonderful samples of pie, Becky found herself alone with Dally's wife, Catherine. They stood together in the clearing between the cabins, where several long tables and benches had been set up. Looking around and finding no sign of their menfolk nearby, Becky leaned closer and asked in a quiet voice, "So you're expecting another?"

Catherine beamed at the question and rubbed a hand over her still-flat stomach. "Number seven." She grinned, her eyes shining. "We hadn't planned on seven, but we're happy."

Taking a second glance around, Becky noticed Isaac approaching. She turned back to Catherine and said quickly, "I want so much to have children of my own." The longing had merely grown since she'd married Isaac. She'd hoped they had an understanding building between them, but over the past week, he again seemed intent on pushing her away. And then there was today. He seemed completely different. Like a new man altogether. He'd gone so far as to hold her hand once on the trip over, when they'd stopped for water. He'd reached down to help her up after she scooped up a drink, and he'd held onto her hand until they retrieved the horses.

She was starting to think the man didn't know his own mind. She certainly didn't. He was a mystery. She just wished she knew where they stood.

Catherine placed a gentle hand over Becky's, perhaps seeing the worry in her face. "God will bless you with a babe when the time is right. I'm sure of it." She smiled and patted Becky's hand. As Isaac passed them, she gave her a mischievous wink and said, "He's given you a good start with such a strapping young man."

Becky realized she'd been watching her husband a little too closely, and Catherine had caught the direction of her gaze. She felt an embarrassed flush burning her cheeks. Although Catherine naturally assumed theirs was a normal marriage, Becky knew better. Not that she would say so. She found herself wondering if her dream of having a family of her own would ever come true.

Little Bess toddled over then, her dress soaked through. "Mama, spilla wawa." Her little lips trembled, and she began to cry in earnest.

Her mother gathered her in her arms. "Come now, Bessie-sweet. Let's get you in some dry clothes." She stood and gave Becky an apologetic smile. "A little too much excitement for this little one, I expect. She needs a change and a quick cuddle, and then she'll be right as rain. You go on and enjoy the festivities. But while we've got the chance, promise me you'll come back and let me know when you have some news of your own to celebrate." Catherine arched an eyebrow and grinned.

Becky nodded. If her face had been hot before, it was positively flaming now.

After her new friend left to change little Bess's dress and put her down for a nap, Becky turned her attention to her husband, marveling at the sudden changes in him. He'd been warmer to her today than he'd been recently, maybe in all the time she'd known him. Today he seemed, well, almost like a suitor. Not quite, but almost. His unexplained about-faces baffled her, not that she was complaining about this particular change. She was reminded of her first meetings with him in the Pearsons' parlor: their awkward conversations, that heart-stopping moment when he'd taken her hand in his. Somehow, he'd changed from that cordial young gentleman into something of a grump over this past week, ever since their first shooting lesson and his wonderful, confusing kiss. It had taken all her strength to stay positive, but the effort drained her.

Today's Isaac was a welcome change.

She followed him at a distance and watched as he approached a group of children playing an unusual game of tag. The children chased each other around in a dirt-packed circle, tickling each other mercilessly with the tips of their branches. One small carrot-topped boy, dodging an attack by an older girl, tripped into Isaac's leg. Spinning around, the boy accidently whacked Isaac in the stomach. Looking way up the entire muscled length of Isaac's body into his face, the boy's eyes grew round with awe. With a gulp visible at a distance, he muttered an apology and fled to hide behind the older girl's skirts.

The older girl swallowed too, but stood her ground.

"He didn't mean nothin' by it, mister." She placed a hand behind her, holding the boy's shoulder bracingly.

"Is that right?" Isaac grasped his stomach in exaggerated pain. Then dropping his arms to his sides, he seemed to grow larger as his shoulders broadened, his stance widened. "Mary Alice, isn't it?"

The girl nodded, but didn't relax her protective stance a bit.

"Well, where I come from, an offense like that deserves retribution." He bent to pick up a willowy pine branch of his own and brandished it with a flourish.

Seeing Isaac's teasing grin, the girl broke into a relieved, girlish laugh.

"Oh, mister, you don't know what you've brung on yourself." She turned to the other children who had circled up behind her, listening to their interchange with wide, curious eyes. "Who's with me?" she asked them.

A roar greeted her words. Looking at them, Becky decided they were gathering courage from each other with each coordinated attack. She watched Isaac with interest. He cavorted about like an eight-year-old boy, yelping at every strike, exacting revenge with answering—though obviously restrained—swats of his pine-needle-tipped stick.

Seeing Isaac laugh and play with the children, Becky grew very still. All the other loggers and their wives who were standing around melted into the forest perimeter. There was only Isaac and the children. He seemed so totally different here. Young and carefree.

Her brows lifted slightly.

And then she wasn't sure what came over her—some spark of mischief maybe. Picking up a branch—a variety with long, pliable needles—she gave chase along with the children. Catching sight of her, Isaac backed away. His smile widened. His eyes twinkled with mirth.

"Don't think you can catch me, young lady." The uneven chuckle in his voice was infectious, and she found herself giggling uncontrollably, sounding like a much younger version of herself.

She darted toward him, her branch extended like a sword, ready to swat him if he got close enough. Several of the children linked arms and formed a wall behind Isaac, bringing him up short. He halted, gasping for air and laughing. He was cornered.

"You're trapped." She mocked as she stalked him. Waving her branch menacingly, she skirted his long-armed grasp. With a quick switch of her wrist, she tickled his side with the tip of the long branch.

He laughed a great, full laugh, which shook his tall frame. Still laughing, he snatched the branch from her and held it aloft above his head, far out of her reach.

Becky's breath hitched in her throat.

There was something about his laugh. It did something to her... Her heart squeezed, and then lightened like a soap bubble floating on the air. She found herself simply smiling at him, bemused.

She couldn't help thinking what an honorable, good man he was.

And he was *her* husband.

Was it possible what she was feeling was the beginning of love?

She made a fist over her stomach and held it there, overcome with the strangeness of it all. After having her heart stuck in a useless place for so long, she wasn't sure if she could love. She'd worried about it many nights, lying awake, wondering if she was still capable of it. And now—more than anything—she wanted quite desperately to be able to love Isaac. She wanted it so badly it hurt, deep down.

Scarcely aware of what was going on around her, she registered that the children's mothers were herding them into a circle around a massive tree stump, one about as big around as a good-sized cabin.

Isaac's friend, Dally, called out, "Come on you two. It's time to heel-and-toe."

Isaac looked at Becky as if waiting for her reaction. With a boyish grin, he jerked his head toward the dance area. "Would you care to dance?"

"They're dancing on top of a tree stump?" She smiled, delighted.

"Makes a perfect dance floor, I guess." He led her over to the base and helped her climb a series of makeshift steps up to the top of the smooth, flat circle.

"We're going to dance *on a tree stump*." She glanced around in wonder as the other couples formed three sides of a square. She and Isaac made up the forth side.

Two fiddlers struck up a rousing medley, and an old wizened-looking man in a gray beard perched on a platform raised above the rest of the stump. He looked oddly like a bird with his round, prominent Adam's apple and spindly legs, encased in slim-fitting denims. A tall gangly-legged bird. A gray-and-blue rooster maybe, Becky thought, tickled by her own fanciful imagination.

The caller greeted the dancers with a singsong chant, "Bow to yer partners!" Then he started calling out his commands, dizzying in their speed and incomprehensible in their meaning at times, like an auctioneer making his spiel.

Becky hadn't ever participated in this particular dance. Little tiny butterflies fluttered in her stomach. What if she took a wrong step? What if she missed her footing and fell right off the edge? It was a good full-length drop to the ground. Then she noticed Isaac was also listening intently to the caller, his brow furrowed in concentration. She scowled at him playfully, and he grinned the same boyish grin that was beginning to turn her insides into mush.

She also decided, looking at him, that she rather liked his dark hair.

His warm, wide palm covered her hand, his fingers gripping hers firmly. It may have been more fanciful thinking, but she imagined it was his way of telling her he wasn't going to let her fall off the side no matter what. They parted and spun, sashaying in a circle along with the other dancers.

"Swing her round!"

Isaac met her as they crossed each other's paths, traveling in opposite directions. He linked arms with her and spun her around. Their eyes met. Becky caught her breath. She'd heard somewhere—church perhaps?—that the eyes were a window to the soul, and she felt very much like she'd glimpsed into Isaac's soul. She liked what she saw: an honorable man. A strong man. A man who worked hard, but wasn't afraid to laugh. A man who wouldn't desert her in times of trouble. And, obviously, a man who'd constantly keep her on her toes.

It was a quick impression, a flash of understanding and no more, for she had to dance, turn the right way...grab his hand.

"Promenade!"

Isaac embraced her loosely then, his arm circling her back, one hand grasping her waist, the other holding her hand. They circled the floor, following the other dancers and laughing helplessly whenever they turned the wrong way. His touch made her heart pound. Each too-brief embrace sent a light bubbly sensation through her heart.

Maybe, just maybe, she could come to love Isaac Jessup.

As Isaac danced, he took pleasure in the feel of Rebecca's slender back under his palm. Seeing Dally and his wife together earlier had stirred up all sorts of new feelings in him, feelings he couldn't shake. Maybe a woman could survive in this wild territory. Sneaking a peek at Catherine tending her brood, Isaac was still amazed to see a woman flourishing in the mountains, with children no less. Lots of them.

But then Catherine seemed the sturdy sort—had probably been brought up out West along with a peck of brothers and sisters. Born to frontier life.

He glanced down at the top of Rebecca's head as she whirled away from him. She twirled back, loose strands of her hair curling around her face, and looked up at him with a delighted smile. Everything about her spoke of grace and refinement. Of tea and crumpets and white gloves. Yet she seemed happy enough today dancing with him atop a tree stump in the middle of nowhere.

All in all, it was almost a perfect day. Well, the best they'd spent in each other's company at any rate. No sooner had the thought passed through his head than the sky turned black. Clouds rolled across the sky, and the heavens opened up with a crack of thunder. Great soaking drops sent the dancers scurrying for cover in whatever building was closest.

"Isaac! Over here!" Dally called, beckoning them to follow. He ran off with his family across the clearing.

Isaac grabbed Rebecca's hand and chased after Dally, as he and his little clan scrambled in through the front door of one of the larger log cabins. Isaac followed after them, hanging onto Rebecca, his other hand covering her head from the beating rain. As best he could anyway. It had sure come on hard and quick. She ducked her head and ran alongside him. He liked the way she leaned into him, using his body for shelter.

As he and Rebecca entered the simple structure, the cluster of wet children parted for them like the Red Sea.

Mary Alice, who Isaac recognized as the one who'd challenged him in the game, stared at him with unabashed curiosity.

"Mama, this night ain't fit for travel." The girl declared with an impish smile. Her twin sister nudged her, and they dissolved in a fit of giggles.

"Looks like you two will be staying the night," Catherine and Dally said in unison. They broke into laughter as their words tumbled over one another.

"That won't be necessary." Isaac couldn't stay the night here. With Rebecca.

"Nonsense, my friend. Look." Dally held the door wide open. A waterfall gushed from the roof overhang onto the ground in a stream of blinding gray.

Looking at the door, Isaac noticed Rebecca's attention seemed oddly fixed above the doorframe, where two rifles were mounted, one man-sized and one smaller— a ladies' rifle decorated with flowers, by the look of it. Must be Catherine's, he thought, wondering at Rebecca's interest in it. He didn't have too much time to think about it though, because a draft blew a sheet of rain indoors, soaking the floor.

"Dally! Close it," Catherine urged as she tugged a sopping dress off the littlest girl, who was drenched and sniffling. "That wind is blowing something fierce. It's getting dark fast, and we may as well get the children in bed. They've had a full day."

Dally closed the door and sent Isaac a look that said, *What did I tell you?*

"You're staying," he said firmly, the way any good boss does, expecting to be listened to. It was much the way Isaac would have spoken to one of his senior men.

"Okay, okay. We're staying." Isaac felt rather than heard

Rebecca's swift intake of breath. He squeezed her hand in a light grip, trying to reassure her with that one small touch. "Thank you," he said to Dally and Catherine.

"Nothing for it but to make the best of it," Dally said. "We haven't much room to spare, as you can see, but our place is always open to friends." He led them to a small curtained-off alcove in the corner, the floor of which was built into a nest of sorts, with a lumpy-looking mattress and a crumpled wool blanket. "This is our oldest son's bed. He's spending the night with the Garretts' oldest son anyway, so you may as well have his bed. It'll be close, but that should serve you lovebirds just fine for a night, shouldn't it?" Dally winked at Isaac and gave him a private little grin.

Isaac stared at the narrow bed and swallowed.

"This'll be just fine, Dally," he heard himself assuring his friend. Even so, sweat dampened his palms and beaded on his upper lip. Sleep here? *With Rebecca?* What if she kissed him again and called him *Jack, darling* in her sleep?

He didn't think he could bear another night like that.

But what could he do?

"This'll be just fine," he repeated and stole a glance at Rebecca's face.

With her bottom lip tucked between her teeth, she looked a mite worried about the sleeping arrangements as well, but "Thank you, Dally" was all she said. She turned immediately to help Catherine get her younger children dried off. To Isaac it seemed like she might be trying to distract herself.

Lucky girl. She had something to do.

He watched silently as Rebecca soothed the smallest girl by holding her in her arms and rocking her from side to side. The child's cries quieted, and soon her head fell against Rebecca's shoulder. She looked up at her with trusting eyes, her eyelids drooping low and her small mouth relaxed in a contented "O," which struck him as sweet. As soon as little Bess's eyes shut all the way, Rebecca tucked her into bed—a small mat in the corner—and kissed her forehead.

"She'll sleep well tonight," Catherine whispered with a gentle smile and laid a hand on Rebecca's shoulder. She bent to kiss the now gently snoring child and pulled Rebecca along by the arm. "Come on in our bedroom for a moment and I'll get you a nice, dry nightgown and wrap."

Isaac heard the woman's words from across the room. He watched as Catherine sent Dally a quick smile, and she and Rebecca disappeared behind a door in the back. He could only imagine what they were doing in there.

"Well, looks like we've got the place to ourselves for a spell."

"How do you figure?" Isaac looked around the main room of the cabin, packed with little sleeping bodies curled up on almost every flat surface.

"What do you mean?" Settling himself into a chair at the long table, Dally looked back at Isaac blankly. "Oh." He seemed to register Isaac's confusion and chuckled under his breath. "Having the children sleeping all around is so normal, I forget they're here sometimes. Don't worry. Once they're asleep, they sleep straight on until morning. Even little Bess."

"I see." Isaac eased his frame onto a chair across the table from Dally and stretched out his legs. As they talked and laughed about old times, he made a conscious effort not to look over at the closed door to the bedroom, where he knew Rebecca was getting changed.

"I'll get you a nightshirt." Dally stood as the women rejoined them and, after ducking into the bedroom, returned to hand Isaac a folded white nightshirt. "It may be a trifle short on you, but it should do for the night." He chuckled. "Come along, wife, let's get to bed. Goodnight, you two. We'll see you in the morning."

"Goodnight." Isaac looked after them dumbly as they went to their room and closed the door.

"Go on and get out of those wet clothes." Rebecca pointed to the alcove. "I'll wait here." She sat at the table and waved him on with a flick of her hand.

Isaac nodded and stepped into the small space, pulling the curtain closed behind him. He swiftly changed into the night-shirt, feeling like a man wearing child's clothes. The shirtsleeves fell several inches above his wrists, and the tail didn't hang nearly low enough. Not low enough to cover his knees anyway. He'd never given much thought to his body before, but the thought of Rebecca seeing him all wrists and knees made him feel foolish and exposed.

Shaking off his discomfort, he pushed back the curtain and picked his way across the darkened room, being careful not to step on any of the children. Rebecca had turned down the lantern, he noticed with a rush of gratitude. He avoided meeting her eyes as he hung his damp trousers, shirt, and socks over the backs of the kitchen chairs. With any luck, they'd be dry by morning.

His chore done, he stared at his clothes for a moment longer. He finally turned to the woman sitting in front of him, not three feet away. Her gaze wandered over him, then she looked into his eyes. He could have sworn her brows lifted slightly and the corner of her lips twitched.

"Are you laughing at me?"

"Who me?" She had the nerve to giggle, muffling the sound with her hand. She had a merry light in her eyes that he found appealing.

"What?" he demanded with mock severity and looked down at his ridiculous attire.

"N—nothing," she spluttered and giggled again.

Her girlish-sounding giggles were so infectious, he found himself chuckling along with her, quietly, so as not to wake the sleeping children. They never stirred. The sound of their slow, regular breathing in the lantern's soft orange glow made the room seem a living thing, warm and homey.

"Come on then. Let's get to bed," he repeated Dally's words for lack of anything better to say.

Her giggles stopped abruptly, and her smile wavered. "All right."

Seventeen

*J*saac gripped the lantern with one hand and with the other led Rebecca to the alcove, holding her elbow to help her keep her balance as they stepped through the maze of sleeping children. The little alcove had seemed confining when he'd changed into the nightshirt, but now, with Rebecca with him, it wasn't large enough for the two of them to stand without touching.

She faced him toe to toe. Gathering the collar of her wrap under her chin, she raised wide eyes to his. She looked sweet—kissable, even—and he found himself almost forgetting about Jack.

He shook himself.

How could he forget?

Frowning, he quickly turned down the wick, casting their little "room" in near total darkness. He set the lantern on the small table wedged into the corner at the foot of the bed. The moon must have broken through the rain clouds, for its soft glow lit the thin curtain. He could just barely make out the outline of Rebecca's face as she stood before him. He could feel her staring at him.

He stretched out on the pallet and pulled the covers up. He was too long for the mattress and had to fold himself up to fit. It would surely make for an interesting night. "Come on then." He silently grumbled to himself about how low and gravelly his voice was. He sounded more angry than anything, when he knew he was simply nervous about their proximity.

After standing in the dark for a moment longer, she curled up in front of him, her head resting on the crook of his arm, her back pressed against his chest. Her closeness made breathing impossible, not simply because she was leaning against him, but her sweet-smelling hair was inches from his nose. He gingerly settled his other arm over her waist and gave in to the urge to hold her a little closer. She snuggled against him with a sigh and didn't say a word about him holding her too tightly.

If he slept at all tonight it would be a miracle.

"Do you have dreams, Isaac?" she whispered, and he was reminded of a time when he was very small and another boy had spent the night with him up in the loft. The two of them had spoken in hushed whispers late into the night. That was back when his mama was alive. She'd called up several times to hush them and told them to get back to sleep. He smiled a little at the memory.

"What kind of dreams? You mean like nightmares—imaginings—that sort of thing?" He was already scouring his mind for those kind of dreams, when she turned her head to look at him over her shoulder. Not that she could have seen much of him in the dark. All he could see of her was the dim outline of her profile.

"No, I mean what did you imagine your life would be, you know, when you grew up? What you wanted most."

"I see." He paused to think about it, but really only one thing came to mind, and it was immediate. "I always saw myself as having a place like this. Making something of myself."

"So you've done it then. You're living your dream." She settled her head back onto the crook of his arm again, as if they were an old married couple used to spooning in a tiny bed.

Living his dream?

176

Was he? Isaac wondered.

No. On one level, maybe he was, but there had to be more. Otherwise he wouldn't feel so not-quite-finished all the time. Would he?

"I guess," he said noncommittally. "What about you?"

"Me?" she asked. Seems like if she'd asked him, she would've been prepared for him to ask her too, but she sounded surprised, like he'd caught her off guard.

"Yes, you," he teased, relaxing more fully. Her hair was soft against his arm—her sweet, lemony scent right there near his nose. He breathed it in.

"Well, I guess I already told you," she said shyly. "You know..."

A baby. She'd told him she'd wanted a baby, almost right off too.

"Oh," he said, and allowed the silence of the night to fall over them. "You mean a baby?"

Great, now she had him thinking about babies and all sorts of other things. Like kissing her, for starters, and how they were—conveniently—already married.

"In a way," she said, startling him. "But in a way not."

"What does that mean?"

"It's not just a baby. I've just always wanted—I don't know—to belong. To have a family of my own."

He pondered that, confused. "Didn't you 'belong' back home?" he asked.

"Oh, no," she said readily, without having to think about it at all.

She couldn't have surprised him more if she'd said she'd really grown up in the circus.

"Why?"

"I guess I was always different from everyone else."

Isaac fell silent, unable to come up with any words to respond to that. Rebecca had never felt like she belonged in her own family? She'd likely built all sorts of dreams around marrying Jack, about starting a family of her own with him. And then Jack had married another woman. No wonder she'd signed up to be a mail-order bride, although he couldn't help wondering if the men back East didn't have eyes.

"Goodnight, Isaac," she whispered and yawned.

"Goodnight," he said. He tried to sleep, but he couldn't stop thinking about what she said. Maybe Rebecca had hoped she'd belong here. Maybe that's why she'd come. But where she'd gotten that idea from, he couldn't imagine. A logging camp was about as far from where she belonged as he could think of, except maybe somewhere even more untamed.

He idly stroked the back of her hand, laying on the mattress so close to his.

He wanted her to feel like she belonged with him.

Fast on the heels of that thought came a sudden rush of icy-cold panic and an almost irresistible urge to run the other way.

Later the next morning, after Becky had returned with Isaac to their own cabin, she eyed him thoughtfully as he cleared off for work like a spooked raccoon running from a pack of hounds.

Mister About-Face.

What's gotten into him? she wondered.

She left soon after, riding Siren through the forest to hunt down their next meal. Thinking about her feelings for Isaac made focusing on the task nearly impossible. Last night in his arms, she'd been all too aware of him as an attractive man. She'd liked the warmth of his solid chest against her back, the weight of his arm across her waist, his thumb smoothing the back of her hand over and over. Her budding feelings for him had made her want him to hold her even closer still and kiss her, but he'd simply lain beside her and slept.

She didn't even think kissing her had crossed his mind, which was a little disheartening. Didn't he *want* to kiss her? That little alcove had practically been made for a romantic embrace. But no, he'd allowed her to snuggle close, only because they'd had to on that narrow bed. And after all that deep eye-gazing they'd done on the dance floor, and the laughter they'd shared—deep belly laughs that had assured her they could have a good life together if they tried.

Maybe it had all been in her head.

Maybe Brody had been right from the start, and Isaac had never wanted a wife.

Several times, as Siren picked her way along the trail, Becky found herself adrift, barely aware of her surroundings. Hearing the distinctive warble of a wild turkey in the brush ahead of her, she came to a standstill. She reached over her shoulder for her gun, pulling it over her head.

"Well, wouldya lookee here."

Becky jumped. Her heart thumped wildly in her chest. Turning to glance in the direction of the hearty male voice, she nearly slipped from Siren's back in her haste. She felt her eyes go wide and gulped to clear her throat.

"Sam."

"Uh-huh. Now why am I not surprised to find my son's lovely little wife out hunting for game?"

"Oh, Sam, please don't tell Isaac. Please?" Becky beseeched him with her eyes.

"I don't know... That's asking an awful lot of a bored old man." His silvery-blue eyes twinkled with merriment.

Becky's heart sank. She had no right to ask Sam to keep her secret from Isaac.

"I just want to be a real lady for Isaac. I'm afraid he'd be offended by my rather—unusual ways."

"Pshaw." Sam choked on a laugh and coughed into his hand. He gingerly rubbed at his ribs as if the effort to quiet his mirth had pained him. "Isaac?"

"Well, I remember Isaac saying his mama was 'a real lady.'"

Sam's eyes turned soft. One corner of his lips lifted in a half smile. "My sweet Emily. Yeah, she was quite a lady."

She breathed a deep sigh at his words. His expression alone would have said it all. A man wanted a woman who was a real lady, not some wild, rifle-toting hoyden.

"Case in point, Sam." Becky dismounted, sliding silently to the ground. She loaded her rifle, pressing a bullet into place, and closed the breech block with a satisfying snap.

"You've got a way with that weapon, gal." Sam's tone was filled with admiration.

"I've been hunting since—well, it seems like forever."

"Your pa teach you?"

She laughed dryly, the irony of his question catching her off guard. "Papa? No. He didn't do much of anything with me—and we both preferred it that way."

"That so?" he said slowly, with a note of disbelief she couldn't miss.

She glanced at him briefly, and then walked slowly along the trail. Siren trailed behind her like a well-trained dog.

"Let's just say he breathed a sigh of relief the day I left," she said softly.

"I can't believe that, Becky." He matched her hushed tone.

Flashing him a look of surprise at the use of her nickname—it caught her square in the heart to hear him say it—she halted for a moment, then continued walking, her pace careful and quiet.

"Believe it," she whispered, scanning the trees, her ears alert to the slightest noise. She put a hand up to warn him.

He'd already stopped, his gaze trained in the direction of the rustling tall grass. Becky brought her rifle up and eased the hammer back. She stood stock-still, ready for any sign of movement. When a turkey broke free of its hiding place and took flight, she paused for a moment to admire the flash of burnished bronze as the morning sun lit the bird's feathers, and then, with firm resolve and a steady aim, brought the turkey down with one shot. She ran over to check on it.

Sam whistled through his teeth. "Good shot." She heard the admiration in his voice as he crouched beside her and looked over her kill. "This here's a beauty," he added. "Never seen a woman bring down a wild tom in flight like that with one shot."

Becky blushed at his unexpected praise. Focusing her attention on preparing the bird for the trip home, she ducked her head and avoided Sam's curious gaze. His easy silence and willingness to lend a hand with the bird meant more to her than he could possibly know. Hunting had become such a lonely occupation lately—whereas growing up, she'd associated the time with companionship. With Jack.

"You're quite skilled with that rifle of yours. Don't see why you're keeping your hunting a secret from Isaac. My boy's no starched-up city fellow, you know. I think you should just tell him." His persistence wore on her resolve.

Becky thought about her visit to Dally's camp and how they'd had two rifles hanging over their door.

One man's rifle. One *ladies'* rifle. And a pretty one at that. Catherine's probably.

It had struck her dumb for a few seconds, mostly because it looked like the rifle had been well-used, not just a display piece. That meant that Catherine *used* it. And Dally had it up on the wall where anyone who wanted to could see it.

She suffered many an uncomfortable squiggle of doubt because of it. This was an untamed country. Maybe men here appreciated a woman with a good aim. Hadn't Isaac taken her out to teach her to shoot?

"I'll think about it. I promise." Becky stopped and placed a hand on Sam's arm. "Isaac thinks highly of you, Sam. And I can see why. You're a good father to him." *And already more a father to me than I've ever known*, she added silently. She stretched up and planted a kiss on his cheek.

He had to bend a little for her to reach, and she noticed his deeply tanned cheeks were growing a little flushed. Crinkles appeared at the corners of his eyes as he grinned at her.

"Well, I'm not sure 'bout Isaac 'thinking highly of me' lately, but I thank you for your kind words just the same. I'd have liked having a daughter like you. Guess I do now. Guess I do." His grin widened. Patting her hand resting on his sleeve, he gave an embarrassed-sounding cough and nodded for her to mount her horse. "I'll bring your bird back for you."

"Thanks, Sam." Becky said, smiling.

She didn't say so, but she was sure Sam simply didn't understand about Isaac. It was one thing to accept her actions as a father-in-law. It was another for *her husband* to appreciate her unorthodox behavior. Isaac's acceptance would mean the world to her, she thought as she mounted Siren and urged her toward the trail.

As her horse picked her way through the forest, unbidden memories of Jack and Melody crept into her mind. She remembered the day she'd found out Melody was expecting. How painful that had been. That bit of truth that had convinced Becky she needed to escape for good. Then, the very next day, Mr. Preston had arrived in town. She'd thought it a sign, a touch of God's own hand. And she'd read the letter from Isaac Jessup, latching onto it immediately. Dreams—foolish mind wanderings at best—had filled her head. Now she knew Sam, not Isaac, had penned the letter she'd read. Did the old man know what trouble his actions had brought on his son and on her too? Looking over at his strong profile, so like Isaac's, she couldn't bring herself to be angry with him.

Her memories of Jack and Melody simply reinforced her determination to keep her hunting escapades a secret from Isaac. Every day her heart seemed more and more tied up in him. She thought about him all the time. Watched the way he moved. Admired the width of his shoulders, his easy, take-charge grace. She was oh-so aware of the way her heart beat a little faster whenever he looked her way. A single smile from him could knock the wind right out of her.

He was much too important to her now to risk disappointing him any further.

No, she'd make every effort to be the kind of wife every man desired—even if that meant acting like a perfect lady for the rest of her life.

Isaac heard the sound of laughter even before he reached the porch of the cabin. He pushed open the front door, his eyes seeking out the two occupants in the kitchen having such a good time.

"Hello, Pop. Rebecca." He took in Rebecca's profile, her flushed cheeks, the plain brown dress. With her reddish-gold hair braided and looped up into a loose knot at the back of her head, she looked so at home. He couldn't believe she was helping Pop truss the wild turkey laid out on the table.

"Isaac, my boy!" Pop greeted him warmly, his voice loud with mirth. "Welcome home."

"Pop, another bird? You're making me feel like the undeserving son," Isaac said, silently adding to himself, *and a husband who hasn't been providing for his wife*. "I've been planning to bring down a deer. Maybe this Sunday after church. There'll be plenty to share."

"Don't you worry about that." Pop shot a look at Rebecca, his brows raised in some sort of message Isaac didn't understand.

Rebecca quickly turned away and washed her hands in the basin. She seemed to be avoiding Isaac's eyes as she dried her hands on a cloth. He wondered what her actions meant. Was she embarrassed about the night they'd had to spend at Dally's, how close they'd had to lie next to each other? Maybe she found his presence discomfiting. If so, the feeling was mutual. If only he knew what directions her thoughts were turning.

"We're grateful, Pop," she said, giving his father a sort of strained smile, and then turned her attention to Isaac. "It's a nice big turkey this time. We'll have a hearty supper tonight. Perhaps your father would like to join us?" She seemed to be asking them both.

"Stay." Isaac added his invitation, glad Rebecca had offered and marveling over the easy relationship that had grown up between her and his father. She'd just called him Pop.

He'd heard her say it clearly, and Pop hadn't batted an eyelid.

Pop wavered, his gaze shifting from Rebecca to Isaac, until he finally conceded, "Thank you kindly, both of you. I've missed sharing a meal as a family."

"I've missed it too." Isaac excused himself and went out back to the barrel to draw a bucket of water so he could wash up more thoroughly in his room. As he was walking back into the cabin, he stopped with one calked boot poised on the step. If he went inside and headed for his old bedroom, Pop would think it awful strange. He didn't want those probing eyes on him, and he didn't want to answer any difficult questions.

So he took a step back and quickly stripped off his coat and shirt, leaving his suspenders hanging, and sluiced the icy cold water over his skin. With a shiver, he pulled his shirt back on, realizing as he did so that it was filthy. He'd need a clean one. He sighed. Now what? He shrugged into his coat and held it closed with one hand. He left the bucket by the back door and quickly marched past Rebecca and Pop. He tried to block out the startled expression on Rebecca's face as he ducked through the door into the new room. Her room. He knew he had at least one clean shirt in the wardrobe.

He'd caught the look she'd given him as he'd hurried past. She'd looked nervous. She must be wondering what he planned to do in here.

Looking around the room, he could see why. There was a pile of clothes tossed in the corner, and the bed sheets and covers were still rumpled. She'd likely taken another nap this morning after he left. There was something cozy and warm about the way the bedclothes formed a little nest, the way her pillow was curved into a letter "C" as if she wrapped it snugly around her head while she was sleeping. He gave himself a shake.

Respecting her privacy, he tried not to gape at her things and quickly found an old dark-green flannel shirt in the wardrobe. He jerked off his damp work shirt, threw it onto the pile of clothes in the corner, and tugged on the one he'd laid out on the bed. He swiftly buttoned the shirt and tucked the tails into the waistband of his pants. He regretted having to invade Rebecca's space and hoped she'd understand his desire to keep Pop out of their private affairs.

As soon as he returned to the kitchen, he immediately sought out Rebecca, sending her a silent look of apology. Her eyes were wide, and he thought the way she swallowed seemed a bit uneasy. When he tried to reassure her with a nod, she smiled slightly and resumed packing the bird with cornmeal stuffing.

"Rebecca's getting quite good with a gun," Isaac said.

His father turned to him with an over-wide smile. "Is that right?" He glanced at Rebecca, who seemed frozen in place, looking at Pop with what seemed outright panic, which was strange. Evidently it was a topic she didn't want openly discussed. "So, Isaac's been teaching you to shoot, eh?" Laughter lines crinkled around Pop's eyes. He seemed to find the subject greatly amusing.

Rebecca's cheeks flushed a pretty rosy color. She flashed a look at Isaac and, with another uneasy smile, replied, "Isaac's a good teacher, Pop. Did you teach him to shoot?"

She'd neatly turned the subject from herself, Isaac realized, but he followed along to ease her obvious embarrassment. How could he have been so insensitive to think a young lady would want to confess to doing something as unwomanly as holding a gun?

"Yeah, but Isaac near grew up with a gun in his hands." At Rebecca's questioning look, Pop added, "Living on the frontier is a dangerous life." His eyes gleamed with a hint of mischief. "His mama was a fair shot herself."

Rebecca fumbled her grip on the bird and nearly dropped it to the floor. Pop grabbed it from her and set it safely back into the pan.

"She was?" she asked, wide-eyed, maybe a tad disbelieving.

Her incredulous tone wasn't lost on Isaac. She probably thought it an unnatural skill for a mother to master a weapon.

Isaac joined them at the kitchen table and sat in a chair, regarding the interchange between the two of them with interest. Pop was up to something, but he wasn't sure what. You never knew what Pop would say or do next.

"Maybe the three of us could all go deer hunting on Sunday, Son."

Aha. So that's what he had brewing in his scheming, interfering mind—God love him. But he was being surprisingly insensitive. Couldn't he see Rebecca had no interest in shooting? Why, she was practically itching to change the subject, at least away from her.

"I'm sure Rebecca's not interested in hunting deer, Pop. It's not exactly a 'ladylike' activity." Isaac sent a sympathetic glance Rebecca's way, but she had her gaze fixed on the turkey or the floor, he wasn't sure which.

Pop scowled at him something fierce. If he'd been holding the turkey at the time, Isaac had the oddest feeling his father would've thrown it at him. What in the world?

"Why are you looking at me like that?"

"Fool son. Thought I raised you to have more brains than that," Pop muttered. He grabbed up the pan and slid the dressed turkey into the oven, closing the door with a decided bang—an irritated kind of bang.

Rebecca shot Pop a look that clearly said, *I told you so.*

Where that came from, Isaac had no idea. Had they been talking about him? Most likely. He watched in confusion as she mumbled an excuse and quickly rushed into her room, closing the door behind her.

"Would someone please tell me what's going on?" Isaac's demand evidently fell on deaf ears, for Pop brushed by him and dropped into the rocker with a resigned sigh.

"You're going to have to figure this one out for yourself, Son." Without giving Isaac a chance to respond, he started talking logging equipment, effectively avoiding Isaac's question.

Isaac listened to Pop with one ear. He responded with grunts whenever his father paused, but his attention was focused on Rebecca's closed door. Why did he have the impression he'd hurt her feelings somehow?

Women. Couldn't understand them for the life of him.

Eighteen

*L*ate the next morning, a good safe time after Isaac went off to the logging site, Becky wandered bareback through the forest just for the simple pleasure of riding Siren and feeling the cool mist on her face. After the night she'd had last night, she was content to allow the horse to wander wherever she wished. Siren led them into a copse of trees. They seemed denser here, and their trunks seemed narrower. Looking around, Becky felt a hush fall over the mountain. As though every animal had stopped and was listening.

Siren stopped too. Her ears pricked forward and back a couple of times, and then she nickered.

Becky listened too. Hearing nothing, she urged Siren on. "Nothing of interest, my darling. Move along."

A strange groaning noise filled her ears. It seemed to be coming from above, high up in the trees.

What in the world was that?

Becky looked up and side to side, straining to locate the source. The hideous screech seemed to grow and have a life of its own, like some tormented beast.

It was loud, everywhere, consuming her. Terrifying and strange.

Filling her ears, confusing her sense of direction.

Where was it coming from?

Seeking escape from the deafening noise, Becky wheeled Siren around, first one way then another, and took off down the path they'd come in on. Spurring the horse on as quickly as she dared, Becky clung to the mare's back. She gripped tightly to the base of Siren's mane, praying all along that they were heading in the right direction.

There was a blur of motion, terrifying. Flashes of green streaking past her.

Branches!

Branches fell around them, whizzing by on every side, scaring the already frightened mare. Siren whinnied—loud as a scream. She reared.

"Hold on! Easy, girl!" Becky's shouts were lost as more branches thundered around them.

Siren reared again. Becky let out a hoarse cry as she felt herself falling toward the ground. Her shoulder hit first, then her hip. *Pain.* A blow to her back drove her rifle into her spine. When she tried to roll to her side, she realized she was pinned. Tears coursed down her cheeks, increasing the maddening blindness of panic. Was she about to be crushed by the falling trunk?

Oh, Lord, please.

There was nothing more to do but lie still and pray. Becky gasped, or tried to anyway. She couldn't move, couldn't fill her lungs the way she wanted to—needed to. Shallow sips of air, not nearly enough. And pain. The pain was blinding. Crushing her. The weight of the branch on her made it difficult to breathe deeply, she realized. And she couldn't get up—there was no way she could roll such a large limb off by herself.

Tears streaked her face, wetting her cheeks, her hair. She told herself to be strong to conserve her energy, but a sob took her by surprise. How could she stay calm? How could she be strong?

How could she?

Isaac had warned her what areas to stay away from, and she *had*.

She'd always been so careful to go the other way. *Always.*

What had she done wrong?

She was sure Isaac and his crew were supposed to be in the opposite direction. On the tail of those thoughts came the realization that she was going to die. She'd die here.

Now.

In the midst of all these wild thoughts, all racing through her head at once, she was dimly aware of one final resounding thud, followed by an eerie silence.

But she had heard a sound.

She'd *heard* it. She was certain of it.

Which meant she wasn't dead. Sobbing and laughing at once, it no longer mattered if Isaac found her in boy's clothing. It no longer mattered if he found out she was an absolute hoyden. Only, please, let him find her and free her!

"Isaac!" Her call seemed barely more than a croak. She tried again and again, but the lack of air was making her weak. Sagging against the dirt, she felt her lungs shrinking. It was like they were shriveling up inside her. Useless.

Her vision turned to gray. She could hear someone cursing loudly, could hear the footfalls of someone running through the fallen brush. A young male voice. Panicked. Not Isaac, but *someone*.

"Oh, dear God," she whispered, "thank you. Thank you for sending someone."

"You all right?" the young man asked, breathing hard, hovering just out of her line of sight. "Just hold on. Hold on. I'll git this off of you."

Excruciating pain knifed her back as the branch shifted, but then blessed relief. The weight lifted away from her and she took a breath. Sweet air filled her lungs. She gasped and gasped again, each breath deeper and longer until she was finally able to lift her head a little.

"Don't move." The voice commanded, and she froze, dropping her chin back onto the ground. "Let me check you first."

Hands ran quickly up her legs and arms. She felt her rifle being lifted off her back and fingers pressing gingerly against her spine.

She groaned as pain shot up her back, radiating up to her neck and down one leg.

"I don't think anything's broke, but you're sure gonna be all bruised up." The voice sounded a little relieved.

The young man gently turned her onto her side. She looked into the face of a boy she'd met in the logging camp, that first day she'd gone to worship service with Isaac. She'd met him outside: a fresh-faced, black-haired fellow with a lot of swagger and attitude. She remembered him chewing on a blade of grass. What was his name? It eluded her. Perhaps it didn't matter. She was too tired now to care.

She did hear him exclaim, "You're a girl!" as soon as he saw her face.

"Urm," she mumbled back, grimacing in pain. Who cared if she was a girl or a boy? She was *alive*—thanks be to God—and that was all that mattered.

The youth lifted her hat off, as if to give her a closer look.

Jem. That was his name. It came to her in a blink as if he'd said it out loud.

"Why, you're Becky," he said incredulously. "You're the boss's wife. Isaac Jessup's wife. I'm a dead man." His eyes, which had held relief just moments ago, were now filled with horror. "I'm a dead man," he repeated.

"Calm down, Jem," Becky said. "Isaac's not going to kill you."

"Oh, he'll kill me all right." His agitation seemed to double, if such a thing was possible. He sank to his knees. "Why? Why did I have to go and do something like this? I should've known." He swore bitterly. His shoulders shook. He began to pound his fist against the ground, again and again. "Why?"

"I'm fine. I think," Becky said, trying to be soothing. The truth was she didn't know if she was fine or not. For all she knew, she'd broken a rib.

"Stupid. Good for nothin'," Jem continued berating himself as if she hadn't said a word.

Realizing the boy was crying, Becky ignored the pain in her back and levered herself up. She could move. It hurt like fire up her back, but she could move. That had to be a good sign. She knelt beside him.

"What did you do?" It was suddenly clear to her that she didn't know the whole story.

"Aw." He slapped his palm against the dirt.

"You're injured!" She touched the back of one of his blood-streaked hands.

"Naw. It's just from the saw." He pulled his hand away from her and looked down at his torn skin with a strangely detached gaze. "Took it into my head that I could fell one of these giants on my own." Looking miserable, he shook his head and swiped at his eyes with his sleeve. "Stupid."

"Stop calling yourself that."

"Well, it was stupid. I'd give anything now to start today all over again. Heck, I'd like a chance to start my whole life over again. Sixteen stupid, wasted years living under Pa's leaky roof."

Those last words slipped out unbidden, she knew, for he pressed his lips together into a firm, straight line.

"Look at me. Cryin' like a girl." He sank back on his heels and gave her a sheepish look.

He really did look like a young boy then, lost and alone. Something about his expression struck a chord with Becky, and she smiled at him in understanding.

"Don't be so hard on yourself." Unwilling to let him off too easily, she added softly, "Just don't ever do anything like this again."

"Oh, there'll never be another time. In fact, after today— if the boss lets me live—I'm pretty certain I'll be looking for a new job."

He looked so forlorn she placed a hand on his forearm.

"You don't know that," she said.

"Oh yeah I do." He met her eyes with fierce certainty blazing in his own. "He pulled me off the felling team first day 'cause a branch fell on me. I can't stand being on peeling crew," he told her earnestly. "A man will never get anywhere on peeling crew."

"Where is it you want to 'get'?" she asked carefully.

He looked at her silently for a long moment before replying, "I want to own my own place. Not some little shanty in the woods either, but a big place, like Mr. Jessup's got here." He swept his arm out to indicate the trees surrounding them.

Most likely he'd never seen their cabin. Becky hid a smile. She gasped as she shifted her weight.

"I've got to git you back home." Jem looked torn.

"I can make it back if I can get my horse to come." She let out a shrill whistle. After a few moments, Siren picked her way through hundreds of fallen limbs toward them. Coming to a stop, she lowered her head and nudged Becky's shoulder repeatedly with her muzzle.

"Ow. Stop it, girl. That hurts." Becky gently pushed the mare's head away. "It's good to see you too, but the bumping has to stop." Becky grinned weakly at Jem. "Do you think you could give me a hand up?"

He jumped to his feet. "Sure thing. You sure you're all right?"

She nodded. "I'll need a soak in a tub, but I think I'll survive."

"I'm following you back," he insisted.

"No, I can make it." But no amount of protesting would deter him.

"There's no saddle on this horse." His voice held a question. He glanced at Becky, frowning as he took in her strange clothing. With a shrug, he grasped her by the waist and helped her crawl onto Siren's back. Every little move brought a sharp gasp of pain.

"How about this whole thing stays our little secret?" Becky asked hopefully as he handed her rifle up.

A doubtful expression crossed his face. "You won't tell the boss?"

"If you don't tell the boss—I won't tell the boss." She arched her brows and waited for his response.

His grin came fast and wide. "You bet!"

Easing the rifle over her shoulder, she smiled in relief. She held out her hand. "Shall we shake on it?"

He took her hand and lifted it, brushing her knuckles briefly with his mouth. "You just saved my life, dear maiden."

She laughed at his antics and pulled her hand back.

Jem returned her hat, then took the reins and walked alongside Siren as she made her way back to the cabin. He helped Becky down, and while she stood leaning against the cabin, he put Siren away in the stable. He returned, following her slow progress into the cabin. His hand hovered near her elbow, not touching her but ready to if she needed it.

"I'll git you a bath," he said.

"You don't have to do that."

"It's no trouble."

She shrugged, too tired to argue. "Pots are next to the stove, on that shelf. Water barrel's out back." She sank onto the rocker and rested her head back, closing her eyes. Soon she heard him clanking around, evidently boiling water in every pot he could find.

"Where to?" he asked, waking her from a daze.

Had she fallen asleep?

She looked up to find him standing to one side of her chair, the heavy galvanized tub dangling from one of his hands.

"In there."

After carrying the tub into her room, Jem filled it with steaming water. He darted glances to the front door, seeming eager to get away, but was obviously reluctant to leave her unattended. If he were surprised what a lowly cabin she and Isaac lived in he didn't show it.

"Go on now, Jem," she prodded him. "I can handle the rest. It wouldn't do for Isaac to find you here, would it? With me in my bath..."

He shook his head, looking horrified at the thought. "No, ma'am."

Becky grimaced at the title. No one had called her "ma'am" before. For goodness' sake, she was twenty, not seventy!

"Becky," she reminded him gently and led him to the back door.

He grinned sheepishly. "All right, Becky. Thanks again

for keeping this all hush."

After saying goodbye to Jem, Becky spent the next hour in the tub, soaking the pain away.

Early in the morning a few days later, Isaac left the house before Rebecca was awake. From her odd behavior these last couple of days, he was a little worried about her health. Moving seemed to pain her, but whenever he asked if she was ailing, she looked at him innocently and brushed his concerns aside. He hated leaving without at least saying "good morning," but she'd slept in again, and he needed to examine the spot he and his father had marked out on the map as their next felling area. Arriving at the new site, he found the trees weren't quite as massive in this part of the forest, but the area was dense, so they could thin a good portion of wood without leaving a bare spot on the mountain.

Satisfied they'd chosen well, he was about to turn his bay for home when he noticed an area with a lot of deadfall. He slid off his mount and bent to pick up one of the smaller limbs, frowning over the fresh tear at one end. This was no deadfall. Within moments of searching, he discovered a felled tree, and from the looks of it, recently felled.

"What in the world?" He scratched the back of his head and made a sweep of the site, looking for clues. Who was cutting down trees on his land?

One area in particular captured his notice. Bending down, he saw two distinct boot prints in the dried mud, one larger, one fairly small, like a man with a younger boy. There were hoof prints everywhere. Maybe a horse had been running loose—spooked by an unexpected falling tree, most likely. Spying a large branch propped up at a strange angle against a nearby tree trunk, Isaac crossed over to it and twisted it side to side. A glimmer of golden red caught his eye. Pulling the string with his fingers, he frowned. It was silky and fine, flexible. Didn't look like any kind of thread he'd ever seen before. Looked more like...hair.

Hair?

With a flash of clarity, he remembered his concerns for Rebecca's health, how the past couple of days she'd moved stiffly and grimaced whenever she rose from her seat or bent over. She'd ignored his concerned questions, but now he suspected the reason.

This was *Rebecca's* hair.

A falling branch had hit her—he was sure of it. Testing the weight of the branch, he felt a chill of fear. She could have been killed.

Why she'd been so far from the cabin was a puzzle, but a more pressing question was who had felled the tree and put his wife in danger? And why hadn't she told him? Didn't she trust him? She could have come to him for help. He would have taken her down the mountain. She needed to be seen by the doctor.

She could have been killed.

Isaac threw the branch aside, willing it far away from him. It fell not a foot away because it was so heavy, not nearly as far as he would've liked. He ground his teeth, frustration and anger welling up inside him, hot as a forest fire.

No one felled a tree on his land without him knowing who, where, and why. No one.

The sun poured in through the window and lit Becky's face. Blinking against the intrusion, she buried her head under the covers. Ugh. She'd missed Isaac again this morning. She hadn't gotten up to milk the goat. She hadn't made Isaac's breakfast. What must he be thinking?

They were small things, maybe, but they were things she could do. Usually.

It was just she was so tired all the time lately.

After the accident, she'd felt tender and sore, but she was moving freely now. She just had some ugly patches of yellowing purple on her back where her bruises were turning color.

That was all.

She was practically better.

But evidently, her body had decided against her will that she needed more sleep. Once again, she'd woken up well past her normal time.

She hadn't even put a toe out of the bed when her door swung wide and Isaac barged in. His face was red, angry. He stopped short at the side of the bed and looked her over.

"You know something about a tree being felled north of the trail?" he demanded.

At least he was giving her the benefit of the doubt, Becky thought wryly.

Not likely.

She could see the way his eyes were gleaming with accusation. The way his presence filled the room.

"Tree?" she croaked. She tried to fix an innocent expression in place, but feared her guilt was written plainly on her face.

"I think you know what I mean," he responded quietly—a little too quietly.

She let out an indistinct little murmur, wishing she were standing facing him fully dressed instead of tucked up like a young girl under her covers.

He came closer, a look of worry crossing his features.

Without asking her permission, he ran his hands over her limbs as if looking for something broken.

Becky felt heat flooding her face. "I'm fine," she protested.

"You're not fine." His voice was so deadly calm. It scared her. Not that he would hurt her. She just feared at some point he'd snap.

"Where are you hurt?" he demanded softly.

"My back," she whispered.

"Let me see."

"Isaac," she pleaded.

He just stood there waiting. He flexed his hands, making her realize he'd been standing there the whole time, his hands in fists.

She quickly wrapped the bed covers around her legs. A kind of mortification filled her at having him see her like this. It wasn't like she was beautiful right now, covered in yellowing purple blotches.

"Here," she whispered. She tugged up her nightgown so he could see just enough of her back to assess her wounds. She knew he'd seen what he needed to see because his face went dark again. Embarrassed, she jerked her gown back down and pulled the covers up to her chin.

"Can you breathe all right? It's not a rib, is it?" he asked, his voice sounding gravelly and harsh to her ears.

She shook her head, miserable.

How had he found out?

She supposed it was only a matter of time before he found out. It was his land after all. She knew he and his father where constantly scouting the area.

Jem should have known that too.

"It was that young fellow, Jem, wasn't it?"

Her gaze flew up to his, her heart thundering against her

breastbone. "Jem?" She could never have been a military spy, she realized, desperately trying to school her features.

"Just wait 'til I get through with that boy!" Isaac slammed his fist against the wall, then glanced at her. "You stay right there. I'm not finished with you yet. You have some explaining to do, but from the looks of it, you had a lucky escape." He stalked away, his caulked boots clattering like hailstones on the wooden floor.

"Where are you going?" Becky disregarded his command and scrambled out of bed. She ran to the wardrobe and, without thinking, yanked on her riding trousers and pulled her old coat on over her nightgown. "Hold up! Isaac!"

But it was too late. He'd already left.

Once Isaac got to the logging camp, he spotted Jem outside the cookhouse alone. The rest of the crew was onsite still: felling trees, peeling bark, transporting logs to the stream. He faced the boy, bracing himself for what he knew he had to do. "You're fired."

Jem stared back at him ashen-faced for what felt like a full minute.

"I want you off my land by sun-up tomorrow. Say your goodbyes and pack your things tonight."

Jem simply nodded.

"Aren't you going to ask me why?"

"No, sir. I know why."

"I can't abide a man going behind my back, Jem. If what I suspect is true, you also put someone else's life at risk. My *wife's* life."

The youth ducked his head and refused to look at Isaac.

"I never meant to hurt nobody."

"I believe that much, but there's no place for recklessness in a logging operation. There's too much at stake. I can't have one of my men—not a single one—going off and taking things into his own hands. Do I make myself clear?"

"Yessir."

Becky hid behind a tree, where she could see Isaac in the logging camp. At first, she'd hoped to catch up with him, but now, from the cover of the trees, she watched him talking to Jem. She was gripping Siren's reins so hard the leather dug into her palm, but she scarcely noticed the pain. Though she was too far to hear what they were saying, she could see the grim set of Isaac's jaw and the stricken look on Jem's face. She knew what was going on. It was like watching a horse-drawn carriage careening out-of-control. And all she could do was stand by and wait for the wreck. Realizing she'd dressed in her hunting clothes and ridden over bareback, she stepped further back into the cover of trees surrounding the logging camp and waited for a chance to speak with Jem alone.

She watched as Isaac stalked into the cookhouse, leaving Jem standing outside like a wounded pup. The boy stood completely still and glassy-eyed. How would he cope without a job? He had trouble back home—she was sure of it. He'd let slip as much when he was talking to her after the accident. She knew what it was like to grow up not getting along with her father. But she suspected Jem's situation was far worse. He hadn't said much, but it had been the way he said it, the misery etched on his face, the bitterness. He'd been hurt bad. He couldn't go home.

Why wouldn't Isaac stop and listen to his story?

She wanted to rush over to Isaac right now and try to make him listen.

It was odd. That day after the church service, she hadn't liked Jem, not one bit. He'd been brash, and his insinuations had embarrassed her. But that hadn't been the real Jem. That had all been bluff and swagger. Him being a sixteen-year-old boy, trying to impress her, no doubt.

The boy she'd seen in the woods was probably far closer to the real Jem—the boy he was inside. He was lost and scared. He wanted a better life. He was impatient and reckless—she could see that clearly enough—but he wasn't bad-hearted. And, well, she just felt bad for him. It was almost like he couldn't help himself.

Her heart broke thinking about it. If only there was something she could do to help. But what?

Isaac certainly wouldn't want her standing up for Jem. He wouldn't understand why. It might even hurt him. Not that he was weak, but he was the boss here. He'd feel she was challenging him, that she didn't respect him. That was a road she didn't want to go down—not now, not when their feelings for each other were so unsettled.

Jem had said Isaac's business was near ruin. He'd told her the men hadn't been paid in weeks. Was it that bad? She didn't know. What she did know was he had enough to worry about right now without her questioning his actions with Jem.

Lost in her thoughts, she almost didn't notice when Jem started to run. Once he got started, he sprinted without stopping. He headed into the trees on the other side of camp and kept going. Jumping on Siren's back, she guided her mare as quickly as she dared in a wide arc around the camp and headed to where she hoped Jem would go. As she rode, she was thankful again that Siren hadn't been hurt by any falling branches that day in the woods. It was a mercy and a miracle that she hadn't been hit by a single one.

When Becky finally found Jem, he was slumped against the trunk of his felled tree. Somehow she knew he'd return here, maybe to relive the incidents that had led up to him losing his job.

He looked up with vacant eyes. "What do you want?" he muttered.

"I came to see if you were all right, Jem. Isaac fired you, didn't he?"

"What do you care?"

"I didn't tell him, I promise. He guessed. He must have come out here, saw all this"—she swept her hand out, indicating the fallen limbs and the great tree lying in the middle of it all—"and he guessed."

Jem turned his head away.

"I'm sorry you got fired. Is there anything I can do—?"

"Just leave me alone. You ain't my mother." He spat the words out.

Becky sank to her knees beside him. He was lashing out at her, but she sensed his anger had nothing to do with her.

"No, I'm not. I'm not your mother. That's true." She paused, noting the twisted expression on his face. Bitterness. Anger. Hurt. "What happened to your mother, Jem?" She wasn't sure where the question had come from, but it came to her as though prompted from an outside source.

"She left when I was little. Couldn't take it no more, I guess—being with Pa."

His eyes never quite met hers, but she could see past his veneer to the hurt boy inside. There was something broken inside him. He was just trying to push her away. Somehow that made him irresistibly vulnerable.

"Where's she now?"

He shrugged as though unconcerned. His fingers played with a pine needle, bending it, watching it spring back. It reminded her of the way he'd bent that sprig of grass between his teeth, bobbing it up and down. "Aw, I don't know. She never wrote or nothin'. Guess I meant about this much to her." He threw the pine needle away and formed an "O" with his thumb and forefinger.

"Surely she loves you, Jem. You're her son."

"She don't love me." He let out a broken laugh. When Becky reached out to place a hand on his arm, he shrugged her off. "She left me there. With him. It wasn't safe. She knew it." He broke his pine needle in two and threw it to the ground. There was something in that action—she could almost picture him as a small boy, left alone with his cruel father.

He swiped his nose on his sleeve, clearly disgusted by his show of emotion. Without looking at her, he sprang up and stalked off, his long strides quickly eating up the distance. Soon he disappeared into the shadows of the forest. Gone. Wanting to be alone. He clearly wouldn't welcome her chasing after him again.

"Oh, Jem," Becky whispered, wiping tears from her cheeks.

After taking a couple of steadying breaths, she headed back to the cabin. She wished Isaac hadn't fired Jem. Couldn't he see the boy needed help? He needed guidance, not another door closing in his face. But she couldn't tell Isaac that—she'd seen the look on his face when he realized Jem had felled that tree. It was an offense he simply couldn't overlook. If there was one thing she'd learned about her husband it was that he held himself to an incredibly high standard. And he expected the same of his men. Of anyone, really. Jem had done wrong—that was true enough—but what about mercy? Why couldn't Isaac have shown him a scrap of compassion?

A chill swept over Becky, sneaking into the opening of her coat. She tugged the fabric more tightly across her body. Jem had run off again, and this time she knew he wasn't coming back.

Where would he go now?

Once she got back to the cabin, she practically tore off her riding clothes and shoved them under her bed. She hung her nightgown on a peg inside the wardrobe and took out some clean clothes. After quickly pulling on a simple work dress—as she was beginning to call her plainer cotton garb—she went back to the kitchen to prepare lunch. She chopped onions with a furious intensity. Tossing them in a big pot with a heaping measure of dried beans, she then covered them with water. She watched the pot, staring into its depths, blind to the world around her.

"See anything interesting in there?"

She jumped at the sound of Isaac's voice.

"No. I don't see anything." Her voice came out a little cooler than she intended.

"Uh, I thought you hated beans."

"I'm not in the mood for anything I like." She turned away from him and stirred the now boiling contents of the pot.

Nineteen

*I*saac chuckled uneasily at Rebecca's comment. Feeling a bit sheepish about his outburst earlier, he'd wanted to smooth things over a bit before he gave her a piece of his mind. Had he actually punched the wall? He shook his head almost imperceptibly as he searched around for a reply. "Is that right?"

Brilliant, Jessup, he chided himself.

"Jem's run off." She spun around, almost knocking him over.

"Whoa, there."

She jabbed a finger into his chest. "And you made him run off!"

"What? Did you *follow* me?"

"He's a *boy*, Isaac. You didn't have to throw him off the crew."

Since when did she know anything about Jem? It almost seemed like she cared about the boy. Had she been spending time with him? When? Where? Here? In the woods?

And why?

"He's a *man*, Rebecca," Isaac said, striving for calm. "And he threw himself off the crew."

"Threw himself off the crew? You *fired* him." She looked strangely hurt, as if he'd somehow disappointed her.

"Only because he was a danger on the job. And you know why." Isaac pushed his hand through his hair. He guessed they was past the point where he could "smooth things over."

"Well, if you'd thought to ask him why—ask him about

his life—then maybe you'd understand him better."

"And how is it you know him so well?" She'd backed him into a corner with her accusations. It was time she answered a few questions.

She took her time selecting a long wooden spoon and started stirring the beans.

Beans she didn't even like.

"Well, I do, and that's all you need to know," she said tersely.

"All I need to know? So now you're an expert on 'all I need,' is that right?" he asked, stung. Why was she questioning his actions, his intentions? This was his operation. If he said the boy needed to go—he needed to go.

He wasn't a cruel man. He was fair. And Jem had gotten what he deserved. He'd go off and find work somewhere else soon enough, and hopefully he would have learned a lesson from what had happened here.

If Isaac had let him stay on...well, the boy would have had no chance of learning anything by that.

Rebecca seemed to shrink a little before his eyes. It made him realize how wound up she'd been over Jem and what had happened. It was still a mystery to him why she even wanted to involve herself with the boy. Jem was a prickly sort of fellow. Not someone Isaac would have expected Rebecca to be drawn to. Maybe it was because he was young. In the whole camp Jem had likely been the closest in age to her. Maybe she related to him in some way because of that?

He was struggling to understand. He hoped she could see that, despite how harsh his last words had come out.

"I'm no expert, Isaac." Her voice was calm now, but husky, thick with emotion. "I don't claim to know what you want. You're my husband but, at this moment, I feel like I don't even know you. The only thing I know is that Jem needs a friend right now."

"You don't know me?" Is that how she really felt? Isaac couldn't let her see how much her comment hurt, so he changed tactics. "You were injured when Jem felled that tree—weren't you? So why are you protecting him now?"

She looked away.

"Tell me." He gripped her chin, gently but firmly, and forced her to look at him. "You got hurt. And that was *his* fault. Although why you were there in the first place, I have no idea. Why were you there...?"

She didn't answer, but the flash of guilt in her eyes made him uneasy. She'd snuck away from the cabin, gone off on her own. Maybe she'd planned to meet Jem?

No. That didn't seem right.

"I was riding Siren," she admitted.

He closed his eyes briefly. "You went off on your own?"

She nodded.

The warning he gave her every morning hung in the air between them unspoken. Every morning, without fail, he warned her to stay close to the cabin. Every morning she promised him she would. Or it was understood anyway. At least he thought it had been.

How could he ever know she was safe if she didn't listen to him? Maybe she didn't take him seriously. Why would she? What sort of dangers had she faced back East? Certainly not bears in the forest or falling trees.

"These mountains are wild, Rebecca. This is no place for a woman, not a delicate woman anyway. You don't belong here—a woman like you." He nearly choked on his words. "Maybe you'd be better off back home with your family." He hadn't meant to say the words aloud, not really, but once they were spoken he couldn't take them back.

Rebecca went absolutely still, her face as pale as snow. Too late, he remembered she'd said there was a rift between her and her father. That she longed for someplace to belong. That was her dream. The one thing she wanted. How could he have been so dense, so insensitive?

"Rebecca, I—"

She jerked away from him, her eyes a little too bright. Without making a sound, she turned and walked stiffly to her room, closing the door silently behind her. She could have said something—told him he was wrong. Told him he was stupid. Anything, but this silence.

Feeling like a heel for upsetting her, Isaac paced about the main room.

Should he knock on the door? Try to go in?

He banged his fist against his thigh, not knowing what to do, and hating this feeling of indecision. If it were one of his men, he'd know what to do. But with Rebecca...what? What did he do to make things up to her?

She was right about one thing, he admitted. Even though they were married, they lived like strangers. What did they really know about each other?

And just how did she know so much about Jem? She hadn't answered his question.

Sinking into the rocker, he leaned his elbows on his knees, dropped his forehead into his hands, and groaned.

He was *jealous* of Jem Wheeler. Some sixteen-year-old *boy*.

He couldn't deny the feeling raging inside him. She wasn't romantically involved with the young man—he felt certain of that—but she'd come out fighting for Jem like a mountain lion protecting her cub.

She *cared* for the boy.

He was jealous because she cared enough to defend Jem and yet she'd cut right through him with one comment: *I don't even know you.* The truth cut. All his wanting it to happen couldn't make his wife love him.

It was time he accepted the fact.

Becky dragged her trunk over to the wardrobe and started flinging dresses inside with total disregard for order.

Isaac wanted her to leave.

He'd said she didn't belong here, and he was right. She didn't belong here. Of course she didn't. She didn't belong back home either, so why should here be any different? Thinking of her father's frowns, she knew she couldn't return to Pepperell. When she'd left, it was with the knowledge that she was going forever. Papa could finally be free of her. He could live the life he wanted to live. Whatever that was.

Where could she go?

Perhaps Meggie's father-in-law would hire her on as a milkmaid. Her hours of practice with Trouble might convince them she could do the job. If she could milk a goat, surely she could learn to milk a cow? A flash of memory brought to mind the worn-down wagon Will had driven out of town that day she'd talked to Meggie outside the general store. She remembered Meggie's words about things being tight, but that they were managing. The last thing they needed was another mouth to feed.

God, why'd you bring me all the way out here if I don't belong here either?

Maybe she didn't belong anywhere.

What was left for her to do, but strike out on her own? Would the general store owner hire her on as a bookkeeper? Unlikely. The man already had a whole family to help him out. She did know how to hunt... Perhaps she could become a trapper. But how long could she survive alone in this untamed territory?

She sighed, defeated. That was beyond what she knew she could do. She wouldn't know the first thing about surviving the winters here, for one. Plus, she'd get lonely. She wasn't the most sociable of women, but she needed some company, even if it was just one companionable soul to talk to.

Regardless of where she went, it was time to let Isaac live the life *he* wanted to live. A life that didn't include a wife. Fortunately, they hadn't let their relationship go any farther than that one sweet kiss. Things would certainly have been more complicated if she was in a family way...

She pressed a hand to her mouth and kneeled in front of her trunk.

With shaky hands, she gathered up the simple red cotton work shirt she'd made for Isaac. She fingered the collar. The red cotton fabric was so soft, but, looking at it now, she could see how far from perfect her stitches were. How had she ever thought she could make a shirt? Foolish girl. She should have known she wasn't wife material. Setting the shirt down in front of her, she dug in her skirt pocket and pulled out the little square of flannel she'd carried with her since leaving Massachusetts. All her dreams for a baby, a family... Her lips pressed into a sad smile. She held the soft cloth to her cheek for a moment, and then tucked it into the pocket of Isaac's work shirt.

She'd likely never have a family to call her own now. The knowledge didn't pierce her nearly as deeply as knowing she'd never have Isaac's heart. All that mattered was *he didn't want her.*

Carefully folding the shirt, she reached over and placed it on the bottom shelf of the wardrobe. Even if it wasn't perfect, she might as well leave it for him. What use was it to her now?

Tomorrow, after things had cooled off between them a bit, she'd calmly let him know she planned to leave.

She plopped onto her side of the bed and let out her breath. She felt so empty inside. As if she'd already left. As if she were already alone.

Her gaze fell on the table next to the bed. The Bible Isaac had given her was there.

She picked it up and held it quietly in her lap.

Surely it meant something that he'd given it to her. He'd seen that she liked reading his Bible. He hadn't berated her for that, as her father would have. He'd simply bought a Bible for her, a gift she could call her own.

He'd bought her a horse too: Siren.

He'd laughed with her at the dance, held her close that night.

That day in the woods, he'd kissed her. And she could have sworn he liked it too.

Maybe they just needed time.

After all, what had she done to convince him she could fit in here?

With a twinge of guilt, she realized all her efforts to appear a "proper young lady" had worked against her. In fact, all she'd done since the first day they'd met was convince him she *didn't* fit in.

She set the Bible back down and drew her knees up to her chest, propping her heels on the edge of the mattress, feeling much like a small girl sitting like that.

If she ever had any hope of belonging anywhere, maybe she needed to be herself. Meggie had said she liked to ride fast too, and *she* was every inch a lady. She'd even said she liked riding astride. Her Will had seemed happy with her. Catherine, Dally's wife, could shoot—and she had her own well-used rifle displayed proudly over their door. If ever a woman fit in around here, *she* did.

Meggie had said something or other to that effect...that the scripture Becky had quoted might not mean what she thought it meant. Maybe Meggie was right. Maybe it did mean more about showing respect and being kindhearted—not forcing her opinions on people, not striking out. Maybe it did.

Becky looped her arms around her shins and squeezed herself into a tight ball.

So what if everything she'd believed up until now was wrong? Or at least a good portion of it?

And what if—*what if*—she could fix it?

By being herself.

The thought was beyond terrifying. Could she do it?

She looked at her trunk, mounded haphazardly with clothes, and wondered what she was doing. There was no way she was ever going to leave Isaac. He'd have to throw her out first. She wasn't entirely certain he wouldn't.

Twenty

*J*em slowly pushed open the door of the little shanty he'd lived in all his life. The dusky shadows of early evening gave him an extra measure of confidence. Pa was never home this time of day. But Jem still hung back, both feet on the porch, ready to bolt. He peered into the window to make sure. It looked deserted, at least from the outside. This might be his last chance to get his picture. Pa had no use for it. If he ever found it, he'd likely just use it as kindling. To Jem though, having that one piece of paper might help loosen the bitter rock lodged in his chest. He'd give anything for that.

As he edged closer, the musty odor of old whiskey hit him, bringing back hard memories. Ready to run at any sign of life, Jem stood in the doorway until his eyes adjusted to the dim interior. He cautiously poked his head through the opening.

Pa's bed was empty.

Jem's old cot stood in the corner, now littered with a pile of laundry and empty bottles. Seeing his bed that way caused his stomach to sink. That was *his* bed, not a table or a shelf.

No, not anymore, he reminded himself with an angry shake of his head.

Pushing his thoughts aside, he dropped to the floor beside the cot and reached his arm underneath. He ran his fingers along the underside of the frame, feeling for the length of twine wrapped around the wood. There. He pulled on the string and a rolled-up piece of paper fell into his palm.

Unrolling it like a scroll, he looked down at a picture

he'd drawn when he was little. It wasn't a good likeness—just a circle and lines scrawled on the page—but he knew it was his mother. And there, up in the corner, written in neat strokes, was his name. She'd put it there. Although he couldn't remember her doing it, he'd always known she had. Sighing, he rolled the picture up and tucked it into his pocket.

He was still on his knees, pushing himself up to stand when the door creaked on its hinges.

"Jem?" The wondering tone in Pa's voice brought Jem around straight away, his pulse hammering.

"Pa." His voice was little more than a croak.

"You come back."

"I'm not staying."

"Aw, Son, you know I didn't mean nothin' by that. I never meant for you to take off." Pa lurched forward.

"I'm not staying," Jem repeated desperately, backing into his cot.

"But ya gotta stay." Pa gestured to the filthy room. "Ain't eaten good since you left."

Jem took in his father's hulking frame. His cheeks did seem leaner, and his belly might have been a little flatter, but Pa was nowhere near starvation—just a whiskey-fed, sickly looking man.

"You don't need me," Jem said. "And—and I don't need you." He threw the words out recklessly, feeling a small jolt of victory when his father flinched as if he'd been struck in the face. But then those eyes of his turned hard and cold. His right hand closed into a fist.

Oh, Lord, what have I done?

Pa swung at his face. Jem dodged, but he was too slow. The blow blinded him. Staggering, he opened his good eye in time to see Pa's boot slam into his thigh. Pain exploded deep in his brain. His vision blurred, but then there was Pa, groping for a log next to the stove. Jem watched, but it didn't seem real. It was a scene on a stage. It couldn't be real.

Then Pa lunged. The log in his hand. Striking Jem in the head.

Jem reeled. He dug deep and threw himself forward with a roar that came from the bottom of his feet straight up through him. The impact knocked Pa backward, and he fell into the edge of the woodstove. He just lay there groaning. Still breathing, but some of the fire seemed to have gone out of him. Before he could recover and take another swing at him, Jem hobbled out as fast as he could.

Where could he go now?

This beat up, with his head bleeding and his leg throbbing, he wouldn't last a full day without collapsing.

The thought of wolves finding his body in the woods spurred him on. Instinctively, he headed up the mountain in the direction he'd come from. He pressed on through the night, stopping at the stream to drink and wash his face as best he could. The throbbing in his leg thankfully eased, and he slept a while under a tree stump, using a pile of pine needles as a blanket.

Twenty-One

$\mathcal{E}$ arly the next morning, Isaac rolled out of bed, intent on a new purpose. His mind had raced all night. Rebecca's comment that she didn't know him had kept him awake. He'd been dealt quite a hand with this marriage. Pop had set the whole thing up without asking him. Then, on top of that, Isaac had found out his bride loved another man. Now she claimed she didn't know him. Having a normal marriage someday seemed impossible.

But didn't God specialize in the impossible?

Until Rebecca had been plunked into his lap, he'd thought a successful business was all he needed to make him happy. Now, he couldn't stop thinking about *her*. He wanted a real marriage and, after the past month, he couldn't imagine living without Rebecca. She'd pretty much turned him inside out, upside down. Though she was undeniably unsuited for rigorous mountain living, she'd managed daily life so far and survived a felling accident to boot. She'd even taken up a rifle and tried her best to learn to fire the unfamiliar weapon, all without a word of complaint. It wasn't her fault she had no skill for it.

Visions of her waving a stick at him at Dally's camp still made him smile. Holding her in his arms at the dance. The sweet torment of sleeping beside her in the small alcove. The kiss he'd stolen in the woods the day he'd started teaching her to shoot. All proved his attraction to her was strong.

So, what was holding him back?

Well, there's her feelings for Jack, he reminded himself as he yanked on his pants and tucked his work shirt in.

One thing at a time.

First, he needed to harness all the ideas that had swirled around in his head and taken shape in the middle of the night. He'd need time to put those into action, and then they could move on to dealing with past hurts and talking about expectations and feelings and such. Feelings. The idea of voicing feelings aloud and talking for any length about them brought on a slight headache. And then, as quick as that, he was back to their wedding night and memories of her confessing her love for Jack.

Determined to cast those thoughts aside, he reached into the trunk at the foot of his bed for a fresh sheet of paper and a pencil. Nothing like a blank piece of paper to settle the mind. He'd make a list. Lists he could handle.

The one thing she'd asked of him was to fix the privy. He'd done that, but he could do better. He'd build her a whole new house, complete with an indoor necessary and all the comforts he could afford. While it didn't make sense to build anything too fancy up here on the mountain, he could certainly pull together something better than this drafty old place.

He pushed through the tattered potato-sack curtain and quickly checked the door to Rebecca's room. Still closed, which was as he expected. It was early yet, and hopefully she wouldn't be up for a while. Paper and pencil in hand, he crossed to the table. Didn't take more than a few strides. Their kitchen was really just a corner of the room after all. And the table had seen better days. So had the chairs, he thought as he straddled one and set the paper on the table in front of him. Pretty much everything had seen better days, which had been fine for Pop and himself, but he couldn't imagine Rebecca caring for their future children here. Maybe a new home would settle her heart, or at least he could hope it would.

Thinking of her face lighting up at the news, Isaac felt a weight lifting off his shoulders. He'd do this for her. He'd make up for the harsh words he'd said yesterday. Surely, once she learned of his plans, she'd realize they could put all that behind them. Better yet, he'd build the new house as quickly as possible and surprise her with the news when he had it all ready.

He liked that. He liked the idea of getting things done. Being busy. Accomplishing something.

Perhaps they could make a go of this marriage yet...

Meanwhile, he'd make a better effort to help her adjust to mountain life. This was no place for a delicate flower, but he had to admit she'd already proven she was willing to learn new things. And she wasn't afraid. Maybe a little too unafraid for his comfort at times, but it helped that she hadn't locked herself up in the cabin and refused to go out at all. As to her inexperience with mountain life, he'd simply have to break her in slowly. He'd persevere with her rifle training, convince her to get rid of that awful sidesaddle, and do whatever else it would take to transform her into a real live frontier woman.

He chuckled at the thought.

Well, he wouldn't go so far as that, but he could hope to better equip her to face the challenges of wild Seattle.

Jem was back on the trail before dawn. The short rest revived his strength a little, but his stomach growled without relenting. He'd need food and maybe a bit of doctoring—but only enough to get him back on his feet again. Then he'd be off for San Francisco. He'd come up with the fare somehow.

For now, he had one destination in mind.

Only one person had shown a shred of concern for him in his whole life: Becky Jessup. He focused on the image of her face and stumbled forward.

By the time Becky got up that morning, Isaac was gone. She'd slept in a little, having tossed all night, but a look at the sky told her it wasn't that late. Figuring he was out tending to the horses, she started on breakfast, her resolution to stay put firmly in place. He'd have to kick her out, she told herself, as she helped herself to the bowl of eggs and pitcher of goat's milk he'd left out on the table.

Didn't belong here.

She'd show him.

When a loud thud sounded on the front door of the cabin, she dropped her spatula, pushed the skillet of eggs to the back of the stove, and rushed across the room.

Jem. How she knew it was him, she couldn't say. She just did. He'd come back.

Opening the door, she gasped as she caught sight of his blood-streaked face.

"Jem! What happened? Was it your pa?"

His response wasn't much more than a groan, but she took that as a yes.

"Why'd you go back?" Ducking under his arm to support his weight about her shoulders, she led him over to the kitchen table and helped him sit in a chair.

His lopsided grin must have hurt, because he winced. "I needed to git something, and I got it," he said with satisfaction.

"Oh, you 'got' it all right. You got beaten up." She dipped a cloth into the water pail and wrung it out. She bent over him and started dabbing at his wounds as gently as she could.

He patted his pocket. "Nope, I got something else. Something I needed. And now I'm headed for California, if I can rustle up the fare." He stopped and looked at her hopefully.

She shook her head. "Sorry, Jem, I don't have a single cent. I'd give it to you if I did though."

Hoping to take the sting out of her words, she served him her share of the eggs she'd cooked. He gobbled them down like a starved man, so she gave him her flapjacks as well.

"Shoulda guessed you wouldn't have any money of your own. Why would you?" he mumbled as he ate.

"What's in California?" Isaac's voice caused Becky to jump, Jem too.

"Boss." Jem sounded so miserable she wanted to put her arm around his shoulders and give him a protective hug.

"Jem's just here to get patched up," she told Isaac, realizing she was actually trembling. The spatula in her hand was shaking. "His Pa lit into him." Her words came out as an accusation.

"*Your pa* did this to you?" Isaac asked. The incredulous look on his face told its own story. His own father was the best of men, the kind of man who wouldn't lay a finger on a child, let alone his own son.

At Jem's nod, Isaac bent to examine the boy's face. He winced in sympathy. "No man has a right to treat you this way."

Isaac straightened. Unable to face Jem's bruised face or Rebecca's accusing eyes, he turned and looked around his simple but comfortable home. Pop had always been kind to him. He'd certainly never struck him in anger.

Jem's father was a snake. He didn't even deserve to be called a man. Stalking across the room, Isaac jerked aside the potato-sack curtain and ducked into his bedroom. He dug in the chest next to his bed and found a stash of bills he kept hidden in the bottom corner. There was enough for a fare to California—if that's where the boy wanted to go—and then some. He stuffed them into his pocket and returned to the kitchen.

Isaac coughed and began speaking, "Jem—"

"I know you're in there, boy!" a man shouted from outside. "You left a trail even that Jezebel ma of yours could have followed. Now, come on out here, Son."

Something crashed against the front door. The sound of glass shattering against wood jerked Isaac into action.

"Stay here." He threw the order over his shoulder as he ran to the front door. Grabbing his rifle on the way, he stepped outside cautiously, closing the cabin door behind him and blocking it with his body. A big man stood about five paces from the porch, weaving on his feet.

"I'm afraid I'm going to have to ask you to get off my property." Isaac widened his stance. Shards of broken glass crunched under his boots. The smell of stale liquor assaulted him. His jaw hardened.

"That's my boy in there." The man brushed a hand over his whiskered chin. His expression seemed vacant. The whites of his eyes were stained a sickly yellow.

A drunk, Isaac decided.

"Well, 'your boy' looks like someone took a plank to his face," he said. Seeing the man was unarmed, Isaac lowered his gun and leaned it against the cabin.

"That's none of your concern."

"It is now." Isaac took a step forward, holding his empty

hands out at his sides in a show of peace. "Now, why don't we talk this out like civilized folk?"

"Look here, mister—" The man staggered onto the porch and stood in front of Isaac. Up close, his foul breath reeked of liquor, a rancid smell, like it was bubbling up from a well deep inside him. The man wasn't nearly as tall as Isaac, but his bulk was impressive, and his eyes gleamed with malice.

Isaac's body stiffened in readiness.

The man's gaze darted beside Isaac, and his eyes took on a hateful gleam. "Git over here, boy."

Isaac registered a presence in the doorway behind him, as Jem's father brushed by and jerked the boy forward by his shirtfront.

Isaac grabbed the man by the back of his shirt and wrenched him away from Jem. "I said—get off my property."

The man spun around and shoveled a ham-sized fist into Isaac's middle.

Sucking in a quick, painful breath, Isaac grabbed the man's wrists and held fast. "Jem's my concern now."

"He's *my* boy."

"He's a man now, and he can take care of himself."

"A father's got rights!" The man pulled with all his might to free himself. His neck turned red, his veins bulging with strain.

"You gave up your rights when you used your fists." Isaac's grip tightened. This drunken brute wasn't getting away without a lesson today. Though his hands itched to fist up and slam into the man's belligerent face, he fought for control.

The bones in the man's wrist creaked under Isaac's grasp. His mottled face took on an ashen cast, and he cried out, "You're gonna break my bones! For pity's sake!"

Appalled at his desire to snap the man's bones in two, Isaac loosened his grip, but continued to hold the man at arm's

224

length.

"You're going to leave the boy alone," he said, nearly growling.

"You got no right!"

Isaac tightened his grip a fraction.

"*Ahh!*" The man yelped and thrashed with both arms, clearly a desperate attempt to free himself. Isaac didn't let go.

"You're going to leave the boy alone," he repeated.

"Okay, okay. Whatever you say—just let me go!"

Isaac pushed the man back and dropped his arms to his sides, breathing hard. His muscles were still tense and ready to lunge forward if the man made another move for Jem.

"Good for nothin'." The man spat at Jem's feet and lumbered off into the forest.

Jem stood frozen, gazing after his pa. He wasn't sure why he couldn't move. His battered face still felt raw, but he didn't think that was why. It was Pa's words—they'd cut deeper this time. Turning to Isaac, he felt a glow of respect and gratitude for the man standing before him.

"Thanks—for what you did." Jem stared down at a hole in the toe of his boot for a moment. Nobody had ever stood up to Pa for him. No one, save for Becky, had ever shown a shred of interest in him. Looking up, he said, "What you said to my pa. Did you mean it?"

Mr. Jessup's brow wrinkled. "Did I mean what?"

"You know. Me being your concern and all."

His former boss's hands came to rest on Jem's shoulders, and he looked intently into Jem's eyes. His expression was warmer than Jem remembered and full of compassion.

"Yeah, I meant it."

Jem's eyes burned. *Don't cry in front of the boss. Don't you dare cry.*

Swallowing, he jerked away from Isaac and began backing away. He stumbled down the porch and righted himself.

"Well, I'll be off now. Get out of your way. Thanks again."

Isaac jumped off the porch and took a tentative step toward the young man. He looked ready to take flight any moment.

"Wait," he urged Jem. Feeling the hairs prick on the back of his neck, he looked over his shoulder to see Rebecca gazing at him from the cabin doorway. How long had she been watching? His face burned, remembering how he'd nearly lost control and pummeled Jem's father. He turned back to Jem, trying to ignore the fact that his wife's eyes were trained on his back. "Wait. You could stay."

"Naw. If he hears I'm around, he'll be back."

Isaac had half expected the boy to insist on leaving, but his reason made good sense. Jem's pa didn't seem like a man given to calm reason. Isaac was certain he could protect the boy to a certain extent, but what if his father returned when Isaac wasn't around? What if he went after Rebecca?

Isaac closed the gap between them and again placed a hand on the youth's shoulder.

"Wherever you go, just remember, you've got a place here—if you want it." At Jem's disbelieving grunt, Isaac continued, "I wouldn't say it if I weren't serious." He reached into his pocket and handed Jem the wad of bills he'd retrieved from his trunk earlier. "Here. Take this."

The boy looked down at them, his eyes widening as he leafed through the stack.

"I heard what you said to Rebecca. It's not much, but enough to buy a corner on a cargo ship to San Francisco Bay— get you down to California, if that's where you want to go. There's some to spare for food too, whatever you need—"

The youth's eyes welled up and one tear slid down his cheek. He flung himself at Isaac, crushing him in a quick but fierce hug. Pushing back, he stood silently, his throat working. He finally nodded, and then with a wave to Rebecca, he spun around and strode off with a hitch in his step, favoring one leg. Soon he disappeared into the trees, the opposite direction from the way his father had gone. Smart boy.

Isaac felt rather than saw Rebecca join him by his side. His heart still thudded wildly in his chest, and his muscles felt strung tight from his struggle with Jem's father. When she placed her hand briefly on his upper arm, he looked down at her.

With an intriguing little smile, she whispered, "That was a good thing you did for Jem."

His heart lightened at the warmth in her tone. Before he could answer, she withdrew her hand and hurried back into the cabin.

Was it possible the look in her eyes had been admiration, or was he seeing what he wanted to see? He straightened to his full height and filled his lungs with air. Whatever the truth, he admitted he wanted her respect. To get it, he'd redouble his efforts to be a better husband.

Something had changed.

It needled at Becky, like a name just barely outside the

edges of her memory, so tantalizingly close she could almost—
almost—latch onto it. But not.

What was it?

She paced back and forth across the kitchen, tending to
Isaac's share of the eggs and flipping the flapjacks over. All the
while she turned over the events of this morning, trying to figure
it out. As soon as Isaac returned, she served him his breakfast.
While he ate the overdone eggs and crisp flapjacks, Becky
sneaked glances at him out of the corner of her eye. He'd been
incredibly generous to Jem.

Maybe that was it—maybe she hadn't thanked him. Had
she said she was grateful? Maybe not...

"I wanted to say thank you—for what you did for Jem."

He gave her a quick, embarrassed smile. "You shouldn't
have been a witness to what went on with Jem's pa. I just hope
the boy gets on okay. He's young, seems even younger than
his years sometimes." Snatching some papers from the table,
he jammed them into his pocket and returned to his breakfast
without further comment.

Now that was odd, Becky thought, her gaze sharpening
on him. "What's that?" she asked innocently, nodding at the
papers peeking out of his trouser pocket.

"Nothing much. Business matters," he said, giving her a
smile. It was a nice smile, the kind that weakened her knees,
but this one seemed a bit too broad, as if he was trying to distract
her.

Business matters. What sort of "business matters" could
he have that he didn't want her to know about? If it had to do
with his troubled finances, she wanted to know. If only he'd
confide in her. She was more than willing to lend a hand.

"Anything I can help with?" She raised her brows in an
inviting manner, hoping he'd open up.

"Not really. Nothing I can't handle," he added quickly, perhaps seeing the way her face fell. "I should be back for supper," he said, "but don't wait for me if I'm late." Pushing back from the table, he was out the door before she could form a response. He didn't even seem to notice when she lifted her hand in a wave.

Now why would he be late?

Becky let her hand fall to her side, struggling with a rush of disappointment and loss.

While she was cleaning up the dishes after he left, her skirt brushed a piece of paper on the floor. Bending, she picked up a list of some sort. She recognized Isaac's handwriting, but the squiggles baffled her. Each item was written in his shorthand, but she didn't recognize any of the words. Probably some new logging equipment for the business. The column of numbers on the right looked to be the prices. Her eyes grew wide as she read down the column to the total.

He'd just given Jem a whole fistful of cash, and now it seemed he was going to place a large order. Where was all this money going to come from? She hadn't discovered any errors in his books, but then she hadn't finished going through every entry. There could be any number of mistakes she hadn't found yet.

His men were going without pay.

Jem had said so.

Some people couldn't manage money. It was a simple fact. Isaac seemed intelligent, but that didn't mean he had a head for numbers. Why, even her papa, a successful businessman, couldn't square a dime.

Isaac was a good man. A generous man. That much she held onto. He wouldn't treat his men unfairly, not unless he had no choice. If she didn't step up and say something, she wouldn't be helping him. Hadn't she been a burden to him since the day he'd married her? The least she could do was prevent him from harming his business.

Her heart gave a painful little squeeze at the thought of anything hurting him.

Because I love him.

I love *him.*

That was it.

That was the feeling that had been nagging at her.

She had changed. Well, her heart had anyway. She wasn't sure when, but it *had* changed. She wasn't pretending. Or hoping. This was the real thing: the rush of affection she felt for him, the respect, the slew of positive thoughts surrounding him, the thump of her heart whenever she thought of him, the way her pulse raced if he just barely brushed up against her, or smiled at her, or looked at her in no particular way at all.

She really *really* loved him.

She felt so lightheaded all of a sudden she had to reach for the back of the chair to steady herself.

She was also aware that the nagging feeling hadn't gone away. There was something else. That's when she had the most awful thought: what if he didn't love her back? She'd seen him looking at her sometimes in a way that made her heart race, but then just as quick his expression would change, like he was disappearing behind a wall of his own making. It could be he had feelings for her, but felt unsure of her. That would make sense. He probably thought she still loved Jack. She'd admitted as much.

But even if he did have feelings for her—and even if she reassured him of her love for him—who did he really love: her or "Rebecca," the proper young lady he thought she was?

The fact was he didn't know her, not the real her.

She'd been hiding the real Becky away since the day they met.

The needling inside her turned to spikes.

Guilt, that's what it was.

Because she had to tell him about the real Becky. She had to let him know who she was. Who she'd always been. That she'd been living a lie, basically.

She'd have to confess that she'd never ridden sidesaddle—didn't know the first thing about it. That she'd ridden like a boy since the first time she'd climbed onto a horse. That she'd pretended she didn't know how to shoot, when she was possibly a better shot than he was—although they might have to have some sort of shoot-off to determine that. She might even have to confess that she'd been the one bringing in all the game for dinner, and not Pop.

Becky went hot and cold just thinking about it.

She rubbed her hands together to warm them and started pacing again.

She had to tell him, didn't she?

How could she?

He'd know then that she was a false kind of person. A person who'd hidden things from him. Deceived him. Even if it was for a good purpose, or so she'd thought. She'd been trying to be a better wife. Surely that had to count for something? But maybe he wouldn't see it that way. Isaac was an honest man. Bible-believing. Hard-working. Straightforward. There didn't seem to be much more to him than what you saw. He might not look kindly on her little masquerade. Maybe learning the truth would change his opinion of her. Maybe it was too much to ask him to forgive.

And any good feelings he might have toward her could completely vanish.

She could lose him before she ever really had him.

Becky bit her lip so hard she drew blood. The room faded in and out—ever so slightly—and she had to grab the chair again. If she was dizzy, she told herself sternly, then it was her own fault. She'd brought all this on herself, and she was the one who had to fix it.

She had to tell Isaac everything. She had to tell him she loved him. And she had to tell him all about who she was. Even if it made her sick. Even if she wanted to die just thinking about it.

She sank onto the chair and buried her head into her arms.

Tonight when he came home. That's when she'd tell him. Until then—until then she'd...

She'd what?

Drive herself crazy chasing after her wild thoughts?

Talk herself out of it and back into it a hundred or a thousand times?

That would be a kind of torture she perhaps deserved—sitting on needles all day—but she didn't know if she could endure it.

If she wanted Isaac to love her—the *real* Becky—then she had to tell him.

But there was no way she could sit around all day waiting to do it, she realized, suddenly on fire with the determination to tell him right away. She had to do it now. She had to get it over and done with. Whatever the outcome.

Shaking herself out of her thoughts, she realized Isaac must be well on his way to the work site by now. She rose, dumped all the breakfast dishes in the basin, and hurried to her room. Discarding her guise as the perfectly proper young lady, she tugged her old hunting jacket over her dress. Then realizing Isaac might need proof about her shooting skills, she slung her rifle over her back too. An attack of nerves swept over her as she stood with the doorknob in her hand, finally ready to go.

This was it.

She took in a shaky breath and let it out real slow-like. No backing out. If she was going to tell Isaac about "Becky," then he might as well see her as she really was: a wild hoyden. And she may as well do it now. What better time than the present? That was something Papa liked to say.

So she'd learned at least one thing from her father: *No better time than the present.*

Isaac was either going to accept her as she was or not.

Becky dashed out of the cabin before she lost her courage. Gathering her skirts up, she jumped onto Siren's back and chased after her husband.

Twenty-Two

As his mount made its way down the familiar mountain path, Isaac was free to think. So, his wife loved another man. He admitted the truth to himself: *he loved her anyway.* Maybe with time, she'd come to love him. He'd just have to try harder. A new cabin would be a good place to start anew. He could almost picture Rebecca someday holding a little bundle wrapped in a white flannel blanket. With any luck, they'd have a peck of boys. He couldn't stand the thought of being responsible for two women, let alone one.

Even as he thought it, an image of a sweet, angelic baby girl made him catch a ragged breath. And that's when he realized the truth:

He wanted a family for himself, not just to please Pop.

In fact, he acknowledged that he desperately wanted a family *now.* He'd been attracted to Rebecca early on and come to care for her fairly quickly, but he'd stuffed his feelings down out of pride. She'd told him up front she didn't expect a love match. He hadn't wanted to believe it, but now he'd have to find a way to make her love him or resign himself to being second best in her affections—no matter how much it stuck in his craw. Either way, she was the mate God had given him, and he loved her. From what he'd seen at Dally's camp that night, he already knew she'd make a wonderful mother.

Stopping for a drink from the stream, Isaac dismounted and crouched by the bank. He drank deeply of the cold, clear water, his thoughts turning to his plans for the new house. He had the perfect site in mind…

Becky rode to the felling site, searching through the trees for Isaac. She heard a logger cry out, "Hold up!" and then another. Soon all the men had halted their work and watched as she rode through the site, their saws in hand, axe heads laid to rest on the ground, all eyes on her.

She recognized big red-haired Brody on a raised footboard of some sort wedged into a tree and called up to him. "Have you seen Isaac?"

He looked at her dumbly for a moment. "Miz Jessup?" he finally said, recognition dawning on his face.

"Isaac?" she called up again. "I'm looking for Isaac."

"Haven't seen him. You might want to ask Sam." He gestured downhill, and she continued on, stopping when she came to Sam. Her skin prickled, feeling the eyes of the men still on her, watching her, gawking. She tugged her skirts down more, worried she was showing too much petticoat.

"Well, what do we have here?" Sam asked, beaming at her in clear appreciation, not in any way that would have made her blush, but with a sort of fatherly pride.

"I'm looking for Isaac."

"In that get-up?" He squinted at her.

"I need to talk to him," she said bravely, ignoring the fact that her hair had loosened itself from her bun and was spilling around her shoulders. No doubt that was one reason all the men were gaping at her. That, and she had clear orders to stay away from the logging site. Or it could have been the rifle strapped to her back. Or the fact that she was riding bareback.

Or all of that put together, most likely.

Sam nodded. "Well, it's about time, I'd say."

"Have you seen him?"

"That I have. He passed by here not that long ago—stopped to tell me he was on his way into town."

"Oh," Becky said, disappointed. She'd so hoped to get this over with. If she had to wait for Isaac to go into town and return back up the mountain...well, she was afraid she'd lose her courage altogether.

"Not that long ago," Sam repeated, angling his head as if waiting for her to catch his meaning. "He'd be following the stream."

"Thanks, Pop." Becky gathered her reins—gathered herself. Yes, she'd follow Isaac down the mountain. She'd come this far. Why not?

She gave Siren a nudge with her knee and continued on, working her way through the trees, more than ever aware of so many gazes trailing after her, tracing her every move. Even if she lost her nerve along the way, Isaac was sure to hear about her appearance here today from his men.

It couldn't have been more than half an hour later when Becky caught sight of a horse through the trees ahead and pulled Siren to a halt. There was Isaac by the stream. His hat lay on the ground beside him, and he was splashing water over his face. She felt a rush of tenderness at the sight of his dark hair brushing the collar of his shirt.

And then a blur of movement upstream caught her eye.

A grizzly on the run.

Becky blinked to clear her vision, sure she was seeing

things, but it still was there. Headed straight for Isaac. And he was still bent over the stream, oblivious to the danger.

Oh, dear Lord.

Isaac.

She drew her rifle and aimed.

"Isaac! Look out!" she screamed as she and Siren surged forward.

At her shout, Isaac jumped up and turned toward her. He just stood there gaping at her.

And the bear—the bear was coming right at him.

"Oh, Lord," Becky whispered, horrified, "he doesn't see it."

Isaac must have sensed the movement then or heard the crack of branches breaking, or the beast grunting, for he looked briefly to the side and tried to stumble out of the bear's reach. A huge paw swiped him down to the ground before he'd moved more than a couple of steps.

Becky brought Siren to a stop. With a racing heart, she tried to calm her breathing and aim.

Please don't let me shoot Isaac. Please don't let me shoot Isaac.

She fired into the bear's thick hide. It didn't budge, didn't even flinch. She had to reload, dropping bullets to the ground in her haste. Fighting the urge to cry out, she bit her lip hard and fired again. Her breath came in short sobs as the beast kept mauling Isaac.

Gripping her last bullet, she loaded as quickly as she could and aimed for the bear's open mouth. The beast seemed to pause mid-roar.

She made her shot.

Oh, dear God, she prayed, *let it die. It's got Isaac. It's got him.*

The bear crumpled in a heap across Isaac's legs.

He lay there unmoving, his head thrown back against the rocks.

"Isaac!"

Please don't let him be dead. Please don't let him be dead.

Becky jumped down from Siren's back, landing with a jarring thump. She raced to Isaac, nearly falling over an exposed root, dropping her rifle at some point. She didn't care. Her blood pulsed through her body. She grabbed Isaac under the arms and hauled him away from the bear, freeing his legs. How she did it, she didn't know. It seemed she had the strength of ten men. His face was so pale and streaked with blood. A gasp caught in her throat.

"Don't you dare die on me, Isaac Jessup," she ordered him, tears running down her cheeks.

Cupping her hands in the stream, she gathered up some cool water and washed his face, then cradled his head in her lap.

"I love you, you hear? You can't die." She repeated the words over and over as she wiped his face and stroked his hair.

Isaac tried to move, but his leg was on fire with pain, and his head hurt something awful too. He must be dreaming, he decided, for he thought he heard Rebecca saying she loved him, but that couldn't be. Rebecca loved Jack.

Yes, it had it be a dream. Only moments ago, he thought he'd seen her barreling toward him. She'd been riding bareback astride her mare, with her rifle aimed high, looking every inch a wild frontier woman. He'd been standing there questioning his vision, when that bear had swiped him to the ground. A bear?

Some crazed grizzly, out of control.

There's a mean bear on the loose.

It sounded like Harper's voice in his head.

A mean bear.

Coming right at him.

Pain.

Gunshots.

Rebecca.

Surely his thinking was all confused. Perhaps the pain was causing him to have delusions, though the pain itself was real enough.

Forcing a breath, he shifted to get more air in his lungs. In his dream, he felt soft lips pressing against his cheek. She was kissing him over and over. His arms wouldn't move. He wanted so much to hold her back, but his limbs seemed nailed to the ground.

"Oh, Isaac, your leg." Rebecca tugged at the leg of his trousers. "The bear got you good. It's badly gouged, I'm afraid."

He forced his eyes open a crack and looked down to find his perfectly ladylike wife ripping some sort of white fabric to shreds and yanking a long strip of it around his thigh, tugging it into a tight knot that made him wince.

"Becky," he whispered. Looking at her now, the name just seemed to fit. She didn't look like a Rebecca anymore at all.

"Shhh. That's right. It's me—Becky. Don't move. Save your strength. I still have to get you on that horse somehow, and I'm going to need as much help as you can give me." She was taking charge of him, bossing him around with a confident air of command that made him want to raise his brows. That is, if he could've moved them.

"I need to get you to the doctor in town." Her panic came to the surface then in the quaver in her voice.

She was really worried about him. The thought sort of pleased him a little. She cared if he lived or died. Not much to go on, but it was a start.

"Okay, now, can you grab my shoulder?" She leaned close.

He wanted to help her so badly. From out of the very depths of him, he managed to lift his arm across her shoulders. The world tilted and faded in and out of black, as she shifted and pulled him and all his great length toward a big boulder. How she expected to get him up on his bay was a mystery. She weighed next to nothing.

Becky held tight to Isaac. He alternately sagged against her with all his weight, threatening to topple her over, and other times, he'd catch himself and surge forward toward the boulder. Her muscles had almost given out by the time she got him up on top of the biggest rock she could find. She urged the bay over to Isaac's side.

Isaac collapsed over the gelding's back with a groan, his eyes closed, his body limp. Once Becky made certain he was secure, she pulled herself astride Siren. Praying she'd get him down the trail in time to get help, she led the big bay down the mountain path. Minutes blurred into hours. It seemed like years passed by until they finally arrived at the doctor's house.

Becky paced around the doctor's office, a small square room with a desk, chairs, and shelves lining the walls. Although she was in his office surrounded by medical books, her heart was just as surely in the examination room with Isaac, where Dr. Sawyer was tending to his injuries. She shivered. Why was she so *cold*? She stomped her feet and paced around, trying to warm herself up, which helped a little and kept her mind somewhat occupied. At the sound of footsteps approaching, she braced herself for bad news.

Dr. Sawyer entered the room and immediately strode to her side. "Mrs. Jessup."

She blinked at him, confused at first by the name.

He gently rested a hand on her shoulder. "Your husband will be fine. He's lost some blood and will have a knot on his head that's going to give him a little trouble. You need to know though, with a head injury like this, he may drift in and out for a few days."

"His leg?" That was her real worry. The images of him lying there so still and the way his leg had looked kept spinning through her mind.

"Stitched up tight. Infection is the biggest worry, but it will mend in time. He's a healthy young man, and I suspect he'll be on his feet soon enough. I've given him something for the pain."

Becky wilted in relief. She felt as if she might float away or fall to the floor, so she gripped the edge of his desk to ground herself.

"Sam," she said, realizing Pop would be worried when Isaac didn't return to the site.

"Sam Jessup? Right. I'll send a messenger up. He'll need to know. I'll inform him of his son's injuries and assure him he's doing fine, and that I'll need to keep him here a few days until he's back on his feet."

"Can I see him?" she asked hoarsely. Her voice sounded odd and her throat was sore. Probably from yelling out to Isaac at the stream. Maybe from the weakness gathering in her limbs. Shock. That's what it was.

"He's in my guestroom—a recovery room, if you will—and you're more than welcome to stay here with him. I'm sure you're going to want to keep a close watch over him."

Before she could answer, he spotted her rifle propped against the wall and bent to pick it up. "What an extraordinary weapon."

"Thank you."

"This is yours?" One dark brow lifted in surprise.

She nodded and felt her lips tremble into a smile. The relief of hearing Isaac would be all right, coupled with this sudden turn in conversation made her want to giggle uncontrollably. Maybe that was the shock too.

"Remarkable. You wouldn't be willing to part with it, would you? No, no. Probably not. It's just I'm a collector of sorts, and this gun looks quite special."

Her prized possession. The gun Jack had given her so many years ago. What did it mean anymore? It was just a gun. Wood and metal. That was all and nothing more. She thought about how she'd considered becoming a trapper. That was a laugh. She would've been dead within a week from some wild animal. She shuddered to think about what it would've been like, being all alone. That was no kind of life. Especially if she couldn't be with Isaac. She wanted to be with him, make a life together. Have a family.

She wanted a place to belong, and she wanted that place to be with Isaac, for the rest of her days. She thought about her rush from the cabin to tell him she loved him, to confess who she really was. It seemed so long ago now, and not nearly as important. But it *was* still important. As soon as he got better, she'd tell him the truth, no matter what.

Lord, I love him. I want him to love me too, she prayed silently. *And, no matter what, I want to know you and be near you always. I know I don't deserve Isaac, not after all I've done— how I came here loving Jack, pretending to be something I'm not—*

but if there's any way...

She realized the doctor was waiting for her reply. As she looked at the gun in his hands, a feeling of peace came over her. She could get another gun someday, one that didn't have memories of Jack all over it. With the money, she could help Isaac pay for his doctor's bill. He'd still have other bills. And there was that expensive order he'd been on his way to place, whatever that was for. There would always be something. But at least by paying this one bill, she'd know she'd helped him a little.

"Will it cover your fees?" she asked the doctor.

He smiled wide. "That it will, Mrs. Jessup. That it will."

Isaac woke in a strange room. Shifting his head to the side, he found Rebecca sleeping next to him. No. *Becky.* It had been a Becky who'd flown toward him on her horse. Bareback? Had his eyes seen right? And she'd brought down a bear. On horseback. A crack shot. And it would've taken more than one good shot, most likely, to do the job. Bringing down a bear wasn't an easy task, especially one charging mid-attack. A bear like that could take bullet after bullet before it went down. Some men died that way: bear and hunter falling dead in a pile.

But *he* was alive.

Where had she learned to shoot like that? Definitely not from him. There was no way on earth she'd learned to shoot from those few short lessons. Which meant *she'd already known how.* She'd let him try to teach her, and all along she could shoot like *that.* And the way she'd ridden that horse. She'd been a blur of motion: her hair free, her skirts flapping around her, clearly riding astride. Like she was born to it.

Who was she?

And why had she hidden herself away from him from the start?

It made no sense.

His head must have gotten a pretty good whack when he fell, because his temple started to throb something fierce from the effort to think about it.

Besides, it didn't much seem to matter at the moment, not with her looking so warm and soft from sleep.

She'd *saved* him.

Isaac gently touched her cheek and whispered, "Becky..."

"Ummm." She snuggled into his hand. "Love you. Don't you dare die on me."

He froze, not daring to move and wake her.

She was sleep-talking again.

"Don't you dare die, you hear me?" she repeated rather fiercely. Her voice held that same tone of command he'd heard her use next to the stream. "Love you."

She loved *him*, Isaac? If that was true—and just thinking it made his blood surge—that must mean, surely, that she no longer loved Jack. Didn't it? He couldn't wait another minute to find out. He shook her awake.

"Becky, wake up." He mustered his strength and hugged her close. Thankfully his arms weren't nearly as heavy as they'd felt earlier next to the stream. "I love you," he said clearly, without the least hesitation.

Becky opened her eyes one at a time. She stared at Isaac, slowly registering that he was awake and looking right at her. He was also breathing in and out with comforting regularity and...

Wait.

"What—what did you say?" she asked, resisting the insistent pull of sleep, but her eyelids were too heavy to keep open. Too much effort. She'd never been so tired. Was it the shock? Why couldn't she wake up?

"I. Love. You," he repeated slowly. He stroked her cheek, and it was the warmest sensation Becky had ever felt. His fingers came to rest under her chin. His gaze drifted down to her lips.

He loves me.

"That's nice." She smiled drowsily at him.

A glow spread slowly through her even as sleep tugged her back into its grasp. She snuggled closer—close enough for him to kiss her. His lips on hers felt like a dream, a wonderful dream that curled her toes in the most delightful way.

After a few days of strict rest, the doctor pronounced Isaac well enough to come to the table for a meal. Dr. Sawyer's wife had served up a hearty breakfast for them, and Becky voiced her appreciation, but her eyes were for Isaac alone. Watching him walk unassisted across the room and sit upright in the chair beside her simply thrilled her. After the meal, Dr. Sawyer whisked Isaac off to the examination room and then returned smiling.

"Take your man home, Mrs. Jessup," he said, beaming.

"Thank you, Dr. Sawyer." Becky turned to the doctor's wife. "Thank you both for your excellent care and hospitality."

"My dear, you're welcome here any time." Mrs. Sawyer, a middle-aged woman with a motherly air, patted Becky's arm.

Dr. Sawyer shook Isaac's hand.

"I'll settle up the bill next time I'm in town, all right?" Isaac asked.

"No need. Your wife here took care of it."

"She did?" Isaac asked, looking confused.

"You're a strong man," the doctor continued, to Becky's relief. "I'd say you'll be back to work in a few days, a week at the most, if I had to guess." The doctor led them out back to his stable, a sturdy two-stall affair, and helped Isaac into the saddle.

"Just make sure he takes it easy for a few more days," the doctor said to her. "And I'll take good care of that gun of yours."

Hoping Isaac hadn't heard that last comment, Becky gave the doctor a smile and accepted his hand up to mount her mare.

He grinned as he noticed the lack of saddle. "You're a remarkable woman, Mrs. Jessup." He chuckled as he waved them off. "Remarkable."

As Isaac rode beside Becky up the mountain trail, he saw her again as that amazing frontier woman who'd barreled toward him in the woods. Gone was the delicate-looking waif he'd first met at the Pearsons' house. Sure, she was still a tiny thing, but now, he could actually imagine her surviving in wild Seattle.

Survive?

She'd done more than *survive* that day with that bear. She'd saved his hide.

"Becky—" He cleared his throat and smiled as she turned to meet his gaze. "You were amazing with that gun. How'd you ever learn to shoot and ride like that? And don't tell me you learned that from me. I know better." He studied her features as if seeing her for the first time, filled with admiration and not a little confusion.

"You mean you don't mind me being an absolute hoyden?"

He tilted his head to one side and let out a laugh. "What?"

"You're not upset your wife's not a proper lady?"

"What good's a 'proper lady' up here? I'm glad you've got some spirit. You'll need it."

"Thank you." Her cheeks colored at his praise.

She seemed to sit her horse more comfortably then, as if a weight had fallen from her shoulders. He sensed he was seeing her as she really was now, and he found her fascinating. How could he have failed to see this, to see *her*?

"I grew up riding and shooting," she admitted, "but men don't want their wives doing those things...at least that's what I thought."

She thought he wanted some prim and proper miss with wide skirts and white gloves?

"Think again." He grinned. "I like you like this, Becky." He reached over and stopped Siren, then lightly grasped Becky's wrist, took her small hand in his.

"And I like that," she said softly.

"What?"

"You calling me Becky. It's so much better than Rebecca. That never quite sounded right to me. The only one who ever called me that was Papa, and only when he was angry with me."

"Then Becky it is." He rubbed his thumb over the back of her hand. Her skin was so smooth and soft...and distracting.

"But you said I didn't belong here," she reminded him,

sounding hurt.

He gripped her fingers. "Look at me, Becky," he commanded.

As she lifted her eyes from their horses, he noticed with brief amusement that his gelding was stoically ignoring the fact that her mare was trying to nip at his mane. He bore it with such an air of grim tolerance, like a longsuffering husband. Which wasn't nearly what Isaac felt for Becky at that moment. He wanted to reassure her. He wanted to hold her.

Isaac waited until Becky met his gaze, then continued clearly, "When I said that...well, I wasn't quite in my right mind. I was so full of fury for what Jem had done. And I was afraid. When I think what could have happened to you..." He shook his head. "I'm sorry I said that. I wish to heaven I could take it back. I want you here with me."

"But you keep pushing me away."

"I thought you still loved Jack. That's what I thought." He pressed his fingertips to the bandage wrapped around his forehead, trying to ease the ache there. "You talked in your sleep on our wedding night and told me how much you loved 'your darling Jack.'"

"I did?" she asked, her face turning slightly pink. "Really?"

"You did. And hummed that blasted waltz tune."

"On our wedding night?"

"The very same."

"Oh, so that's how you knew about Jack."

Isaac nodded once, struggling against the weariness eating away at his strength. He hated being so tired. Hated feeling weak. Knew he'd probably have to lie down as soon as they got back. It was in no way what he wanted though. He wanted to appear whole and strong, like he could take on the world. Like he could protect her and not the other way around. There was also something bothering him that he knew he needed to air. He'd never felt comfortable talking about feelings or bringing up incidents from the past, but he forced himself to go on.

"Becky..." he began. When she looked at him, his heart gave an unsteady bump. "I heard you sobbing in your room one night. Not that long ago."

How can you say you love me when I heard you crying over another man?

He didn't say it aloud, but the question hung in the air between them.

She hesitated, seeming to gather her words. She closed her eyes for a second as if bringing back the memory of that night. "It was kind of a ceremony, I guess you could say. Saying goodbye to old memories. I'd grown up with Jack. And I guess I always loved him—ever since we were children. Then he came back from the war, and he had a wife, and all my dreams dried up to nothing. I wanted more. I wanted something new. A fresh start, maybe. That's why I signed up to come here. That's why I married you."

Her hand was trembling, Isaac noticed. As he listened to her story, he wondered why it hurt so much to hear her tell him again that she loved Jack. She was staring at him, her eyes so huge, so earnest. He pressed on his temple again and tried to think clearly. He couldn't very well expect her to say she'd never loved anyone else. That would be a lie. She'd been honest from the first that she hadn't come here with dreams of falling in love with him. She'd told him straight out she didn't expect a love match, that her heart wasn't free.

He cleared his throat. "You talked in your sleep again the other night. You said you loved me. Please don't tell me I was dreaming."

"I do love you," she said, and her smile turned his insides

all soft. "I was coming to tell you. That's why I followed you that day. I was coming to tell you everything, honest. That night...that was the night I let Jack go. He wasn't the man for me. I know that now. I was young, I guess, and it wasn't meant to last. Do you know why I chose your letter? Or I guess it was Sam's letter." A brief frown marred her brow. "It was because of your name. I thought it was a sign: an Isaac for my Rebecca. Silly, I guess, but maybe it really was a sign. I was meant to come here. I was meant to marry you. What I felt for Jack was just calf love and nothing more—I can see that now. I love *you*. Like a woman loves a husband. Fully and completely, with all I have inside."

"Is that right?" If Isaac weren't so weak still, he might've pulled her off the saddle and into his arms right then.

She must have sensed the direction his thoughts had taken, for she blushed and nodded.

"I love you too, Becky. You can't know how happy it makes me to hear you say those words to me now, but you will soon... I promise."

"Oh," she said and gave him a shy smile that made him wish he wasn't still recovering from an accident.

Every morning now it seemed Becky woke up with a happy heart. Looking back over the past week, it was as if she and Isaac had found a wonderful peace with each other. He'd made startling progress, healing quickly, as the doctor had predicted, and his leg only seemed to give him trouble when he was tired. She marveled at how much had changed between them. All the strain of living like strangers had melted away to a warm closeness. Even now, as they ate breakfast together, she kept glancing over at her husband, liking the way he looked in the morning, all smooth-cheeked from a fresh shave, ready for the day. She liked how he looked in the red flannel shirt she'd made him—remembered his surprised pleasure at her gift. It wasn't perfect by any means, but he seemed to like it nonetheless. With a warm rush of embarrassment, she also remembered the wonder of the marriage bed. Mama's awkward pink-cheeked talk hadn't prepared her in the least for the experience. She hid a smile.

Isaac leaned over and gave her a peck on the cheek. "You're looking good enough to eat, Becky, but I have to go to town to place an order."

An order?

Becky nearly choked on her milk.

"Isaac, don't. Save the money for your men."

"What?" The look he gave her made her pause. Like she'd lost her senses. "What are you talking about?"

Hurrying to his old trunk, she grabbed up the ledger resting on top and returned to his side. She plunked the book down on the table and flipped through the pages.

"There has to be a mistake here, Isaac," she insisted.

"There's no mistake, I promise. There's no mistake with the numbers." He sounded so firm, so sure.

Could she have been wrong?

"But Jem said the men have gone without pay for weeks." She looked up at him and wondered how he could possibly explain that away.

Isaac pulled himself up, his shoulders stiff and proud. "Gone without pay? Never. The only truth in that is *Jem* went without pay for a while. I had to dock his pay because he wasn't doing his work. But I assure you, my men are well provided for, and they always have been."

Becky gazed around the cabin, taking in the ragged potato-sack curtains, the worn furniture. Nothing matched. It was so *small*. Why, the porch was even crooked. It sloped downhill.

What he was saying made no sense.

Why would they live this way if they had as much money as his records said?

Isaac rubbed the back of his neck, clearly embarrassed by her inspection. "I guess I never explained things properly," he said. "I can't blame you for thinking we're poor. It's just, well, Pop and I never cared much what the place looks like. It's just a place to sleep, mostly. Always has been. In fact, the only thing that means anything is that old cook stove. It was my mother's."

Becky looked at the stove with new eyes. "It was your mother's?"

"Becky," Isaac said, claiming her attention. He seemed a little anxious now, as if he had a secret to share. Which made her anxious too. "I wanted it to be a surprise, but I've got plans to build you a house, one with an indoor pump. With all the things a woman needs to raise her children."

A house?

For her?

It was a dream come true. An answer to a prayer she hadn't even realized she'd prayed.

Looking in Isaac's eyes right then, Becky felt like every dream she'd ever had just came true. Except for one. He'd said children—plural—which was interesting and made her heart race a little too quickly. That was one dream she was still waiting for. Although for all she knew maybe it had been answered too. Maybe even now, a baby was growing inside her.

The open ledger lay before her. All those neat columns and rows. All perfectly balanced.

"I'm sorry, Isaac. I should've known better—I should

have asked you sooner, but I—"

Before she could finish, he bent to capture her lips in a long, drawn-out kiss—a full-fledged, knee-buckling kiss that made her wish he didn't have to leave for work.

"I'll be back before dark," he promised.

"I'll be here." She followed him outside and stood on the porch, waving goodbye as he rode away. A warm glow of contentment washed over her simply from watching him. She loved the way he moved. Like he owned the place. Which was appropriate, she thought with smile, since he did. Looking up at the bright blue sky and the sun glinting off the snow-topped mountains made her feel as close to heaven as she could ever be here on earth. It reminded her of the day she'd prayed in the farmer's field back home. How desperate she'd felt. It seemed so long ago now. Her prayers had been answered after all. Not like she'd expected, but even better.

This was where she belonged. Right here.

Her home was—and always would be—here with Isaac in wild Seattle.

Epilogue

*I*saac loaded up the skid with Becky's trunks and all the remaining items they'd be taking over to the new house today. Tying everything off with one last yank of the rope, he stepped back. Today, he'd bring his wife to her new home. Fighting a nervous tightening in his chest, he reminded himself she was sure to like it—anything was better compared to this drafty old cabin she'd lived in for the better part of a year. He felt eyes on him and glanced back. There was Pop on the porch, watching him with a distinct air of fatherly satisfaction.

Isaac raised a hand in a welcoming wave. *Meddling old man*, he thought with affection. Pop would never let him live this down now, not after it turned out to be the best thing that had ever happened to him. Isaac sighed, resigned to the fact that he was going to have to put up with Pop's meddling in all sorts of other ways in the future.

"Mr. Jessup?" A tall, broad-shouldered young man with black hair and fair skin approached, a knapsack slung over his back. He was on foot, no sign of a horse. And he looked weary, his feet dragging a bit, as if he'd come a long way.

"Jem? Is that you? It's been a while." Isaac greeted him warmly, recognizing him as he drew closer. He shook Jem's hand and grasped his shoulder.

"Spent time with a crew of loggers outside Sacramento. Learned a lot about the business—and myself." Jem smiled, but his eyes were sober. He looked years older. "You seen my pa?"

"No sign of him," Isaac assured him, but from Jem's creased brow he knew the young man was worried his father would return to take revenge.

"I came back to ask if I could join the crew again." Jem rushed on quickly without waiting for Isaac's response, "I know I acted the fool—'kicking against the goads' so to speak—but I'm willing to work wherever you feel's best. I felt called to return. I'm hopin' you'll take me back?"

Isaac looked the young man over thoughtfully. He did seem willing to take direction. Time would tell, but after seeing how Jem's father had treated him, Isaac felt the young man needed more than a second chance.

"How'd you like to learn the business from a real expert?" He directed a questioning gaze at Pop, who walked over and stood beside him.

"I've got an extra room in the cabin that needs a body," Pop declared. "Don't need no shenanigans though." He fixed Jem with a steely-gray stare, the one Isaac had heeled to his whole life.

"No, sir."

"Well, then, I 'spect we could use an assistant."

"You don't mean it?" Jem looked back and forth between the two older men, his gaze incredulous.

"Do I have to ask twice?" Sam shrugged and started to walk off.

"No, sir!" Jem stepped closer and offered his hand. "You've got an assistant."

"Well, then, let's get you started." Pop led the young man toward the current logging site, talking to him as they went. "Enjoy your new home, Son!" he called back with a cheery wave. "I'm expecting to hear all about it tomorrow."

"Make it the day after. I'm taking tomorrow off," Isaac

shouted back. He could hear Pop chuckling as he continued walking on. His father bent his head in toward Jem, no doubt settling in for a lecture on the dangers of the logging business.

After a short ride though the forest, Becky followed Isaac until they reached the edge of a clearing.

This was it.

He was finally going to show her their new home. Countless delays had cropped up to keep the project going for months longer than Isaac had planned, but several days ago he'd declared the new house ready, and she'd packed for the move in a flurry of activity.

With her mother's letter tucked in her pocket, she felt everything in her world was right. He father had even scrawled a note at the bottom saying simply, "Miss you. Hope all is well, Papa." Those few words made her cry every time she read them. Simply thinking about them now made her eyes smart with tears. Who would've guessed that leaving home and moving to the other side of the country would have the unexpected side effect of bringing her closer to her father? That, in and of itself, was a miracle. God had brought her here and given her a home—a place to belong. He'd given her a wonderful husband to share it with. She looked at Isaac with a contented smile.

He helped her dismount and immediately covered her eyes with his hand.

She leaned back against him, felt his arm slide securely around her waist.

"Do you trust me?" He whispered close to her ear, making her shiver a little, in the best way possible.

"Of course." She smiled. "That's a silly question."

"Glad to hear it." He pressed a quick kiss to her cheek and guided her forward. "Just a little farther now."

Her heart skipped along a little faster, and she laughed from sheer excitement.

"Here we are." His voice sounded a little deeper than usual, like he was nervous. He dropped his hand, but she kept her eyes shut, delaying the suspense.

"I can't wait to see it."

"Then open your eyes, woman." He playfully tickled the small of her back.

"All right." She popped one eye open and then the other. "Oh, Isaac." A quaint little cabin with a covered porch stood in the clearing before her. "The windows are so big! And you planted flowers?" She glanced over her shoulder at him, a smile nearly bursting from her face. "It's perfect."

"It's no mansion," he said, with a self-deprecating smile. "But there's a real barn." He pointed to a large wood-beam structure behind the cabin. "And we've got an indoor pump, and one of those indoor necessaries."

"That's lovely." She teased him with her eyes and looped her arm through his. "Almost as lovely as my birthday present. I still don't know how you got Dr. Sawyer to part with my old rifle."

"He has a soft spot for you, I think. Plus, I convinced him that gun was sized just right for you." He took her hands in his and squeezed lightly, guiding her gaze to the new cabin. "So, you like my surprise?" he asked, obviously fishing.

She nodded and squeezed his hands back. "I love it. And—and I have a surprise for you too," she said in a little singsong voice.

"Do you now?" His eyes twinkled.

"It's a good thing you made the cabin plenty big…"

His smile wavered, and his dark brown eyes grew serious. "Are you saying what I think you're saying?"

"Are you going to be happy about it?"

He grinned and swung her up in his arms, spinning her around. Holding her aloft, he jumped up onto the front porch.

"Isaac!" she protested, as her feet dangled uselessly off the ground. She squirmed. "Put me down."

He simply hitched her more securely into his arms, looping his arm under her legs and cradling her to his chest. She immediately stopped protesting and snuggled in close. Perhaps it wasn't so bad being carried, just this once. It was almost like she was a new bride and he was the groom. As if they'd just come from repeating their vows.

Now there was a thought she hadn't considered until now...

"I think it's time to show you the rest of your new home," Isaac said. "And I think you'll especially appreciate the rug in front of the fireplace." He carried her inside and set her on her feet.

She took a few steps forward and turned in a slow circle, a smile splitting her face.

It was perfect. Wide pine floors, heavy beams, all in earthy tones of caramel-gold and brown. Warm and welcoming. There was a generous kitchen area to one side, with a big red cast-iron cook stove. Cabinets and shelves that went from floor to ceiling. An ice box. And a great big kitchen table with eight wood chairs and an extra bench sitting against one wall—so she guessed they'd be entertaining a fair bit. Plenty of room for Pop to come visit. Plenty of room for children some day.

She rested her hand on the back of a soft-looking sofa—not some stiff settee like the Pearsons', but one with a sturdy wood frame and deep leather cushions and a couple of fluffy red pillows. A pretty quilt in red, gold, and evergreen—stitched in a spiky star-pattern—hung over the back.

That certainly looked cozy.

"Oh," Becky whispered, turning once again, all too aware that Isaac was watching her with an air of expectation, his stance proud—like he owned the place, of course.

Her eyes reluctantly left his, and she turned her gaze to the best part of all: a big bear rug spread out over the wood floor between two comfy looking rush-seat rocking chairs. Side-by-side rockers. It looked like the perfect place to stretch out after a long day and warm your toes in front of that big stone fireplace against the far wall.

Warm. Homey.

Isaac had outdone himself.

"Anyone I know?" she asked, nodding at the rug. A little giggle escaped her lips as she sidled over to Isaac and bumped her shoulder against his arm.

"The same." He paused and looked down at her. "I like having a reminder that you 'saved my hide.'"

"You can't know how glad I am that you don't mind me being a complete hoyden." With a contented sigh, Becky slipped her arms around his waist and tugged him close.

"I wouldn't want you any other way." He chuckled and with the slightest nudge of his boot, kicked the front door shut.

Author's Note

I was intrigued by the true story of Asa Mercer, who was rather loosely the inspiration for my Melrose Preston. Two hundred women, with hopes of employment or marriage, sailed with him around the tip of South America and up the West Coast to Washington Territory in 1866.

I was also inspired by the Bible story of Isaac and Rebekah. Genesis 24 tells the tale of an aging Abraham, who sends a trusted servant back to his homeland to get a wife for his son Isaac. The servant goes and prays for God to reveal just the right girl to him. He meets Rebekah at the well, and when he asks her for a drink, she gives it to him and brings water for his camels as well. This is the sign he had prayed for. So, amazingly, Rebekah leaves her family to go with this stranger, the servant of their kinsman Abraham, and becomes the wife of Isaac. "Then the servant told Isaac all he had done. Isaac brought her into the tent of his mother Sarah, and he married Rebekah. So she became his wife, and he loved her; and Isaac was comforted after his mother's death." —Genesis 24:66-67 (NIV) The story always struck me as intriguing and somewhat romantic. Then at some point it occurred to me that Rebekah was a very early example of a "mail-order" bride, but not.

Finally, I've quoted from the *New International Version* of the Bible within the story even though this translation was unavailable in the time of my Isaac and Rebecca (1866). I request the reader's latitude in this, as I've used this version solely as a matter of personal preference—for readability and because it's the version I'm most familiar with.

—*Lena Goldfinch*

Also by Lena Goldfinch

THE BRIDES
The Unexpected Bride (Book 1)

ROMANCE FOR ADULTS & TEENS
Songstone
Aire
The Language of Souls

BOOKS FOR TEENS
Haunting Joy
Chain Reaction: A Short Story (Prequel to *Haunting Joy*)
Haunting Melody (Sequel to *Haunting Joy*)—Coming Soon
Take a Picture : A Novelette

Acknowledgements

To my mom and dad, and sister and brother—and to all my family and friends, with love and appreciation for your support and encouragement.

To my editor, Amber Stokes, for your excellent editing skills, your long-distance friendship, and the many ways you help with my writing and publishing. Much appreciation!

To Kim Hanson for your expert eagle eyes for catching "dings" in a manuscript, for your friendship, support of my writing, and encouragement. Thanks!

To Eliza and Evan for encouraging me to keep writing. Lots of love!

And last, but far from least, to my wonderful husband, Paul. You are my biggest support. With all my love.

About the Author

LENA GOLDFINCH writes sweet historical romance and books for teens. She's always been a sucker for a good old-fashioned romance, whether it's a novel or short story, young adult or adult, fantasy or realistic, contemporary or historical. Lena has been a finalist in several national writing contests, including the RWA Golden Heart and ACFW Genesis contests. She enjoys life in a quiet, small-town with her husband, two kids, and a very spoiled Black Lab.

You can reach me at Lena@LenaGoldfinch.com or visit me at www.LenaGoldfinch.com.

Would you like to receive updates about new books?
You can join my free author newsletter on my website.